D0823726

Acclaim for *Devil in a Blue Dress*

Winner of the John Creasey Award for the best first crime novel of 1991

'A magnificent first novel by Walter Mosley in which, from the first page, it's clear we have discovered a wonderful new talent . . . the most exciting arrival in the genre for years.'
J. D. F. Jones in the *Financial Times*

'An original, beguiling creation. One of the most impressive first crime novels.'
Marcel Berlins in *The Times*

'His strength is in speech rhythms rather than slangy signifying, in understated pacing, in the precision-tooled plot which really does sink its hooks in and is over before you know it . . . This is great stuff. Roll on the next in the series, *A Red Death*.'
Jim McClellan in *i-D*

and *A Red Death*

Short listed for the 1992 Golden Dagger Award

'This novel is so hot it burns your fingers with blistering dialogue and multi-coloured images. Highly addictive food.'
Frances Fyfield in the *Evening Standard*

'Mosley's second novel confirms him as one of crime writing's finds of the 1990s.'
Mike Ripley in the *Daily Telegraph*

and *White Butterfly*

Short listed for the 1993 Golden Dagger Award

'In the crime field this is unquestionably the novel of the year. But Mosley is already outstripping the genre. Stay with him while you can.'
Literary Review

'Rawlins moves intimately through Los Angeles' menacing mid-fifties black low-life, accumulating threats, violence, clues and the disintegration of his marriage, Mosley captures the era with masterful dialogue, subtle social comment and a total command of place and time. Even Clinton can be right.'
The Times

Other Mask Noir titles

Alex Abella	*The Killing of the Saints*
Susan Wittig Albert	*Thyme of Death*
Jerome Charyn	*Maria's Girls*
Didier Daeninckx	*Murder in Memoriam*
Stella Duffy	*Calendar Girl*
Maxim Jakubowski (ed)	*London Noir*
Elsa Lewin	*I, Anna*
Walter Mosley	*Devil in a Blue Dress* *A Red Death* *White Butterfly*
Julian Rathbone	*Sand Blind*
Derek Raymond	*The Crust on its Uppers* *A State of Denmark*
Sam Reaves	*Fear Will Do It* *A Long Cold Fall*
Manuel Vasquez Montalban	*The Angst-Ridden Executive* *Murder in the Central Committee* *An Olympic Death* *Southern Seas*
David Veronese	*Jana*

BLACK BETTY

Walter Mosley

First published in 1994 by W. W. Norton & Company Inc.,
New York

A catalogue record for this book is available from the British Library on request

This edition first published in 1994 by
Serpent's Tail, 4 Blackstock Mews, London N4

Phototypeset by Intype, London
Printed in Great Britain by Cox & Wyman Ltd., Reading, Berkshire

This book is dedicated to my father, who died on New Year's Day, 1993.
I miss you, Dad.

Ghetto Pedagogy

"Dad?"
"Yes?"
"Why do black men always kill each other?"
(long pause)
"Practicing."

They were standing under a hard yellow light in the alley behind John's bar. Big Hand Bruno Ingram was large and powerful, and he had the ability to swagger even when he was standing still. He wore a brown mohair suit with no hat and no shirt. The smaller man's suit was close-fitting and silver, imported, I knew, from Italy. I stayed in the shelter of the doorway listening to their small talk; hidden.

". . . Dodgers lost it," Mouse, the smaller man, was saying. He sounded fine. "You owe me twenty-fi'e cent."

"Come on, Sooky," a bodiless voice said from the street. It was a man's voice. A young man.

"Uh-uh, Alfred," a woman answered as clear as you could want. But I didn't hear the rest of what she said.

Bruno's bass voice was rumbling, "Get outta my face, motherfucker." I turned again, a sense of dread so deep in my body that it felt like the oldest thing in the world. "You could suck my big black dick."

He didn't mean it. That's what I wanted to shout out. But I couldn't make a sound. Mouse pushed against the big man's chest, not to move Bruno but to push himself far enough away so that he could get out his long .41-caliber pistol.

Bruno's manly sneer turned into an eight-year-old's wonder at what he'd done wrong. The impact of the first shot knocked him four feet backwards, big hands thrust out in front of him like a cartoon sleepwalker. He wanted to fall, to get down on the ground out of harm's way, but Mouse just kept on shooting, throwing Bruno up against the pork butcher's back door again and again.

There was a scream and I was stumbling backwards into the doorway.

CHAPTER 1

I awoke with a start in almost complete darkness. I didn't know where I was. The mattress was too soft. I reached over to get my watch but the night table wasn't there. I almost fell off the lawn chair onto the porch. Then I remembered how hot it was in the house. The kids, Jesus and Feather, had taken the only working fan to blow air from the window into Jesus's room. I'd come outside to the screened-in porch at two A.M. after waking up to find myself sweating in the bed.

I sat up trying to throw off the nightmare. It had been almost five years, but Bruno died in my dreams at least once a month—more often recently. I'll never forget him being nailed to the wall by my best friend's gun.

I tried to think of better things. About our new young Irish president and Martin Luther King; about how the world was changing and a black man in America had the chance to be a man for the first time in hundreds of years. But that same world was being rocked almost daily by underground nuclear explosions and the threat of war.

Across town an old friend of mine, Martin Smith, lay dying. He'd been the closest thing to a teacher that I ever had. I knew that I had to go see him, to say goodbye, but I kept putting it off.

And through it all blew that hot September wind. It wouldn't let me rest. It just got hotter and hotter while my temper wore thin.

I wanted to feel better but all I had was the certainty that the world had passed me by—leaving me and my kind dead or making death in dark causeways.

A strip of dawn light showed above the houses across

the street. A better day might have been coming, for some people—but not for everyone. Bruno was in his grave almost five years now, while Mouse languished in the state prison at Chino for manslaughter. I was in a kind of prison too. A prison of guilt, a prison of my mind.

"Mr. Rawlins?" a voice said.

My hand went straight for the pistol in the night-table drawer again. But I wasn't in my bedroom. I was naked, not even under a sheet, outside in the dark. I grabbed a ceramic ashtray that Jesus had made me at summer camp.

"Whoisit?" I tried to sound calm. The silhouette in the screened doorway was a man—somewhere between five foot six and six foot five. With my free hand I took the sheet from the floor and held it to my crotch.

"Saul Lynx, Mr. Rawlins." A white man. "Can you talk?"

"Huh? What?" I clutched the misshapen slab of clay so hard that it cracked in my hand.

"I know it's early," the white man said. "But it's important that I speak with you. I got your name last night, but by the time I got a chance to come over it was too late. I was going to wait outside until later, but when I came up to check the address I heard you talking in your sleep. You see, I have to talk to you this morning."

"Then why don't you get-ass away from here and call me in the mornin'?" I could feel the strength in my arm build to the point where I could have hurled the ashtray through the screen. If he had touched the latch on the door he would have been a dead man.

But instead of taking any chances he said, "I've come to offer you a job. But you've got to start today—this morning." Then he said, "Can we turn on a light or something?"

I didn't want him to see me with no clothes on. It was like I was still in a dream, as if I was vulnerable if someone could see my skin. I wanted to linger in those shadows, but I'd learned that you can't hide in your own house—if somebody knows where you live you've got to stand up.

I wrapped the sheet around me like an African robe and reached inside the front door to switch on the porch light. Mr. Lynx was still hidden in the faint light beyond my screen.

"May I come in?" he asked.

"Come on then."

He was a smallish man in a light brown cotton suit and a loose dark brown tie. His nose was the only big thing on him—protruding and somehow shapeless. If you'd forgotten his name you would have said, "You know, the guy with the nose." His cap was brown. He had on a white shirt to go with his pale skin. His eyes were brilliant green.

Saul Lynx smiled and bobbed his head, but I didn't take his hand.

"You won't be needing that." He was looking down at the ashtray. "I don't blame you for sleeping outside on a night like this. In the summers back in the Bronx when I was a boy I spent more time on the fire escape than I did in the apartment."

"What do you want, man?" I didn't have patience for his small talk.

"Like I say," he answered, unperturbed, "I've got a job for you. There's a woman missing and it's my client's desire to find her quickly."

The shadow of night was lifting from Genesee Avenue. I could make out the shapes of large carob trees across the street and the neat little lawns of my neighbors.

"Can we sit down?" Saul Lynx wanted to know.

"Say what you got to say, man, and then get outta here." I had children in the house and didn't want this stranger too comfortable in their home.

Saul Lynx had a smile that was just about as sincere as

the kind of grin the undertaker puts on a corpse. "Have you ever heard of a woman named Elizabeth Eady?" he asked.

Her name struck a dark chord at the back my mind. It fit with the humid September heat—and with my dreams.

"She's lived in L.A. for almost twenty-five years, but she's from Houston originally," the little man was saying. "From down in your old neighborhood, I think. The only picture I have of her is this one." Lynx handed me an old brittle photograph. Its colors were rose-brown and tan instead of black and white. It wasn't a posed portrait, but a kind of snapshot. A young woman on the front porch of a small house. She was smiling at the time, leaning awkwardly against the doorjamb. She was tall and big-boned and very dark, even the rose coloring couldn't hide Betty's blackness. Her mouth was open as if she were smiling and flirting with the photographer. It brought a sense of intimacy that few amateur photographs have. Intimacy but not warmth. Black Betty wasn't your warm sort of homemaking girl.

Betty was a great shark of a woman. Men died in her wake.

If you heard that a friend of yours was courting Betty you could start crying then, because he was bound to come to harm. She had something about her that drove men wild. And she wasn't stingy with her charms. If a man could afford her supper, and her drink, she was happy to be with him. She'd go out with him on Monday, Tuesday, Wednesday, and Thursday nights—all night. Betty wasn't the kind who sat home, so if Friday came and his pockets were empty—Betty was gone. Because when the sun went down, Betty and Marlon (Marlon, that was Betty's fancy half brother), they hit the streets. And if one man couldn't pay, another one was happy to take his place.

Back then there weren't too many of your colored men who could afford a steady diet of Betty. Many a night, yesterday's boyfriend went up against tonight's man. Betty could draw blood three nights in a week, and if it ever bothered her she never let it show.

I had seen her sashaying down the wooden sidewalks of Houston's Fifth Ward. I was a raggedy twelve-year-old and she was more woman than I had ever seen in one place. She wore black lace, gloves, and fur and smelled so good that I forgot who I was. It was out in front of a bar called Corcheran's on Blanford Street. I guess I was looking pretty hard, my nostrils were probably flared out too.

"What you lookin' at, boy?" she asked me.

"You, ma'am."

"You like what you see?"

I had to swallow before saying, "Uh-huh, yes'm. You 'bout the prettiest woman I ever seen."

"About?"

I was crushed. I should have said the prettiest. She was the prettiest. I had ruined my chances of her ever talking to me again.

"Come on, honey," her date said.

But instead of listening to him Betty came over and kissed me—right on the lips. She pushed her tongue out but I was too slow to open my own mouth. When she pulled back from me I fell on the ground from leaning into the embrace that didn't come.

They all laughed at me, all the men standing outside. But Betty didn't laugh. She was moved by her power over me. I would have fallen down for her anyday. I would have jumped out of a window for her kiss.

"Do you know her, Mr. Rawlins?" Saul Lynx asked.

Dawn had come while I studied the picture. A car drove by and tossed a newspaper onto my lawn and the lawn next door. Almost immediately a spidery white woman came out of her house to retrieve her paper. Mrs. Horn was insomniac and impatient. She'd probably been waiting for hours just to get the news.

"I don't remember her," I said.

"Well . . ." He took a long time with the word as if to say that he didn't know whether to believe me or not. "That doesn't matter, not really. You're known for finding people in the colored part of town. That's why we need you."

"Who's we?"

"I'm the only one you need to be concerned with."

"What's she done?"

"Nothing as far as I know. She worked for a woman almost the whole time she's been up here. But something happened. Miss Eady quit and left her job and now her boss wants her to come on back." Saul Lynx smiled and caressed his nose like it was favored pet. "She didn't leave a forwarding address and there's no Elizabeth Eady in the book."

"Who she work for?"

"I'm not at liberty to say."

"Uh-huh. And how much you payin' t'find her?"

"Two hundred dollars now and another two hundred when you find her." He pointed his baby finger at me. "But the job has got to be done quickly. From what I understand, the woman who's paying is very upset and wants to find Miss Eady soon."

"From what you understand?"

"Well, you see," he said, almost apologetically, "I haven't actually met the woman. She doesn't deal with dicks. It's her lawyer who hired me." He took a small fold of bills from his pants pocket and handed it in my general direction.

I had the ashtray in one hand and the picture in the other.

"Two hundred dollars up front," he said.

It was more than I had in the bank. At one time I was flush with the income from apartment buildings I owned. I'd bought them with a windfall I'd come upon in 1948. But since then I'd stretched myself pretty thin trying to make it in the real estate game. I was almost bankrupt. The house I lived in was rented. We ate beans and rice for dinner three nights a week.

I put down the ashtray and took the bills. They were damp from being in his pants.

"I might look," I said tentatively. "But I'll want to talk to this lawyer guy myself before I give you anything I find. What you say his name was?"

"We'll talk about that when you've got something. I'll let him know that you'll be wanting to see to him, though." He couldn't have cared less about what I wanted. "How can he get in touch with you if he wants to talk?"

I told him my number and he nodded. Mr. Lynx was the kind of man who didn't write things down.

"How did you find me, Mr. Lynx? My address ain't in no book."

"You're famous, Mr. Rawlins." He took a cracked leather wallet from his back pocket. From this he produced a creased and soiled business card. It was damp too. It had a phone number and a Venice Beach address printed in black letters that had run slightly with the moisture. There wasn't a name, though.

"That's L-Y-N-X," he said. "Call me when you find something. And call me soon."

"How do you know that I won't just take this money and say you owed it to me for somethin'?"

Saul Lynx looked me in the eye and stopped his placid smiling. "I might be wrong, but I bet that you're the kind of man who does what he says, Mr. Rawlins. Anyway, there's still two hundred dollars to be made."

"Well, maybe so, but how do you expect me to find this one woman outta two and a half million people? You must have somethin' t'tell me about her." I already knew how to go about looking for Betty, but I wanted to know what that white man knew.

And he saw what I was about. A smile that bordered on respect grazed his lips. Then he shook his head. "Sorry, Mr. Rawlins, but all I know is that she has friends down in the Negro community. Maybe somebody you know will recognize her from the picture."

I would have given him the money back but I had an idea of how he found me—and an itch to see Betty when I was a man.

"I'll be talkin' to ya," I said.

Lynx touched his forehead in a mock-friendly salute.

"Don't forget," he said. "I have to know about this soon."

He smiled and walked out. I watched him get into an especially small and tinny brown car. It was something foreign, I never knew what. As he drove off Mrs. Horn came out—just curious, I suppose. When she saw me standing outside dressed in my toga her white face paled even more. I don't know what she thought. I smiled and called to her but she was already hurrying back into her house.

I picked up my own paper and read the headlines. Russia had just set off their third nuclear blast that month.

CHAPTER 2

The house was hot even in the early morning and I was a little light-headed from dehydration. I knew that the shabby little detective had been there but the memory was like my dream about Bruno's murder—not quite real.

The kids were still asleep in Jesus's room so I put on my

housecoat and took up the empty time with a book. I'd picked up *Huckleberry Finn* at a used-book store in Santa Monica. A few liberal libraries and the school system had wanted to ban the book because of the racist content. Liberal-minded whites and blacks wanted to erase racism from the world. I applauded the idea but my memory of Huckleberry wasn't one of racism. I remembered Jim and Huck as friends out on the river. I could have been either one of them.

Before I found a home in Houston I was a wild boy riding the rails. No mother, no father. Just enough clothes to keep me decent and ten cents less than I needed to survive.

I sat down next to the window and read under the soft light of morning. I entered another dream—of con men and criminals and ignorance too. Mr. Clemens knew that all men were ignorant and he wasn't afraid to say so.

After about a hundred pages I still hadn't got the urge to go burn books, so I went to the kitchen instead and started breakfast. Grits with eggs and bacon were on the bill of fare. Coffee for me. I knew that the odors would wake up Jesus and that he would get Feather out of the tiny cot at the foot of his bed. They'd be washed up and dressed just when the table was set.

It was a rhythm more satisfying than good music. I could have spent a whole life watching my children grow. Even though we didn't share common blood I loved them so much that it hurt sometimes.

I seemed to collect children in my line of work; doing *"favors"* for people. I took Jesus out of a life of child prostitution before he was three. I'd caught the murderer of Feather's white mother. It was Feather's grandfather, who had killed his own daughter for bearing a black child.

"Hi, Daddy!" Feather screamed. She was so excited to see me after all those hours asleep that she ran right for me, banging her nose against my knee. She started to cry and I picked her up. Jesus slipped into the room as silent as mist. He was small for fifteen, slight and surefooted. He was the star long-distance runner at Hamilton High School. He smiled at me, not saying a word.

Jesus hadn't said a thing in the thirteen years I'd known him. He wrote me notes sometimes. Usually about money he needed and events at school that I should attend. The doctors said that he was healthy, that he could talk if he wanted to. All I could do was wait.

Jesus took over the breakfast while I cooed to Feather and held her close.

"You hurt me," she whined.

"You want peanut butter or salami for lunch?" I answered.

Feather's skin was light brown and fleshy. Her stomach rumbled against my chest. I could see in her face that she didn't know whether to cry or run for the table.

"Lemme go! Lemme go!" she said, pushing at my arms to get down to her chair. The moment she was on her stack of phone books Jesus put a slice of bread covered with strawberry jam in front of her.

"I dreamed," Feather said, then she stared off into space lost for a moment. Her amber eyes and crinkled golden hair were both made almost transparent from the light through the kitchen window. "I dreamed, I dreamed," she continued. "There was a scary man in the house last night."

"What kind of man?"

She held out her hands and opened her eyes wide to say she didn't know. "I didn't see him. I just hearded him."

"What did he sound like?"

"He sounded like a crocodile in the Peter Pan book."

"Like a clock?"

Jesus rapped his knuckles on the table to sound like

Captain Hook's enemy. Feather laughed so hard that she dropped her jelly bread on the floor.

"Watch what the hell you doin'!" I yelled. Immediately I regretted it. Feather's face collapsed into terror and tears. Jesus crouched down as if he was about to take off. Maybe that's what he thought about when he was racing—escaping from evil men.

Feather's cry started low like the wail of an air-raid siren. I picked her up out of the chair and hugged her.

"I'm sorry, honey, but it's just so damn hot that I get mad sometimes when I shouldn't."

Her chin was still trembling. Jesus had another jelly bread on the table and he cleaned up the mess while I put Feather back in her chair.

"Daddy got a hot head," Feather said. Then she laughed.

I put together the lunch bags while the kids got on their shoes.

"I got to do something this mornin', Juice." Juice was the nickname the kids had given Jesus at school. Nobody except the Mexican kids felt comfortable calling somebody after the Lord.

"I want you to take Feather to school."

"Nooooo!" Feather cried. She loved to ride in my car.

Jesus nodded and looked as if he were about to say yes. But I knew that that was just another dream.

Hope is the harshest kind of dreaming.

I roughed up my son's hair and went into my room to dress for the day.

The house was the same. Large picture windows on either side of the front door. An old dog was sitting lazily on the front step. The last time I had been at Odell's house that dog was a puppy. Bougainvillea was planted along the fence and there were succulent shrubs instead of grass for lawn. Odell Jones didn't like to cut grass, so he never had it. There were tangelo trees rising up from the shrubs laden with fully formed fruit. The house had a deep stone porch with timbers for pillars.

The door was open and the screen shut. I could see the back of Odell's head as he was seated in a chair turned away from the door.

I knocked and said, "Hello? Odell? It's me—Easy."

Odell didn't move, at least not at first. After maybe thirty seconds he turned the page of his newspaper and continued reading.

"Easy?" a voice came from behind me.

Maude, Odell's wife, had been working in the garden somewhere out of sight. She wore a pink sun visor and carried a dirty trowel. Her mouth was smiling but her big eyes showed concern.

"Hi, Maude. I was knockin'."

"Odell in there but he can't hear too good lately," she lied. We both knew that he could hear me. It was just that Odell had cut his friendship off from me years ago after he'd done me a favor once.

I had wanted to get to somebody through Reverend Towne, the minister of First African Baptist Church. Odell made the introduction and Towne wound up dead—his pants down around his ankles and the corpse of one of his parishioners on her knees at his feet. Odell blamed me and I never argued with him. It was a tough life that we lived and I couldn't deny my own complicity with the pain.

"What can I do for you, Easy?"

"Why you send that man to my house?" I asked simply.

"What man?"

"Com'on, Maudria, don't play me."

Odell's wife had a large body with only tiny shoulders to hang it on. When she hunched those shoulders she looked a little like an overfed pink-eyed frog. "I don't know what you talkin' 'bout, Easy."

"Then I'm gonna stay knockin' at this here door till Odell tells me." I made like I was going to turn, but, as large as she was, Maude beat me to the door.

"Let him alone now, Easy. You know it hurts him enough that he cain't talk to you." She took me by the arm and pulled me down the front steps.

"I ain't never said he couldn't."

"I don't know what come between you two, Odell won't talk about it. But I told him that whatever it was happened, you two was friends and friends don't do like that."

I'd given up on talking to my old friend. At least before that morning.

"If he don't wanna talk, then why he send that man to me?"

"I told you, Easy. We didn't send no man."

"Yes you did," I said loud enough to be heard in the house.

I held out the picture Lynx had given me. "This picture was taken on Elba Thomas's front porch and Elba was Odell's girlfriend back then. And we both know that Betty's Odell's cousin."

Maude clasped her hands and begged without words.

"Maudria." Odell was at the screen. He stared straight at his wife and addressed her as if she were alone. "You come on in here and get my breakfast ready," he said. He was wearing a house robe on a Thursday morning. It dawned on me that he must have retired.

He turned his back and walked away into the house. Maude was drawn to him but I grabbed her arm.

"Talk to me, Maude, or I will be here all day long."

"I don't know hardly a thing," she said. And then, when I didn't let go, "This man Mr. Lynx come over yesterday and says that he's lookin' for Elizabeth."

"So she does live up here?"

Maude nodded. "Marlon had TB and they said that the

California climate would help. They come up before the war, before we did. But we hardly ever seen 'em. She worked for this rich white woman and didn't ever even tell Odell who she was or where she lived. If it wasn't for Marlon comin' by 'bout two weeks ago we woulda thought she was dead."

"What did Marlon come for?"

"He said that he was going to go away soon. That if Betty asked we should tell her that it was sudden but that he was okay and he'd get in touch."

"Why couldn't he tell her that himself?"

"I don't know." Ignorance was a virtue where Maude was weaned.

"What else did Marlon have to say?"

"Nuthin'. We just had some lemonade and talked. He said that he retired like 'Dell did."

"Retired from what?"

"He didn't say."

"What did Lynx want?"

"He said that Betty had left her job but that her boss wanted her back. He said that he'd pay fifty dollars for any information we had. Dell let him have that picture but he told him we didn't know where she was. Then that man Lynx said that was too bad because she would probably lose some kinda retirement from the rich family and how she was gettin' older an' that could hurt. Huh! He don't have to tell us about that. We could use that fifty dollars.

"That's when we said about you, Easy. I said that you knew Betty when you was a boy an' that you might be able t'find her because I heard you do that kinda thing sometimes. Odell give him your address. He had it from those Christmas cards you sent." Maude paused for the memory of my ten-cent cards. "It's nice 'bout how you was thinkin'a us, Easy. You know Odell always looked at your cards."

We were quiet for a few seconds then, thinking about a friendship gone by.

"Mr. Lynx said he wouldn't tell where he got your address and then he said thank you very much."

Maude was the kind of woman who took manners seriously.

"How did Lynx know to come to you?"

"Betty had give the people she work for our address—in case of emergency."

"Where did Marlon go when he left here?"

"I don't know," she said, making her impression of a frog again. "He was real nervous and jittery. He wanted Odell to lend him some money, but we just retired now," she apologized. " 'Dell ain't sick but he's weak-like. If I didn't go out and clean houses part-time we couldn't even make the tax on this house."

"So you say Marlon was sick?"

"Yes he is, but he ain't bad as Martin."

Just the mention of Martin's name hurt me. I had stayed away from him partly because I knew that he and Odell were good friends. Seeing Odell ignore me and Martin dying at the same time was too much for me to imagine.

"I heard about that," I said. "How's Martin doin'?"

"He hackin' an' coughin' an' he got a pain in his back so bad he ain't slep' in nine weeks. Doctor says that it's cancer but you know them doctors wrong half the time."

"I better get over there after I look for Betty," I said. "You know how I could find Marlon?"

"No, baby." She was looking back up at the door.

"He had a nickname, right?" I snapped my fingers trying to remember.

For the first time Maude showed me a friendly smile. "Bluto. They used to call him Bluto."

"From the Popeye cartoon?"

"Uh-uh. I mean, yeah, that was the name, but Marlon got

it because he used to wear them old alligator shoes he got from this white guy he did some work for. Marlon won a bet and got them shoes but the white man was so mad that he had to give'em up that he dyed'em blue before he let Marlon have'em." She even laughed! "But you know them was forty-dollar shoes and Marlon wore'em anyways. So they called him Blue Toes after that."

We both laughed and smiled. Where I had been holding Maude's wrist she twisted and took my hand.

"Don't you let nuthin' happen to Elizabeth now, Easy. Odell won't say it but I know he wants you to find her."

"What could happen?"

Maude stared dumbly up at me. Over her head I saw Odell standing silently at the door.

CHAPTER 3

One thing I knew about Marlon Eady was that he loved to gamble. Horses, numbers, or cards—it didn't make any difference to him. So I went out looking for him where people laid down bets.

There was a Safeway supermarket and a Thrifty's drugstore over off of Florence. Their parking lots were back to back. Not much business at ten in the morning. Two busboys were hustling wire grocery carts off of a truck that picked up strays around the neighborhood. The driver was seated sideways behind the wheel with his bear-sized legs and woolly head hanging out of the open door.

"Yeah," he was saying to the hardworking young men. "That yellah house on Sixty-second had fi'e wagons right up front. No tellin' what she got out behind. I told Mr. Moul that we better get some law out over to there or she gonna have his whole fleet."

The older man wore gray cotton pants and a stretch T-shirt of the same material and hue; a kind of makeshift uniform. I'd never seen him before. He looked old enough to be retired.

Retired. Back in 1961 that meant you worked "part-time" forty hours a week and paid your own insurance.

"I thought maybe you boys wanna show some initiative and go on out there with me," the bearish man was saying. "Shit! We come up wit' some extra carts an' Mr. Moul prob'ly give us a bonus."

"Three'a these is Vons," one of the young men said. He was light-colored and tall, muscular in his shoulders like a football player. "We gotta take 'em back there."

"Back?" The old man shook his head. His blubbery black cheeks were lightened by gray stubble. "Shit! I ain't goin' back nowhere. Let 'em go'n get they own carts. Shit! I wouldn't even spend a dime callin' nobody for no carts."

"Drop it, DJ," the other busboy said. His name was Spider. He was as dark as the old man but cut from a cat instead of a bear. His grin came off easy. I'm sure his father would have been upset to see Spider smoking a cigarette. Yes, Mr. Hoag would have come after his son, with a gun if he had to, to make sure that his boy grew up to be a right man.

But Mr. Hoag was in state prison for shooting his wife's lover, Sam Fixx, who was also said to be Spider's real father.

"Easy," Spider hailed. "How you doin'?"

The young man waved and grinned. He loafed over to where I was. The truck driver turned around quickly and revved his engine. After all, I might know the boss. The other busboy went into the store.

"Hey, Spider." I shook out a cigarette from my pack even though the boy was already smoking.

He took the offering and asked, "What's up?"

"You still takin' down numbers for Willie?"

Spider put the cigarette behind his ear and took a tiny diary from his shirt pocket.

"No, no," I said, looking around. Spider was seventeen. He wasn't worried about jail. "I wanna know if you know somebody."

"Who?"

"A man, older guy around fifty. His name is Marlon Eady but we used to call him Bluto."

That brought a grin to Spider's face. "Like the cartoon?"

"You know him?"

"Naw, Easy. Ain't never had no cartoons buy no numbers. Uh-uh."

The football player came out of the store followed by a tall white man in a bright blue suit. Probably the store manager.

"See ya later, Spider," I said. "You take care now."

He leaned over with his hand out, already a politician of the street. "I gots it covered."

If Spider was my son I would have slapped that cigarette and that grin away. I would have made him stand up straight instead of slouching like some gangster or pimp. But I didn't have the right to criticize. Spider was the natural product of the streets I lived in. He made up his own manhood and I had to respect that.

Jackson Blue's apartment was on the second floor of the Eighty-eight Building. There were only two floors. It was a long white stucco building that had walls you could scrape through with a tin spoon. I walked up the single flight of stairs and down the slender balcony to his door. I knocked loud and hard, don't ask me why, just mean I guess.

Jackson Blue had a brilliant mind, he might have been a genius, but he was cowardly and blustery to the core. If he could have put it in a jar, Jackson would have sold his soul for tonight's dinner or, even better, for fifteen minutes with a whore.

If there is a God he was drinking or mad the night he put Jackson together. Scrawny, lying, and afraid of his own footsteps, Jackson was one of the many friends who would never abandon me—he had nowhere else to go.

I was still banging on the door when it swung inward quickly.

"What the fuck you think you poundin' on, motherfucker?" The same God who made Jackson Blue took a crocodile to make the man I was facing. He was every bit as tall as me, over six foot in cotton socks, and bumpy. He had rough skin that shifted hue now and then over his corded bare chest. His muscles weren't big but his shoulders dropped in a boxer's stance and the damage that time had done to his face hadn't wiped the bitter dare from his lips.

"Jackson Blue here?" I gave just as mean as I got. One of the things the street teaches you is that if you bend over you're bound to get kicked.

"Who axin'?"

His eyes were swamp-colored. I could smell the ancient decay on his troglodyte breath.

" 'Sup, Ease?" Jackson came from behind my new friend. "You meet Ortiz?"

"You might say that."

"Come on in." Little Jackson pushed at the man called Ortiz, and to my surprise the croc gave five inches. Enough for me to get into the dark apartment and still keep my dignity.

The darkened room was foul with cigarettes, coffee, stale food, and the odor of two men who've been locked up in a cell for a month. Both of them were bare-chested with only loose trousers on. The band of Ortiz's boxer shorts rode out over his belt. He was watching me and I was trying to show that I didn't care.

But I did care. When I crossed the door into this man's domain my life was in danger. Jackson's new friend was a deadly force. I imagined that he ran a fever as a rule, and as he burned, he wanted everything else to wither with him.

"What you want, Easy?" Jackson was smiling and comfortable, more comfortable than I had ever seen him. He seated himself without offering me a chair. Ortiz slammed the door and then slumped up against the wall for his seat.

I'd heard that Jackson had gone into the bookie game. He got sent away to the county jail for selling stolen batteries out of the trunk of his car. On his release he went right into the horses. It surprised me, because there were some big men who didn't want competition with the game they already ran.

"Been a while, Blue," I said.

"What the fuck you want, man?" That was Ortiz acting up. He pushed himself away from the wall and put his right hand in his pocket.

"Relax," Jackson said in his high whiny voice. "Easy here is my friend. He all right." Jackson's grin showed a sense of power that all cowardly men yearn for. After a whole lifetime of running scared they can hardly wait to show off their strength when they get it.

"I thought you was a bookie," I said. "I guess I was wrong about that."

"Why you say that?"

"Well here you are, right?" I pointed at him in his chair. "I don't hear no phones ringin'."

Ortiz thought that was funny enough to get a cough.

When he took the hand out of his pocket I realized that I hadn't been breathing.

"They ringin' though, Easy," Jackson boasted. "They ringin'!"

I looked around the rank-smelling room. My gaze stopped at the TV tray in the center of the squat coffee table. There I saw a brass plate piled high with marijuana and a carton of stale onion rings showered in ashes. The decor didn't fit with the diamond ring on Jackson's pinky finger or the mink coat lying on the floor beside the couch.

"Don't look like no penthouse, Jackson."

"Cain't let'em know what you up to, Easy. I learnt that from you, brother. But we got it, man. We got it all right."

"Got what?"

Jackson went toward a door on the other side of Ortiz, but before he could get there his friend grabbed him by the arm.

"What you doin'?" the crocodile asked.

Jackson shook off the grip like a brave man and said, "It's okay. Easy family, man."

Jackson left for only a moment and then returned with a wooden box that was a dark reddish brown, made from telephone-pole wood. The box was a foot high and wide, and maybe three-quarters of that in depth. On one long side of the box there was a latch to secure a little door. Inside was a telephone receiver connected to a bunch of tiny blue and red electric wires, a dry cell battery, and one of those new transistorized tape recorders that they made in Japan. The whole thing looked professional, well made. Jackson's life was always a sloppy mess, but his work, when he cared to do it, was a dream.

"What's this?" I asked.

"Forget you!" That was Ortiz. If he and I were ever to find ourselves alone in a room there'd come a dead man soon after.

But Jackson ignored his friend. "This is my bookie box, Easy. Ortiz here used t'work for the phone company 'fore he got sent to jail. He give me some numbers. I give out one'a them numbers for this here box and put it up on the pole. Now my clients got this number and they calls it. All Ortiz gotta do is crawl up on the pole an' get the tape."

"What if they get yo' box? What if it breaks?"

"That shit ain't gonna break. I made it strong and put rubber in the cracks."

Jackson was smart enough to be the first man murdered on the moon.

"Ortiz here collect and I do the books. We gots twelve hundred reg'lars and a bankroll that'a choke a mule. An', man, you should see all the pussy we gets up here." Jackson held up his hands as if he were amazed by his own story. "I got me a brand-new red Caddy right downstairs."

"White boys ain't gonna like that, Jackson."

"How they gonna find me?"

"On a pickup."

Jackson's eyes darted toward Ortiz for a moment. A quick grin crossed his face, and suddenly I knew the whole story. Jackson never built anything that would last. He couldn't hold down a regular job. He never had a girlfriend for long. So he meets this crazy-in-a-rage man and comes up with a plan to take a thousand dollars a week. When the cops or the white mob catch on they grab Ortiz, maybe even kill him. Ortiz loves little Jackson. Jackson was probably the first man he met who was like him but didn't try to take something. Take something? Hell! Jackson was making him more money than he knew how to count. He'd die for Mr. Blue without ever giving him up. And then Jackson would move to another hole—not leaving even two dimes to mark his friend's eyes.

I wanted out of that room. I stood up so fast that Ortiz was taken off guard. He fumbled at his pocket.

"Take it easy, brother," I said. "I just gotta get outta here. I came 'cause I needed t'find somebody likes to gamble." As I said it I wondered if I was going to do to Betty what was certain to happen to this scaly fool.

"Who?" Jackson asked.

"His name is Marlon Eady but the street calls him Bluto. Bluto." I said it twice just to be sure that I wasn't dreaming.

Jackson got a cagey look about him. "What you want him for?"

"Don't fuck wit' me, Jackson," I said. "Either you know or you don't. Either you gonna tell me or you ain't. So let's get down to it, 'cause I got places to be."

I was getting tired of Ortiz, all stiff with his hand on his pocket. Jackson was scared. He never liked it when I got mean. He had the coward's sense of survival.

"Never heard of him," he said. "But I could look around."

"Yah," I said. "Maybe you should."

CHAPTER 4

You could tell by some people's houses that they came to L.A. to live out their dreams. Home is not a place to dream. At home you had to do like your father did and your mother. Home meant that everybody already knew what you could do and if you did the slightest little thing different they'd laugh you right down into a hole. You lived in that hole. Festered in it. After a while you either accepted your hole or you got out of it.

There were all kinds of ways out. You could get married,

get drunk, get next to somebody's wife. You could take a shotgun and eat it for a midnight snack.

Or you could move to California.

In California they wouldn't laugh at you, or anybody. In California the sun shone three hundred and more days in the year. In California you could work until you dropped. And when you got up there was another job waiting for you.

In California you could paint the slats of your house like a rainbow and put a smiling face on your front door. You could have a caged rabbit and chickens right out in the yard and big granite animals for children to climb on. You could, like Georgette Harris, put a sign on your wire gate saying "Little Animals Nursery School and Day Care." Nobody cared. Nobody asked you, "What makes you a schoolteacher?" They'd just take you at your word. And if the law came down and asked for some papers you'd just move a mile or so further on, hang up the same sign, and collect children like a crow taking in glass.

Georgette was sitting on her front porch smiling down at her family of kids. Next to her on a slender black table sat a telephone that led from the house on a long, knotted cord.

Little black boys and girls, a dozen of them, ran ragged in their dusty pen. There was a rubber pool that overflowed with six children and about a cupful of urine-laced, tepid water. Everybody was screaming for joy. That's what children do—they scream because life is just too much for them but they don't know it yet.

When I walked into the yard everything went quiet. The kids all stopped and stared at me. Crusty-nosed boys and girls with their short skirts turned up over their underwear. A couple of them were bleeding from fresh scrapes on their knees. All those little bright eyes on me were just waiting to get back to the business of noise. Not one of them looked hungry or tired. And I'm willing to bet that they all would look back to the days of Mrs. Harris's yard with the greatest pleasure. Running wild with the animals before the hunters started tracking them down.

"Easy," Georgette called.

I said hello back but I'm sure she didn't hear me. The children took her greeting to me as a sign that they could go back to calling up the dead.

I made it up to the porch and nodded. There was no extra chair up there so I leaned against a porch beam.

"What you want, honey?" she asked me.

I didn't really know Georgette. She lived in my old neighborhood, down near Watts. But I had moved away from there, with Jesus and Feather, to West Los Angeles.

I decided on a new neighborhood soon after my wife left me. My old friend Primo and his family took my old house over. And I took my kids to an anonymous place where people didn't know me; where no one asked painful questions about my wife and daughter; where no one knew enough about me to question my legal guardianship of Jesus and Feather. The only agreement between us was love and mutual need—not the kind of agreement they like in courts.

So I left Watts. At first I'd bought a house in a middle-class black neighborhood. But then my money problems forced me to sell and rent the place on Genesee.

Georgette lived on McKinley between Eightieth and Eighty-first. The nursery school had been her dream ever since she was a little girl in Minnesota.

You had to have a better education than Georgette was ever likely to get to have that kind of school, so she came to L.A. She took in the children of a man I knew and sometimes I'd pick up one of his boys to play with Feather.

Georgette had her dream, but as so often happens, her dream didn't pay the bills.

The big black telephone barked and Georgette was quick to snatch it up.

"Animals," she said. Then, cupping her hand over the mouthpiece, she shouted, "Leo, get outta that dirt, boy!

"What's that?" she asked into the phone. Then she wrote something down on a sheet of paper that she kept on a clipboard in her lap, and hung up.

"Yes, Easy?"

I was stumped. It seemed to me almost crazy that I was standing there among all those wild shrieks, next to this placid bookie. It didn't make any sense. I actually forgot what I was there for.

"Um," I mumbled. "You, uh, you been doin' okay?"

"Yes?" Georgette wondered what I wanted.

"I, uh, um, ah," I faltered, then I laughed and sat down on the stairs like I was one of her charges. "I'm sorry, Georgette. You know, I got outta bed at five and I been all over town since then. I seen people don't even want me in their house. I been with bad men and gamblers and . . ." I remembered what I had to ask. "And seein' all these beautiful babies you got here just didn't fit."

Georgette smiled. If you said something about her kids she was happy. California worked for some people.

"I'm lookin' for a guy called Bluto," I said. The slant of the sun was coming right down at my eye because there were few trees landscaped in Georgette's neighborhood.

Georgette shook her head. It didn't surprise me. Maybe Marlon had gotten tired of throwing his money away.

"What's his real name?" she asked.

"Marlon," I said. "Marlon Eady."

"Oooooh, you mean Ed Sullivan."

"You know'im?"

"Oh yeah, I know Marlon. We ain't never called him no Bluto. He had some kinda accident that got the bones in his neck fused. I think he said that it was a cop beatin' him that did it. They called him No-Neck at first and then, after that show started, they called him Ed Sullivan. He really kinda looked like him. Yeah, baby, he been puttin' down bets with me since 1946. Mmm-hm. Marlon give the spread mo' money than any other po' soul out here." Georgette looked out over her children as if they were the ones who called in their bets. Who knows? Maybe they would all grow up calling their old nanny to put two dollars on some nag's nose.

"You know his sister?"

"Betty?" Georgette got wistful. "All I know is that Marlon's sun rise and set on that girl. You get him talkin' 'bout his sister an' he could go on for days."

"You know her?"

"Uh-uh. Marlon said that she lived at some rich people's house up in them canyons somewhere. She stayed up there all the time."

"You know where I could find him?"

"No, baby. He was workin' doin' civilian work at the navy yards down in San Diego for a while but he got sick. He had somethin' wit' his lungs and the work just got too much. He moved out in the desert. I don't know where." But there was a thought brewing at the back of the schoolteacher's brain. I waited to hear its conclusion.

"Yeah," she said. "Yeah, that's right. . . . Linda! You get up offa Darleen! She done told you she don't wanna play!" Georgette stared at a little girl who was standing astride her prone playmate.

When the girl moved off, Georgette, still staring hard, said, "Marlon was bettin' pretty thick wit' Terry Tyler there for a while not too long ago. Terry used to stay here wit' me when he was a baby."

"That's the boxer Terry T?"

"Mmm-hm. That's him."

"You know where I could find Terry?"

"No. Uh-uh. I don't go to the fights. An' his parents both done passed away. But you know Marlon was like Terry's godfather. He used to always be takin' him around. Half the time he'd come over to my old house to pick him up."

I didn't want to move. If Georgette had offered me a glass of milk and a graham cracker I would have toddled off to her living room and napped the afternoon by.

But I was a grown man. No more sweet cookies and sweet dreams for me.

"You take care now," I said, pulling myself up to a standing position. A small boy wearing tiny little overalls and no shirt stared at me. He was two and a half feet tall and I was a giant. I relished the moment of his gaping awe. I wasn't going to be that powerful in the world that waited for me.

CHAPTER 5

I drove down Manchester to La Cienega, then up La Cienega to Venice Boulevard. When I got to Robertson I went northward. I cruised up past Jesus's high school toward Airdrome and the small branch of the L.A. library there.

It was a solitary library, barely used on weekdays. Miss Eto was the librarian. She'd been living in the wine country up north when her family was relocated to a concentration camp during World War Two. Her parents both died while detained. Miss Eto came down to work in L.A. after the war. She was a pleasant woman. I'd helped her out once when a man, Charles Emory, kept coming around the library and bothering her.

One day when I was there to pick up Jesus I noticed that she was upset. I asked her what was wrong, and she told me that a man had been bothering her. I don't think she would have mentioned it except that Emory had just been there and she had the feeling that Jesus was in danger too.

Emory would come around when the library was almost empty and whisper about things he had done to Japanese women and children during the war.

"Why don't you go to the cops?" I asked her.

"Oh, no," she said. "Never go to the police."

Maybe that's why I helped her.

I hung around the library for a few days until Emory came back. He was a short and pudgy white man sporting brand-new jeans, turned up a full six inches at the cuff, and a white shirt. His face was flaccid and mean.

I followed Emory out to a small house on Venice just a little west of National. When I was sure that the house was his I called an acquaintance named Alamo Weir. Alamo was a scrawny, beat-up old white man who had saved my life once when I was in jail on false charges. Because he'd saved me I threw work his way now and again.

As I got to know L.A. over the years I found myself roaming outside my native black community, a community that had been transplanted from southern Texas and Louisiana. When I had to work in the white world, Alamo was the perfect tool. He was crazy and naturally criminal. He would have hated Negroes if it wasn't for World War One. He felt that all those white generals and politicians had set up the poor white trash the same way black folks were set up.

He was right.

I told Alamo to check Emory out and I spent all of my extra time hanging around the library.

I thought that we were going to have to try to scare Emory. I didn't like the idea, because that kind of thing can backfire. But as it turned out we had a better bet.

It only took about a week. Emory had been in the army

and now he was dealing in stolen arms. He was moving M1 rifles and handguns through his garage.

Alamo bought Emory some drinks at a bar the white man frequented, and before you know it Alamo was buying U.S. issue for seventy-five dollars a weapon. I made a call to a man I didn't like in Washington, D.C. He gave me twenty-five hundred dollars through his agents in L.A. and I gave him Emory's address.

It made the papers. Senior Agent Craxton of the FBI announced the predawn raid on the house.

The day before the raid I told Miss Eto that she didn't have to worry about being bothered anymore. The next morning I showed her the article in the library's copy of the *Examiner.*

"That's your boy," I said.

Ever since that day I had a friend in the library. Anything I wanted to know, any little piece of information at all. Miss Eto loved me. She loved me in a way that wasn't American at all. If I had fallen and broken my back, little Miss Eto would have fed me with a spoon in her own house for fifty years.

"Does Mr. Eady have a phone?" Miss Eto asked me.

"Maybe so, but you know, I kinda doubt it. Marlon always lived close to the bone. It used to be a coin toss if he could pay the rent."

"How about some job? Who did he work for?"

"That's what I was thinkin' too," I said. "I heard he did civilian work for the navy yards down in San Diego. He quit because of his lungs."

"You just sit," she told me. "Read something."

I tried to make like I could help her but she wouldn't hear of it. So I sat at one of the long tables and put my head down on folded arms.

For a long time I just sat there, enjoying my eyes being

closed. But after a while I fell into a kind of half-sleep. There was Bruno again, laid up in his pine-veneered press-board coffin; innocent, with all the swagger gone. His face and crossed hands were waxy, like artificial fruit. I stood behind his sisters, five of them, all in black and crying over the only son born to their parents. They swayed back and forth with their knees so weak I was afraid they'd fall.

I couldn't bear their grief.

The sounds of women crying followed me down into sleep. It was like being lowered into the grave myself. Darker and darker. The crying turned into shouts and suddenly I knew that it was me yelling, "Don't put me down there with him! Let me up!"

"Mr. Rawlins." A little mouse was eating at my fingers. "Mr. Rawlins?"

When I opened my eyes I saw Miss Eto pushing a scrap of paper at me.

"I got it." She was smiling. I smiled too because she had saved me from the dream.

"He lives in Mecca," she said.

"Where?"

"Mecca. It's out around Joshua Tree National Monument. I don't know if he lives in the town. I don't think so. His address is RFD."

"How'd you get it?"

"I called the navy in San Diego and told them that our letters come back from down there. I said that we needed to write to him. Then they said that if he quit because of medical problems maybe I could get the information from Washington or from the insurance company they use—Patriot Trust in San Diego." She smiled. "I knew that with Washington you have to work through the mail. But I talked to a nice lady at Patriot."

"Mm," I said like a barroom intellectual. "Thanks, Miss Eto." I had the strange urge to kiss the tiny woman. Maybe she even leaned toward me a shade. But kissing wasn't in the program between us. I shook her hand, gave her a quick military nod, and marched out of there.

There was still space in southern California in those days. The desert was an old place inhabited by people who were original Californians. Desert men and women in pickup trucks stopping at diners that had bottomless cups of coffee for a nickel, or at the occasional oasis where piped-in water fed date palms and lush flowering cacti. Railroad tracks ran along the side of the flimsy ribbon of a highway and the trains went so fast that they seemed to come barreling out of nowhere and then, just as fast, they were gone.

Civilization was scant out there. You drove for hours seeing nobody and nothing. The air was thin and the only water for miles around was in the three glass jugs on the seat next to me in the car. I refilled all three in Mecca's sole gas station.

The postal clerk didn't know where Marlon lived but she said that he got his mail at a general store about forty miles away.

"He told me once," the jowly white woman said, "that he just had one'a them tar shacks. You mostly got yer tar shacks up to the north. You could just take the road out that way and ask at the crossroads store. That's where he picks up his mail. I bet they know right where Mr. Eady lives. An' if'n they don't you could just suck down sodas and camp out a couple'a days—he's bound to show up sooner or later."

She wasn't joking.

On either side of the road there was nothing for as far as I could see. The nothingness ended in lifeless hills. I had both of the windows open and was through my water supply before I was half the way there. The radio said that it was one hundred and sixteen degrees. My light green pants had turned dark green with sweat. The desert is like the worst felon in San Quentin. It's a senseless killer barren of any sign of intelligence.

But the desert is also beautiful. It's hard to tell at first sight. It stays in the range of the lighter shades. Buff and yellow and gray like a clear sky a minute after sunset. Most life forms are small and hard out there. Tiny little bugs with long legs to keep them off the hot sod or with giant gaudy red claws to fight off a world far larger than them. Once every four or five years it rains enough for little puddles to form. In the mud hump-backed crustacean shrimp, who had reached the end of their evolutionary trek before the first dinosaurs appeared, hatch from pebble-hard eggs. They mate and die quickly. A week later desert blossoms, so tiny that you have to get on your knees to see them, break out everywhere. They're bright and strawlike; dry and rough because the desert will suck any moisture right away like some insane god pulling the souls out of his children before they've had the chance to live.

I reached the general store and gas station after thirty-seven miles. The weathered wood walls of the structure didn't stand up straight anymore. Instead they leaned inward around a once flat tin roof that had buckled and now looked like a wave threatening to roll right down the front of the store.

The only sign was a round Coca-Cola poster that, once red, had bleached out into a weak pink color. The gas pump next to the front door looked like something out of a 1930s movie.

I stopped and got out, waiting for the attendant to come running from inside.

Nobody came.

There was no shade on that side of the building. I hoped

that there was air conditioning inside the ramshackle house. A fan maybe, or just one of those Coke machines.

I stopped at the door. Maybe this wasn't even a store at all. The sign and the gas pump were old. There was no other outward indication of a working business. Maybe this was just someone's house with just a few leftovers from the old store.

I looked out over the horizon. There wasn't another structure in sight. So I rapped my knuckles on the front door. It was fabricated from many layers of wood. So many layers that I couldn't get a sure knock. The sound I did make was nothing more than the rustling of kisses in a close hallway at night.

"Yeah," he said from inside. "Come on in."

The voice sounded relaxed, so I wasn't surprised to see the man reclined on a sofa chair in the middle of what looked like a parlor. A refrigerator hummed happily in a corner of the shapeless room. There were open shelves that ran along the uneven walls. On the shelves were dry goods and some bottles and cans. It might have been a store and then again it could have been a careless man's home. There was an electric fan blowing over him. He wore only boxer shorts, a T-shirt, and a ruffled fisherman's cap. He was long and skinny but not too tall. When he saw me he got immediately up. At the back of the room was a large podium-like piece of furniture. It wasn't until he was behind this whitewashed stand that he said, "Can I help you?"

I froze dead in my tracks. I was sure that he had a handgun or worse back there and I didn't want to make any move to cause him to use it.

"Afternoon," I said in a voice far too happy for the heat.

"What can I do ya for?" He even smiled at me. I was more afraid of his robin's-egg eyes than I was of the gun I suspected.

"All I want is about a dozen'a them Cokes you got," I said, hearing the scared voice of a small homeless boy in my throat. "And some directions."

"Three to a customer," he answered. He nodded toward the small box refrigerator. We both knew that he wasn't going to move.

I walked over to the box and lifted the lid. As nervous as I was, I enjoyed the cold coming out at me. I lingered, taking the Cokes out from between homemade ham sandwiches and an old-time bottle of gin that was stoppered with a cork.

"What kinda directions you need, son?"

He was from the south. If I hadn't been able to tell by his accent I sure could have from the liberties he took with my age. But I had to remember—I was out in the middle of nowhere, a black spot against a white backdrop. Even if I could have moved quickly enough to keep from being shot, what was the value of killing a white man for belittling me? I'd killed white men before in my life and that hadn't changed a thing.

But still, I hated him. I even hated the air because it reeked of his sweat.

"Marlon Eady," I said through tight lips.

"The nigger?" The crooked grin made his leathery gaunt face into a kind of evil crescent.

I'd been out of the south for too long. The hate for this man must have shown from deep down where we all learned as children to keep it hidden.

"Oh." The sparse beard and mustache bristled around his mock smile like brier thorns. "Don't get me wrong, son. We all call him that around here—he likes it. They call me Dickhead. Now wouldn't you druther be called Nigger than Dickhead?"

It was the heat; that's what made me a fool.

If I had thought about moving he would have had the

time to shoot me. But I didn't think. I ran right at him, turning over the podium and wresting a sawed-off double-barreled shotgun from his grip. He fell back against a peg-board and down into a variety of hand drills, screwdrivers, and hammers that hung there.

"What the hell?" Dickhead tried to get up, but I put my foot in his chest and pressed until he gave.

"Stay down, brother," I said as if I were talking to somebody from my part of town. "And tell me where I can find Mr. Marlon Eady."

"You in trouble, boy," Dickhead informed me. And for all that I was on top right then I felt a thrill of fear down through my testicles.

I swung the barrel of the sawed-off toward his head, firing one round at the end of the arc. A hole the size of a shotput appeared in the floor next to Dickhead's shocked face. He shouted and tried to jump up, clapping his hands over his ears. I flipped the gun around and slammed the heavy butt into his cheekbone. Luckily he had the good sense to fall down and be still, because if he had stayed trying to get up I would have hit him again.

"Stay down!"

Dickhead cringed. Saliva and blood came from his mouth, mucus poured out of his nostrils, and baby tears welled in his eyes. But I didn't enjoy it. One of the problems with so many oppressed people is that they don't have the stomach to give what they get. I hurt that simple white man because I was scared of him. If he'd called me boy or nigger one more time I might have started gibbering myself.

"Just tell me where I could find Marlon Eady and I'll leave you be." My tongue was reverting back to southern ways. This man had defeated me and didn't even know it.

All he could do was shiver and nod on the floor.

I went over to the refrigerator and got the bottle of gin. I pulled out the cork and handed it to him.

"Drink it."

He poured the stuff at his mouth but most of it just dribbled down his face.

"Do it again."

The second drink was better. He probably thought it was his last. He sobered up a little and sniffed back the snot in his nose.

"Tell me where I could find Marlon Eady."

"The road don't have a name," he whined. "But it's the third one on your left about six miles back the way you come."

"Gimme the shells for this thing," I said. And when the fear came back into his eyes, "I'm just takin' 'em with me."

He led me to a small room behind where the podium lay. It was a closet with a shelf that he used for his kitchen. On it sat a toaster, a two-burner hot plate, and a slice of white bread that had curled into a hard chip in the heat. Behind the toaster was a partly full box of twelve-gauge shells.

He handed them to me.

"Why you pull that gun on me, fool?" I was shaking with rage at this man who had come close to making me murder him. I was so mad that I had to take my finger from the live trigger. "You pull a gun on everybody come in your store?"

"I thought you wanted to rob me."

"Rob you? Rob what?" I yelled.

I swung the barrel over his head in frustration. Dickhead ducked down low.

I took him outside, pushing and shaking him from behind so that he wouldn't have the time to note my license plate. I made him get on his knees while I took off the rear plate. Behind his store there was an old Studebaker station wagon, painted yellow like a taxi. The key was right in the ignition. I took the key, the distributor cap head, the battery, and the steering wheel and made Dickhead put them all in my trunk. Back in his house I tore the phone out of the wall and brought it out to my car.

"You can't leave me out here with no car and no way to call," he wailed.

"I'm gonna go out to where you said Marlon's place was, and if his house is there I'll leave your stuff at the turnoff you gave me. Now sit'own an' wait till I'm gone."

We were both happy that I didn't have to kill him.

CHAPTER 6

As soon as the little store was out of the range of the rear-view mirror I thought, "Suppose one of his friends or a customer drives by when he's trying to get down to the turnoff?" And "What if he had a pistol hidden in there and he lays at the road for me?"

But then I put my fears away. Sure, something like that might happen, but there was nothing I could do about it. I had a shotgun and thirteen cartridges. I was ready to die if that was the way it had to be.

Poor men are always ready to die. We always expect that there's somebody out there who wants to kill us. That's why I never questioned that a white man would pull out his gun when he saw a Negro coming. That's just the way it is in America.

The third turnoff went on for miles. On either side of the road were great stands of cactus that seemed to quiver with the desire to stab. Every once in a while a pile of stones loomed off the road. These piles were up to twenty-five feet high and didn't seem to follow any logic in the plan of the desert. Just a stack of stones that might have made a halfway decent shelter against the hard sun. But nobody put them there.

Nobody put me there either.

The shack was tar paper and chicken wire tightly wrapped around a box frame that stood away from the ground on stumpy cement blocks. There was one big step up and the door didn't even have a knob. Instead it sported a brass handle like you'd put on a kitchen cabinet.

First I tried knocking on the plasterboard door, but that didn't make much more noise than rapping on sponge. The window was too high, so finally I banged on the wall and called out, "Marlon! Marlon Eady!"

No answer. As a matter of fact there wasn't any sound at all. The afternoon desert was so quiet that I could hear the blood pumping in my ears. Sweat trickled down my chest and legs. My head hurt and I felt light-headed from the heat. Somewhere out behind me was a crazy white man maybe on my trail.

I walked into Marlon's house cursing myself for a fool.

It was a neat little place. Nothing fancy. The uncured wood floor was clean and well-swept, which is saying something in the desert, where sand and grit find a way in everywhere.

The chairs were wooden crates, the bed was just a mattress on the floor. On a cardboard box next to the bed was a bell-topped alarm clock that had run down at ten-thirteen—no telling whether it was morning or night. There was also a picture of Betty. A more recent portrait in a smart flowery dress sitting in a photographer's modeling chair. It was in a gilded stand-up oval frame. I put that in my pocket and looked around a little more.

He used a big copper bowl for a sink. No running water

at all. I figured that the water had been standing in that bowl for more than two days because of the dozen or so crickets and desert beetles who'd drowned themselves in it.

Across the room from the bed was the only real furniture. A maple-stained cedar chest of drawers that sported a four-foot mirror of real glass on top. Next to that was a metal rack from which hung Marlon's clothes. He might have fallen on hard times but he still had nice clothes. A dozen suits of every hue. Gabardine, straight wool, sharkskin, and silk. There were only two cotton suits designed for the desert heat. He had seven hats suspended from hooks that were jabbed into the tar-paper wall.

In the chest I found silk handkerchiefs, silk undershirts, and even silk underpants. There was one small drawer with only jewelry in it: ruby cufflinks, a gold ring decorated with five diamond chips, a silver money clip with a roll of two-dollar bills (each one with a corner torn off to avoid bad luck) in its clasp, and various overlarge belt buckles as a Texan is liable to have.

There were sweaters and socks and a stack of magazines that exhibited scantily clad black models in blurred black-and-white photographs.

Under these I found a stack of letters, but none of them were from Betty. I was almost sick from the heat in that house. Marlon had probably left because of the heat. It was too hot for anybody out there.

But I didn't come all that way for nothing.

There was a pair of pants on the floor next to the cardboard box. Work pants. The kind of threadbare trousers you wore around the house. At first I thought that Marlon had left them when he'd dressed up to leave. But his wallet was in the back pocket. He didn't have much cash. Just eight dollars and three nickels in the change pouch. But he made up for that with a personal check for five thousand dollars made out to him—not the kind of thing I'd leave just lying around.

Outside again I went to look around back.

There was a tin outhouse behind the shack. When I pulled open the door a pack of leaping mice came racing out around and between my feet, followed by the foul smell of rotted human waste. The toilet seat was an aluminum funnel that thickened toward the rim so as to provide a seat.

I had no desire to sit there. Not only did a terrible smell come out from the hole but the commode was fouled with dark black drippings that had flowed both in and out of the bowl.

I noticed that the black dollops were all over the room, dried by the sun beaming down into the roofless toilet. In one corner, behind the funnel, was a thick glop of the stuff festooned with a white boil.

I sank to my knees then. If someone had seen me I would have told them that it was to get a closer look at that white pustule. But the truth was closer to the fact that I had just realized the depth of my troubles.

With my pocket knife and handkerchief I teased the tooth out of its cake of dry blood. A full molar with long, hungry-looking roots. It could have been used for a dentist's display. It was so perfect that you would have thought it was plastic. But who would put a plastic tooth in a pool of blood under their toilet?

Nobody was waiting for me at the turnoff. I stopped there long enough to put Dickhead's auto parts and phone out in the road. I kept the sawed-off along with a few of Marlon's personal items: his letters, his wallet, and a magazine with the blurred photographs of naked black women.

CHAPTER 7

It was late by the time I'd made it back home. Almost seven. The sun was throwing its last long shadows across the city. I pulled up into the driveway but before I got past the front lawn a man ran out in front of the car. I hit the brake and cursed.

He was a tall white man with long black hair generously streaked in gray. He had a thick black mustache that was a triplet brother to the hair over each of his eyes.

Roger "Lucky" Horn was a retired air force officer. He'd run the PX at Norton Air Force Base for fourteen years. Before that he flew supplies in behind enemy lines to the partisans for most of World War Two.

Lucky was from California originally. His wife, April, and he had been high school sweethearts in Santa Barbara. They married a week before Black Friday and the beginning of the Great Depression.

Lucky had deep-set eyes that were dark and dull; impenetrable, like a religious zealot's. I never heard him badmouth anybody and he held an open invitation for me and the kids to go with them to their church on Olympic Boulevard any Sunday. April baked sweets for Feather and Jesus at least once a week, and her back door was always open for a bruised knee or for lemonade and a few moments' rest.

When I was away the Horns looked out for the kids. They were real people and so I rarely thought about them being white.

"Don't go back there, Easy," he said in my window.

"Why not?"

"Come on over in my backyard and I'll show you."

I didn't want to go anywhere, but we were friends and

neighbors. So I followed the stooped ex-pilot down the long driveway to his backyard. Every once in a while he'd turn to me and put his finger to his lips.

Instead of a fence separating our properties there were planted all kinds of trees and shrubbery. Jacaranda, kumquat, magnolia, and trimmed bamboo made our borderline. Ferns and honeysuckle closed up any gaps that might allow you to see from one yard to the other. I kept my side of the yard cut back and trim. I liked the sun shining down on us. But Lucky let the trees hang over the driveway so that you had the feeling that you were entering a jungle path, some dark tunnel into another time.

Mrs. Horn was standing next to the wall of leaves in the backyard. She was very excited, almost jumping up and down, batting a finger against her lips so that I wouldn't make a mistake and break out into a rendition of "What'd I Say?"

Solemnly Lucky brushed his bony wife aside. Then he carefully parted the wall of ferns and gestured with his head for me to look through the hole.

As tired as I was, I had to smile when I gazed out into my own yard. It was an open plot of grass surrounded by bushes that sported large mottled red-and-yellow roses. It was a picture-perfect yard in my opinion, but that's not what made me smile. Jesus and Feather were there. They both had on swimming trunks and were reclining on a big cardboard box that they'd flattened for a sun blanket. Near them the green water hose sputtered, the nozzle turned closed with the water still on. Whenever I was late and Feather started to get scared that I'd never come home again, Juice would do something like let her play in the water.

Juice had his hands behind his head with his eyes closed. Feather copied his pose but I couldn't tell about her eyes, because she wore a pair of Snow White black-lensed glasses we'd brought home from Disneyland.

I made up my mind to be a better father to them. What was I doing way out in the desert dueling with some strange white man? I was all they had, and here I was squandering my time on needless danger when they were so beautiful right there in our own paradise.

I made to turn away. I was going to go home and hug those children, call Mr. L-Y-N-X, send him his money, and go out looking for a regular job that would have me living right.

But before I could turn, Lucky held out a hand for me to keep on watching. And as if he had magic in his hands, it happened.

"How high is the sun up in the sky, Juice?" Feather asked. And when the mute boy didn't respond she insisted, "Huh?"

"I don't know. But it's real high, all right. I bet you wouldn't want to fall down from way up there."

"No sir!" Feather shook her head so hard that the little sunglasses went askew on her head. She was so beautiful that I almost forgot that Jesus had talked.

Jesus reached over and tickled Feather under her arm. She squealed and squirmed. "Stop! Stop!"

"I got you!" He laughed with her. "I got you!"

It was the only time I ever cried from being happy. I staggered away from the wall, and Lucky caught me around the chest, afraid that I might fall I guess. And maybe I would have fallen. I could have let go of myself, because I didn't believe in the laws of nature right then. Gravity might have let me loose, let me soar up over my house.

"He talked," April whispered in my ear.

And I didn't feel like she was some kind of fool telling me

what I already knew. She could have said it a thousand times.

I went into the house after that and started dinner. I wanted to run right out in the yard and ask Jesus to say something, but I controlled myself. About ten minutes later Feather came in shouting, "Daddy! Daddy home, Juice!"

She came running in the back door and right into my leg, hugging me and grinning with the kind of love only children can feel. I tousled her light walnut hair and thought for a moment about the daughter that I had somewhere down in Mississippi. The daughter I'd lost.

My wife Regina took Edna, our only daughter, and went down to Mississippi. Sometimes I thought of how Edna was calling my onetime friend Dupree Bouchard her daddy. When I thought about it too long I began to understand how some men say that they were driven to murder.

Jesus came in a minute after Feather. He looked at me, and my heart skipped with anticipation. Then he walked over to us and hugged me. He looked up into my eyes and smiled the same silent greeting he'd given me for years.

"Hold on!" I shouted and turned away to the stove as if my oil were burning in the skillet. Maybe I should have let him see me cry—but men didn't cry where I survived childhood.

I made hamburgers and an avocado salad with tomatoes, onion, and minced garlic for dinner. The kids ate up every bite and sent me back to the kitchen to make more.

Feather told me all about her day at school. How she got mad at some little boy for not liking her and how they saw big hairy elephants in a book and then they made one.

Jesus nodded, smiled, and hunched his shoulders to answer my questions. He'd won the meet that Hamilton High had against Dorsey; was the only runner from Hami to take first place.

I spent many long and tense hours talking to the boy's vice principal about Juice before he got into running. Other boys would make fun of him because he was Mexican and silent and small. But in spite of his size, Jesus was completely fearless. He'd never stop fighting until his opponent quit. And he wasn't afraid to bleed or face more than one in a fight.

They wanted to put him in a correctional high school, but I said no. I was prepared to keep him home rather than let them make him into some kind of delinquent.

But then Coach Mark had him run the mile one day—and that was it for correctional school. Hamilton had a star, and they made sure the other boys left him alone.

He was my son. A son of preference. We weren't blood, but he wanted to live with me and I wanted to have him—how many fathers and sons can say that?

But still I was hurt that he wouldn't talk to me.

"Feather?"

"Huh?" she answered. Jesus had already gone up to bed, tired from his long-distance race.

Feather and I were on the couch in the TV den watching Dobie Gillis. She loved Maynard G. Krebs, and I liked how the father was such a cheapskate about what went on in his store. He knew that no matter how much somebody wants to make something in this world there's always somebody else who wants to take it away.

"Why won't Juice talk to me?" I asked.

"He talk to you, Daddy. He just don't say something."

"But why won't he say something?"

"Because," she said. And then Maynard came on the screen. Somebody said the word "work" and he was having a conniption fit. I had to wait for a commercial until I could ask her again.

"So, Feather?"

"Um?"

"Why won't Juice talk to me?"

"Because he don't like you to talk to, Daddy," she said as simply and easily as you please. "But that's okay because he love you too."

"But I'm sad that he won't say anything to me." Somewhere I knew that I had crossed a line, that I was asking my little girl to be older than she was. But I wanted so much for Jesus to talk to me. He'd been abused as a child, as a baby, and I didn't want the evil to have won and taken his words from me.

Feather put her hand over my thumb, causing me to look down at her.

"That's okay, Daddy," she said. "But he can't right now."

I heard my own words from her lips. Then she stood up and put her arms around my head and held me like I had held her a thousand times when she was crying and sad.

"It's time for bed," I told her, just to get some kind of control back in my life.

On the coffee table in front of me lay an old photograph and a newer one, a bus schedule, a bloody molar tooth, and a check for five thousand dollars written out by Sarah Clarice Cain of Beverly Hills. According to the date on the check she had written it two and a half weeks before.

I didn't have to do a thing. I didn't have any contracts with anyone. I hadn't been convicted of any crime.

That's when Martin Smith came back to me. His peanut head and his big hands that seemed to have too much flesh around the fingers. If it hadn't been for Martin and Odell I would have died when I was a boy. They had taken me into their homes and fed me when there was nothing but cold and hunger outside.

I knew that I had to go visit Martin before he died. I *did* have to do that.

So I decided to go see Martin—right after I took care of the things on my table.

CHAPTER 8

I awoke in a cold sweat. Bruno had been laid up against the butcher's door with his eyes open. He wanted me to help him but I couldn't; I couldn't leave the shelter of the doorway. He was muttering my name under his ragged breath. His dying was more important than any other death I'd known. But I couldn't go out there and face Mouse though. I couldn't.

I dropped Feather off at her school on Burnside and then headed south. I was upset about my dream and the job I had to perform in the late morning, so I decided to take care of some business first. I thought that if I could get some money I wouldn't have to find the owner of that tooth.

Down near Crenshaw and Santa Barbara I came to a little prefabricated building that had a large sign set up on the roof. The sign was twelve feet high and forty feet across, as if designed for a much larger building. It had a big yellow background covered with giant red letters that spelled out ESQUIRE REALITY INC.

The inner office was no more than a room with four tan metal desks on a concrete floor. The desks were arranged in a diamond—one at the center of each wall. Renee Stewart sat at the desk that faced the front door. Her sister, Clovis MacDonald, was seated at the back of the office.

"Can I help you?" Renee asked as if she had never met me before in her life.

Her hair was arranged in bright gold curls and her skin was black as skin could get, but her lips and nose were strangely Caucasian. Renee was skinny and unhappy. Her red nails needed a touch-up and her dark blue dress might have given you the impression that she was naked if you saw her from afar.

"I wanna talk to Clovis."

Clovis was within earshot, but Renee jumped up and said, "I'll see if she's available."

Renee had no butt to speak of, though she moved like she did. She switched-walked to Clovis's desk and rested both hands there, indicating that if she had to do one more thing she might just pass out from exhaustion.

"Somebody to see you," I heard her say. She pointed behind to indicate what she meant.

Then she came back to her own desk, sat down, and looked up at me. "You can go on in," she said as she picked up the telephone and started to dial.

Clovis didn't stand to greet me. She didn't even reach out a hand across the desk in common courtesy.

"Mr. Rawlins," she said.

"Clo," I replied. "You plannin' t'put some walls in here?"

"Huh?"

"Well, you got Renee actin' like she cain't even see you. I figure you practicin' for some walls."

Clovis didn't have much of a sense of humor. Her life had been too hard for laughs. She was a short, stout woman whose skin was the color of burnished bronze. Her blunt face jutted out from her head, making her appear like a boxer after he's delivered a chopping blow, expecting his foe to crumple any moment. Her eyebrows were dense and mannish. The thick shelf over her eyes was furrowed as if she were angry down into her bones.

"What can I do for you, Mr. Rawlins?"

"I came to see about when we can start movin' on Freedom's Plaza. You know my money's gettin' kinda low."

Clovis stared at me like I was a hobo instead of being a member of her investment consortium.

She hailed from Dallas, Texas—not a part of the state I had ever visited—and came to L.A. after the violent death of a man named "Jammer" Jerry Redd. Seems Jerry was trying to force his affections on Clovis's youngest sister—Antoinette. But he gave up that enterprise when Clovis dissuaded him with a twelve-inch pipe that she carried around in a sack. Jerry died three days later, and even though the judge called it self-defense the Redd clan wanted Clo's scalp.

Clovis was on a bus to Los Angeles twenty-five minutes after the verdict.

Clovis didn't have but sixty-five dollars to her name when she came to L.A. in 1955. She took a room on 103rd Street and got a job serving ham hocks and collard greens at a nameless diner that Mofass, my money-hungry real estate agent, and I used to frequent. Clovis was civil to us whenever we ate there but she was especially deferential to Mofass, because he was the boss—at least that was what she thought. I liked to pretend that I worked for Mofass and that he was the landlord. That way I got most of the money and none of the complaints. And people were only nice to me because they liked me. Nobody ever greased me up the way Clovis used to butter Mofass's cornbread.

Mofass was already sick by then. He had wasted away to a mere two hundred and thirty pounds and his breath came faster than a small dog's. He'd finally given up cigars but the emphysema still moved through his lungs like thick glue. Even then his breath was high and musical, like the chatter from domesticated dolphins at Pacific Ocean Park.

One day Mofass was complaining that the only home-cooked meals he got came from Clo's table. At that time he lived in a rented room on Spruce, the opposite direction from Clo's. But she told him that she'd be happy to drop by with a hot meal now and then.

"Important man like you shouldn't have to be eatin' out no cans," she said, bending so far down across the counter that we could see her stomach down between her breasts. "I could bring you somethin' hot if you want it."

Mofass's fast breathing picked up its pace. I thought he was going to keel over dead right then.

They had a house together in less than three months. Before the year was out, Esquire Realty was formed and Clovis had started drumming up business all over south L.A.

Clovis had a real flair for the real estate business. She put together a group of middle-class workingmen and started them investing in apartment buildings. She and Mofass managed the properties and then Clovis started making deals with wealthier white landowners. She told the white men that she could represent their investments better in the black neighborhoods because she had her ear close to the ground out there and because she had the trust of the tenants.

In three years, Freedom's Trust, which was the Negro investment group's name, owned twelve buildings and Esquire Realty represented them all, along with another twenty buildings owned by outside whites.

Esquire still represented me, in a limited way, but Clovis wasn't happy about it. Even once she'd found that I owned all the property that Mofass had represented she still couldn't shake the notion of me as a handyman.

"We cain't move on Freedom's Plaza," she said.

" "Scuse me?"

"They done put a freeze on our permit. Cain't even put a shovel in the ground out there."

"What about the lawyer?" I asked.

Clovis twisted her lips to the side in a sour kiss. "Ain't nuthin' he could do. They got a injunction on the whole place. City says that they wanna build a sewage treatment plant out there." Clovis's gaze kept going back to the papers on her desk. She was trying to give me the hint that she was too busy to spend much time discussing a foregone conclusion.

"But they granted us a permit. If they granted us a permit then they got to honor it—right?"

Freedom's Trust looked like a good idea to me when Clovis started it. Everything she touched turned to cash. So I brought her an idea that got her to smile—even at me.

I owned a large lot of property down in Compton and I had an option to buy even more. Clovis gathered the assets of Freedom's Trust to buy an adjacent lot and then we all got together a proposal to build a shopping mall called Freedom's Plaza. There'd be a supermarket, an appliance store, and a dozen smaller shops owned and patronized by black people.

We had the plans drawn up and all the permits we needed. I had gone deeply into debt to do my part, but I knew that you had to spend money in order to make it. Everything had been moving fine up until that morning. It had been a slow process, so I was hurting, but I never imagined that our permit would be disallowed.

"What's gonna happen to the property if they go through with this?"

"City'll foreclose for the development and pay us whatever the land is worth."

"But we're in debt over the plans and all those fees and taxes," I said. "The undeveloped price won't even half cover what we owe."

"That's the chance we took, Mr. Rawlins," Clovis said as if she was talking about a ten-dollar bet laid with Georgette. "We got to pay for the plans and the lawyer—and the management fees."

"Management fees? You expect me to pay you for losin' my money? I don't have no money left."

"You got them buildin's, Mr. Rawlins. If you sold off a couple'a them you could pay what you owe an' still have some money in your pocket."

"What?" I reached for the edge of the desk, and at that same moment the front door opened. I didn't need to turn around to know that the heavy footfalls were Tyrone, Clavell, Grover, and Fitts—Clovis's younger brothers. I knew Renee had gotten on the phone to call them. Whenever Clovis needed their help they were just waiting for the call—all four of them.

"You heard me, Mr. Rawlins."

"I wanna talk to Mofass about this." A hum had started at the base of my skull. The heat in that room turned into hatred for them.

"You talk to me, Mr. Rawlins. I'm the one run this here office. I'm the one you gotta talk to."

I stood straight up out of my chair, knocking it over. Then I turned on my heel, walked straight past those big men and right out of the door.

The hot Santa Ana wind hit my face like a wall. Sweat was coming down my legs by the time I reached the trunk of my '56 Pontiac. Dickhead's sawed-off was still there. I broke it open and replaced the spent cartridge. Two blasts would wound everybody in the room, after that they were mine. I reached for the box of ammo in case I needed to reload. It was lying in the corner of the tire well. When I picked it up I saw Feather's little rubber Tweety-Bird doll jammed underneath. She'd been looking for that doll for two weeks. Three different nights she went to sleep crying because her Tweety was lost and scared somewhere and nobody would feed him. For a second I forgot my anger and felt the flash of joy sure to be on her face when I returned the oil-stained toy.

"Rawlins." The smug voice was Fitts. He was at the front of the car.

I peeked out over the open trunk and asked, pleasantly, "Yeah?"

"I just wanna tell you that you better be leavin' sis alone, man. An' I ain't fuckin' wichya."

Fitts was young and hale. No matter how much he tried to make his face into a scowl he just looked like a little boy. Smooth skin and round eyes.

I put the gun down and closed the trunk.

"You don't have to worry 'bout me, man," I said. "I'm the one who got to worry."

Fitts didn't know what to say to that.

I went around the boy-faced man and got into the driver's seat. Fitts was staring at me through the open window, a look of confusion on his face. He watched me as I pulled away, his brothers coming around, gathering up in a group around him like wolves and dogs do.

The thought of that boy exhausted me. He didn't have the slightest concept of what was going on in the world around him. He was young and strong and he had brothers to run with and sisters to clean his clothes and serve him.

I could have killed him—for nothing. Somebody would kill him one day. Like Mouse had killed Bruno.

I wanted to kill Clovis too, but there wasn't any reason for it. She hadn't done anything. It was me. I had reached out for the white man's brass ring and got caught up short, that's all. They taught me when I was a boy to stay in my place. I was a fool for forgetting that lesson, and now all I was doing was paying for that foolishness.

Deep inside I knew that the world wasn't going to let me

be an upright businessman. It was just that I had worked so hard. Since I was a child I worked the daylight hours; sweeping, gardening, delivering. I'd done every kind of low job, and I wanted my success. I wanted it—violently.

But the violence didn't sit easily in me anymore. Every time I felt it I remembered Bruno and Mouse and how easily we come to die.

Back home in Texas and Louisiana, shootings and stabbings and beatings were commonplace. A man would kill you with his bare hands if he didn't have the right tools. Women died giving birth, men drowned trying to do logging jobs that no man should have been expected to do. There was syphilis and pneumonia and tuberculosis everywhere you turned.

And then came World War Two. People died by the millions there. They died in their own homes and on lonely winter landscapes. In Europe they built giant factories to kill people in. In Europe they made you dig your own grave before putting a bullet in the back of your head.

In Europe I'd have days where I saw more dead people than I did live ones. In one town, in Poland, I came upon a hole, six by six by six, that was full to overflowing with the corpses of infant children, not one of whom had grown old enough to speak a word.

But through all that time I had hope. Hope that I'd come to a place and time where death would no longer haunt me. It's not that I thought people would stop dying one day. I knew that death was always coming. But not this senseless kind of death where men killed from boredom or because of a child's game they played.

When Bruno died I realized that I'd always be surrounded by violence and insanity. I saw it everywhere; in Fitts's innocent face, in Dickhead's diseased gaze. It was even in me. That feeling of anger wrapped tight under my skin, in my hands.

And it was getting worse.

CHAPTER 9

The drive northward was a monotonous landscape of one-story houses except for an occasional office building and the palm trees. The sky was dense with smog, gray all around, with a deepening amber color hugging low at the horizon. If I took a deep breath I felt a sharp pain in the pit of my lungs. I welcomed it. I had one more thing to take care of before I could go out and earn Saul Lynx's money.

L.A. has always been flat and featureless. Anybody could be anywhere out there. The police arrested you for jaywalking or because you didn't have the brains not to brag after you hit a liquor store for the day's receipts. But if you wanted to hide from the law, L.A. was the place to do it. There was no logic to the layout of the city. And there were more people every day. Sharecroppers and starlets, migrant Mexicans and insurance salesmen, come to pick over the money tree for a few years before they went back home. But they never went home. The money slipped through their fingers and the easy life weighed them down.

I drove over to the old bus station on Los Angeles, parked across the street, and killed the motor. It was hot in the car, but that didn't matter. Actually it felt right being scorched by the sun. I enjoyed it so much that I even lit a cigarette to burn up my insides too.

After the Camel I laid back behind the wheel and closed my eyes for a moment.

No matter where my mind wanted to go in that half-doze my heart wended its way back to that alley behind John's.

It was quiet with Bruno slumped against the butcher's door. Blood dripped down his chest and he made a gurgling sound. A bubble of blood kept bulging and receding from his nostril. Blood seeped across the alley toward my bare feet. I didn't want to get blood on my feet; didn't want a dead man's blood on me.

Then there was Mouse again. He walked right in the blood and stooped over to see Bruno up close. He listened to the ragged breath for a moment, then pulled his long pistol out of the front of his pants and leveled it at Bruno's eye. It was the same way he killed Joppy Shag all those years ago.

The shot exploded and I jumped awake. Across the street the glass doors of the bus station swung open and Raymond "Mouse" Alexander walked out in the same silver suit and gray shoes he wore while killing Bruno Ingram. His shirt was a deep smoky color, his hat was short in the brim. Most men do a jolt up in prison and when they come out they're behind the times. But not Mouse. His tastes were so impeccable that he would have looked good after fifty years in jail.

The only thing different from the night he laid Bruno down that I could see from across the street was a pencil-thin mustache that Mouse sometimes grew and sometimes cut off.

"Hey!" I waved through the window.

He carried a drab green bag down at his side. It was almost empty. You don't collect many keepsakes in prison—at least not the kind you can carry around in a bag.

He jumped into the passenger's seat all excited. "Easy, lemme have your gun."

"What?"

"Couple'a motherfuckers on that bus wanna get the news. They was laughin' at me, Easy."

Any other man, even the craziest killer, I could have talked sense to. I could have said that there were policemen in the station, that they'd throw him back in prison. But not Mouse. He was like an ancient pagan needing to celebrate and anoint his freedom with blood.

"Sorry, man," I said, thinking about the shotgun in my trunk. "I didn't bring nuthin'."

"You go around wit' no gun?"

"What I need a gun for?"

"S'pose you gotta kill somebody, that's why."

I used the pause to turn the ignition and take off.

We'd been driving for a few minutes before either of us spoke again.

"How you doin', Raymond?" I asked lamely.

"How you think? They got me locked up in a pen like a pig wit' a whole buncha other pigs. Make me wear that shit. Make me eat shit. An' every motherfuckah there think he could mess wit' me 'cause I'm little."

I imagined the hard lessons brought about by that mistake. Mouse wasn't a large man. I could have picked him up and thrown him across a room. But he was a killer. If he had any chance to put out your eye or sever a tendon, he did it.

He told me once that a white sheriff in west Texas had taken him in for vagrancy.

"You hear that shit?" Mouse said. "Vagrancy! I told him I was lookin' for a job!"

But the sheriff took Mouse to jail and chained his hands behind his back. That night, when they were alone, the sheriff came into the cell.

"He was gonna kill me," Mouse said. "Go upside my head an' get me up an' hit me again. I knew I had ta do sumpin', so when he hit me one time I pretend like I'm out. . . ." Mouse closed his eyes as in a swoon and fell forward on the street corner where he was telling his tale. I grabbed him almost like an embrace and he bit me! Bit me right on the big muscle of my shoulder.

Mouse threw his arms around my neck and chortled in my ear, "Heh-heh-heh-heh-heh. That's just what he did, man. Stooped down a little an' grab me. It's what you call a reflex. But I didn't bite his arm. Uh-uh." Mouse showed me his big teeth. "I clamped down on his windpipe an' I didn't pull back until my teefs was touchin'."

Mouse ripped out the sheriff's throat and then took his keys. I always thought of him stopping at the sink to wash the blood from his mouth and clothes. He didn't tell me about that, but I knew Mouse better than any brother I could have ever had. He was closer than a friend and he'd saved my life more times than a man should need saving.

He was the darkness on the other side of the moon.

"I'ma kill me somebody, Easy," he said.

"Who?"

"I don't know yet. But I do know that somebody give me up to the cops and that somebody was at John's bar the night I cut Bruno down. Somebody got to die behind that shit."

The police were waiting for Raymond when he got home from killing Bruno Ingram. That's why he was wearing the same suit. They knew he'd done the killing and were laying for him; he still had the murder gun hooked in his belt. It sure seemed that he was set up. As a matter of fact, if he'd known that I was in that doorway, I was the most likely candidate.

"How you gonna kill somebody if you don't know who did it? You don't, right?"

"No. But I remember who was there. You and John an' three other men: Malcolm Reeves, Clinton Davis, and Melvin Quick." He recited the names as if in a trance.

"But if you don't know now how you gonna know?"

"Either I find out or I'ma kill all of three of 'em. But one way or another I'ma get the man who did it."

Mouse's ex-wife, EttaMae, lived in small white house surrounded by lemon groves, in the city of Compton. It was a tall single-story house that had a latticed skirt of crisscrossed green slats. The yard was big and unruly. Long shaggy grass grew around a rusty old slide left out there to remind Etta of when their son, LaMarque, was still a small child. In the center of the yard stood a half-dead crab-apple tree that was covered with some kind of splotchy blue-and-white fungus. Around the dying tree grew a garden full of eggplant, snap beans, and bushy tomatoes. Etta liked to be surrounded by things that were bountiful, but she didn't turn away from hard times. When Etta was only a child, barely sixteen, she nursed her bedridden grandmother until the suffering old woman began to hate her.

EttaMae was standing in the yard when we drove up to her solitary home.

I never minded seeing EttaMae Harris. She would have been Rodin's model if he were a black man and lived in the south. She was big and strong like a man but still womanly—very womanly. Her face wasn't beautiful so much as it was handsome and proud. "Noble" is too weak a word to use to describe her looks and her bearing.

Mouse and I walked up to the fence. Etta wore a simple cotton dress to do her work around the house.

"Easy," she said in greeting to me, but I could tell her full attention was on him.

"Hey, Etta. House looks good. You painted it?"

"I'm'onna start payin' you back for the loan just as soon as I could get ahead on this here mortgage," she answered.

I nodded. I didn't care. One of the reasons that I was broke is that I gave my money away to friends who had less than I did. That's a poor man's insurance: Give when you got it and hope that they remember and give back when you're in need.

"Hey, Etta," Mouse said. His grin was a caged laugh.

"What?"

I could have been the twin to that dying tree for all they knew. Mouse was standing straighter by the moment, his smile getting deeper. I noticed then, for the first time, that Raymond was aging. You could see it around his eyes, a network of wrinkles that shivered with his grinning.

Etta didn't exhibit feelings like he did. But her silence and solemnity showed that she had been thinking about this man for her whole life. He was down in the core of her. Mouse had once told me that he was drawn to Etta because, as he said, "She's a hungry woman." I could see the hunger in her.

I don't know what might have happened if the door to the house hadn't come open.

"LaMarque," Etta said, not taking her eyes off of Mouse.

Mouse gave a whoop and let the laugh come out. "LaMarque!"

I looked up and saw the shy boy, dressed all in farmer's green, coming down the stair. He had inherited his mother's big bones and her sepia hue. He was sullen and bowed as he came near to us. But Raymond didn't notice. He grabbed LaMarque in a rough hug around the neck and said aloud, "I missed you, son. I missed you."

Raymond kept his arm around the boy's neck, almost like he had him in a headlock. He jerked him sideways so that they were both facing me.

"That's my boy," he declared.

And you could see it when they were side by side. Something in the eyes. In LaMarque it was a kind of softness, a childhood that Mouse never knew.

Etta touched my arm. "Stay for supper, baby."

"Naw, Etta," I said. "I got a job t'do. Anyway you three should spend some time."

She didn't argue. I shook LaMarque's hand. He was twelve then and wanted to be treated like a man.

I was all the way to the car when Mouse yelled, "Easy!" and ran to me. He came up with a big smile on his face.

"Thanks, man," he said. "You know, I got pretty sour in there. They try an' keep a brother down."

I smiled. "Nuthin', man. We friends, right?"

"Yeah . . . sure." Mouse's glassy gray eyes went cold even though he was smiling.

"John's."

"Hey, man," I said.

"Easy."

I'd known John for over twenty-five years, from Texas to L.A.; from speakeasy to legitimate bar.

"Mouse is out."

"Yeah?"

"He's lookin' for the men was in the bar that night. Thinks one'a them put the finger on him. There was three men there," I said. "Melvin Quick—"

He cut me off. "I know who was there, Easy."

"Well, maybe you should tell'em to lay low awhile."

"Uh-huh."

"In the meantime I'll try to set it right."

"Somebody better do somethin', 'cause I ain't gonna take no shit outta Mouse."

We both knew that Mouse wouldn't stop just because those men hid from him.

CHAPTER 10

The next morning I was on the road to Beverly Hills. Loma Vista Drive was clear and beautiful. I couldn't even imagine being rich enough to live in any of the mansions I passed. I mean, even if I was white and they would have let me stay up there I didn't know where so much money could come from. All the houses had more room than anybody needed, with lawns big enough to raise livestock in. As I went on and on the houses got bigger, making the drive seem even more like a ride in Fantasyland.

When I got to the gate that said "Beverly Estates" a uniformed guard came out. I stopped and rolled down my window.

"Can I help you?" the half-bald man with spectacles asked. He didn't mean it. His job was to keep out those who had no business in the land of the rich. He was a white nigger hired to keep other niggers, both black and white, out.

"Yeah, yeah," I said slow and easy. "I got to see a woman called . . ." I hesitated while I went into the glove compartment and pulled out an old grocery list. "Let's see now, um, uh, yeah, here it is. Sarah Clarice Cain. Lives at number two Meadowbrook Circle."

"Let me see that." The white nigger reached for my list, but I shoved it back into the glove compartment.

"Sorry," I said. "Confidential." I loved using that line on white men.

"I can't just let you in just because—"

"You cain't stop me," I interrupted. "This road here is public access. So stand aside."

I revved my engine and zoomed past. In the mirror I

watched the guard go to his little kiosk. That was okay by me. I didn't care who knew I was coming.

The Cain mansion, first seen through bars of wrought iron painted pink, looked like heaven. It was on top of a hill of sloping grasses, dotted now and then with various fruit trees. The structure rose high in the center with giant pillars that looked from the distance to be made of marble.

"May I help you?" an electronic female voice asked.

To the side of me at the gate there was a speaker box. My driving up must have set off some kind of alarm.

"May I help you?" the voice asked again.

"Um, I'm here to see Sarah Clarice Cain."

"What is your business?"

"I have to talk to her," I said. And when the robot woman didn't answer I added, "About Marlon Eady."

"What do you . . ." the voice started to ask. Then, "Come in."

The gate rolled to the side and I drove up the long lane to the house. To the right was a tall evergreen hedge that was there to muffle the sound of traffic. To the left was the lawn leading down to a line of Greek statues that couldn't be seen from outside.

The lane led to a circular drive wide enough that visitors could park there while other cars could drive past and let passengers off at the front door.

The building, you couldn't call it a house really, was three tall stories high. The marble pillars flanked a front door that was at the center of a wall of glass. You could see the long staircase that led upward to floors above. The entrance hall was pink stone.

I wasn't surprised that a Negro woman opened the front door. Her skin was definitely brown but on the lighter side. Freckles were scattered around her upturned nose. It's always strange to see a black person's nose turned up.

Instead of me being put off by her arrogant stare I just wanted to get to know her better.

"Hi," I said, smiling and hoping that she'd like me.

"Hello," the pretty young woman said, devoid of any emotion. The black dress defined her as a maid, but she wore large gaudy earrings and the material of the dress was a fine cotton, maybe even silk. She might have been an employee but she was secure in that position.

"Can I talk to the lady?"

"It would be inconvenient at the moment for Miss Cain to receive anyone." She sounded just like a white woman. There wasn't a hint of down home in her voice. "So if you'd like to leave a message I'll make sure that she gets it."

I let my head loll forward while I leered. "No," was all I said.

"Why not?" She was indignant.

"You go tell the lady that if she wants to talk to me about Marlon Eady and a certain check that she wrote to him then she could un-inconvenience herself and come on down here to see me. I don't have to sit on her good chairs or nuthin'. I'll be standin' right here, waiting for her t'come on down."

"Have you spoken to . . . to . . . Mr. Eady?" she asked instead of running my errand.

"That depends," I answered.

"Depends on what?"

"Do you know him?"

"His sister worked for us. She left recently."

"Us?"

"I mean here, at the house," she answered, slightly flustered.

"We talkin' 'bout Betty, right?"

A light went on in the maid's eyes. "Do you know Elizabeth?"

"Can I talk to the lady?" I smiled.

The maid's nostrils flared and her eyes widened. She was definitely a pretty woman. "Can't you answer a question?"

"Can you?"

She was put off balance by my manner. It was as if nobody had ever refused her anything. I was some strange beast to her; and she was either going to cut my throat—or ride me.

"Wait here," she commanded. Then she slammed the door in my face.

I waited about five minutes or so thinking about all the people who've slammed doors on me. I had counted up to twenty-three, with a couple of good chuckles, when the door opened again.

This time there was a real white woman. She was in her early forties, light-haired—blond going gray—and slight. Her expression gave you the impression that she was thinking about something very far away and very beautiful—if sad. All in all she seemed like one of those otherworldly heroines in the romantic novels of the Brontë sisters.

"Yes?" she asked as if to someone behind me.

"Mrs. Cain?" I was noticing the gold band on her finger.

"The Mrs. I am is Mrs. Hawkes," she said. The name seemed to cause a bitter taste in her mouth.

"There must be some kind of mistake, ma'am. I'm here to see Sarah Cain."

"Yes?"

"Is that you?"

"Hawkes is my married name. I don't use it, but if you're going to call me Mrs. that's the name to use."

"So . . . you're Sarah Cain?"

"Her name is Mrs. Hawkes." A pale young man came up beside the woman. He had a delicate build for a man and his chin looked as though it had never sprouted a hair.

They were definitely related.

"Arthur." The lady patted her thigh and Arthur moved closer to her—a quarter step behind.

"I'm Miss Cain," she said. "Ronald Hawkes is Arthur's father." Then, almost as an afterthought, "He doesn't live with us anymore."

"But he's still my father," Arthur said, more to his mother than to me.

While we spoke, Sarah Cain's gaze had slowly come into focus. "And you are, sir?"

"Rawlins, ma'am. I'm a . . . an old friend of Marlon Eady."

"Yes." She gave me a watery smile. "He was Elizabeth's brother, her half brother actually."

"Was?"

"Did I say was? I hardly knew the man. He came to stay with Elizabeth now and then. That was until my father put his foot down." Distaste twisted her lips again.

"Is Betty here?" I asked.

"No," she said. I got the feeling that she was about to say more, but then changed her mind.

"Is your father in?"

"Heavens no. He died two weeks ago Saturday." There was no sorrow in Sarah Cain's declaration. She didn't actually smile, but her posture improved.

The boy, Arthur, wore white linen pants and a red short-sleeved shirt. His belt was corded cotton and his moccasins were drab green. His mother sported a thickly embroidered Japanese-style orange silk jacket that hung down over loose black pants. Her feet were bare except for the bright red lacquer on the nails.

The sun was hot on my back but the air coming out of the house felt like church; cool and angelic. I reminded myself that Satan was an angel too.

I was trying to frame my next question when I heard him.

"Boy," a heavy masculine southern drawl declared. I

couldn't have been more shocked if someone had slapped me across the face. "What business you got here?"

Coming across the entrance hall was a white Texan. A large-framed man with lots of meat to fill out the bones. He wore a cowboy hat, sandpaper jeans, and a blue checkered shirt.

Behind the Texan came the maid again. It was a regular party.

"Mr. Rawlins came to speak to me, Calvin," Miss Cain said.

I appreciated her words but the cowboy was a commanding force.

"Rawlins," I told him. "Ezekiel Rawlins. I came here because I found something that Miss Cain gave to a friend of mine."

"And what is that now?"

Everyone was waiting for me to answer the Texan's question. I would have preferred to be alone with the lady but that didn't seem possible.

"I was lookin' for my friend Betty, but I couldn't find her so I went over to Marlon's place. But then Marlon wasn't around neither. I went back a couple'a times and when he wasn't never there I got scared and went inside to see if he left somethin' to say where he was. All I found was this here." I held up the five-thousand-dollar check. "It's written to Marlon. I couldn't find him but I found this check at his house. And I couldn't imagine anybody as poor as he is leavin' this kinda money around." I paused a second. "You'd have to kill Marlon for this kinda money."

"He's daid?" Calvin asked.

"That's what the lady seems to think . . ."

"I said no such thing," she piped in.

"... but I don't know," I finished my sentence. "All I found was the check. Marlon wasn't nowhere to be seen." I spoke in a dialect that they would expect. If I gave them what they expected then they wouldn't suspect me of being any kind of real threat.

"So you really don't even know that he's missin'," Calvin said, and I knew for a fact that he was a lawyer in spite of his rough clothes. "He could be off with some girl."

I had better things to do with my breath than to waste it arguing with a lawyer. He was an immense man, resembling a demon out of Hindu mythology that had been sculpted from a big square rock. He looked vital, like he could take it if it came down to that. He was rolling two small black stones in his hand.

"You better get out of the heat, Mom," the pale boy said to Sarah Cain. "We can take care of this."

Sarah smiled at her son and nodded. "Thank you, Arthur."

"Miss Cain?" I asked before they could leave.

"Yes?"

"Why'd you give Marlon five thousand dollars?"

"It is mine," she said, peering at the check in my hand. "But I didn't write it. And it would have bounced if I had. Father never let me have much money, and now that he's dead the estate is in the hands of lawyers." She gave Calvin an evil stare. "Until they figure out the will."

"Let me take a look at that," Calvin said.

"Excuse me." I snatched the check away. "But who are you?"

"My name is Calvin Hodge, boy. I'm the family lawyer."

Sarah Cain bridled out of her fey stance when Calvin said that. She looked as if she was about to protest. But Calvin gave her an evil grin and her complaint withered.

I was standing two feet from the Texan. Between his rank pipe smoker's breath and sweat I felt like withering myself.

"Are you the one who hired me to find Elizabeth Eady?"

"What? Calvin, you did that? I thought you said . . ." Sarah started saying.

"I haven't hired you for a damn thing, boy. Now let me have a look at Miss Cain's property."

"This property," I said, pocketing the check, "belongs to Marlon Eady. I'm trying to find him and his sister. I was hired to find his sister by someone claiming to represent Miss Cain."

"You, Calvin?" Sarah Cain said. She even pointed a finger at him as if she were a witness to his crime.

"Nonsense. I never heard of you before this minute."

"Have you found Elizabeth?" Miss Cain wanted to know.

"No, ma'am. Just your check."

I was looking right at the woman, but then Calvin Hodge pressed his reeking bulk in between us.

"Will you give me that check, son?"

"Do I look like one of your relatives?" I asked instead of hitting him in the face.

"We can make it easy," he said. "You hand me that check now and there won't be any difficulties down the hill."

"This here check belongs to Marlon. I'd think about givin' it to ya if you said that you were the one hired Saul Lynx."

Calvin Hodge shook his head at me. Behind him the maid and boy were holding Sarah Cain's hands. They all seemed to be afraid, but I couldn't tell who was the source of their fear, me or Calvin Hodge.

"I'll be seein' ya," the cowboy lawyer threatened.

I took a full step backward before I turned my back on him.

Twelve blocks away I began to feel safe. Once I was past danger I started to wonder; Calvin Hodge had to be the man who hired Lynx.

"It's her lawyer who hired me," Lynx had said.

Didn't he?

And if Hodge wasn't the lawyer then it was Lynx who was lying. Maybe Lynx was lying anyway.

When I was a younger man I would have had to figure that puzzle out. But at forty-one I knew when to call it quits. I had certainly earned my two hundred dollars.

When the siren sounded I figured that it was some overzealous cop who didn't like the idea of a black man cruising around in Beverly Hills. I pulled to the curb at Wilshire and Doheny. A black-and-white car careened to a stop right in front of me. Its two brothers braked behind.

Six men! Policemen. They were around the car and in the doors before I could even think.

I was dragged from the front seat and thrown to the asphalt.

"Spread'em!"

"Get the keys. Search the vehicle."

They went through my clothes and cuffed my hands behind my back.

"Hey, man! What'd I do?" I shouted.

That got me a nightstick pressed hard across the back of my neck.

"You just shut up," an angry voice whispered in my ear.

I glanced up to the side and saw a young white woman pull away a small child who was staring at me. The child was trying to ask her mother a question but the woman gave no answer.

I heard the trunk of the car come open and breathed a sigh of relief that I had the sense to store the shotgun before braving Beverly Hills.

Sawed-off shotguns were illegal in the state of California.

They picked me up by the armpits and threw me into one of the cars. Two men got in the back with me. Grim men with flawless white faces.

I remember thinking that a man who's never been scarred doesn't have any mercy. He doesn't know what pain really feels like.

CHAPTER 11

They put me in a sort of meeting room with bars. There was a long beech table surrounded by beech chairs on a buffed parquet pine floor. Through the bars on the window I could see down onto Santa Monica Boulevard. The cars were going about their business. Not one of those drivers knew that I was bunged up in jail for no reason. And if any of them had found out they wouldn't have cared. And even if they did care there wasn't any help for me.

The meeting room didn't have a toilet. There was a tall aluminum ashtray, though, it was a freestanding cone that had a shallow dish of sand nestled up top. When I took the dish off I saw that the cone was hollow, so I relieved myself there. I had to move my bowels too but decided to wait for my jailer's generosity.

I waited for hours.

Nobody entered the room until almost night.

I sat at the window thinking about what a fool I was to get into a mess like that when I had children who expected me home.

I watched the sun go down and the car lights come on. I banged on the door and yelled a couple of times but nobody came and nobody answered. I knew that all this was designed to frighten me.

It worked.

Mouse came into my mind with the sunset. He'd spent almost five years in a cell worse than this one. Here I was running after shadows and dreams when I should have been trying to keep Mouse from killing whatever poor fool turned him in.

I thought about Jesus talking. About Feather crying over where her daddy had gone to.

Something had happened to Marlon. Maybe he was dead. Betty was still missing and I didn't have a clue where she might have been. All I had was some half-truths from Saul Lynx and a check written out to Marlon for five thousand dollars. Actually the cops had the check. They had everything I owned.

And I still didn't know a thing.

The cops came in when I'd given up trying. My gut felt like there was a bowling ball lodged inside. My tongue was dry. My stomach had given up grumbling and died.

There were three of them. A little man in gray trousers and a white shirt with the sleeves rolled up past his bony elbows. He wore gold-rimmed glasses and had thin, milky skin with blue veins just below the surface. There was a uniformed cop dressed in a black uniform. He had ironed his uniform that day. By the way he held his hat under his left arm, military-style, I believed that he ironed it every morning. He was a tall man, well-built and self-assured. His brown hair and brown eyes jarred slightly with the paleness of his skin.

But it was the third man whom I paid attention to. He was at least six and a half feet tall. Broad-shouldered and redheaded, he had the kind of swagger in his body language that reminded me of Bruno Ingram. His dark blue pants might have been police-issue but his white shirt was spun fine and tailored. His collar was open at the throat.

His face was busy. His eyes moved over me quickly and

then around the floor, then back to me. His lips went between the beginning of a friendly grin and a sneer.

If I had seen this man walking my way on the street I'd've crossed to the other side.

"Styles," the jumpy-faced giant said, pointing at his own chest. "Commander Styles."

Commander.

The little man in the gray pants was carrying a small suitcase by the handle. He put this down on the board table and opened it up to reveal a tape recorder. He took a rolled-up electric wire from the box, unraveled it, and plugged into a socket underneath the window that looked down onto the street.

I weighed my chances. No matter how big a man is, a hard toe to the testicles would lay him low. The uniform was only three steps further on. Beyond him? Who knew? Freedom maybe. I could get the kids and be out of the state before midnight. Plane tickets to New York or Hawaii were eighty dollars a head, I could get that from John. We could disappear in an evening.

But what about the little guy? The commander had to go first, then the cop. I could come back for the little guy. But what if he shouted?

Commander Styles could see everything I thought by the way my eyes traveled from man to man.

"Sit down, Rawlins," he said. The .45 he pulled from his pocket looked like a cap pistol in his big hand.

"Sit down," he said again.

I pulled a beech chair from the table and did as I was told.

He sat on top of the table to my right, then put the pistol down in front of me.

I had to go to the toilet so bad that I could have cried.

"We don't appreciate our citizenry being hectored," he said.

"Yessir," I answered quickly and contritely, trying my best to keep the hatred out of my voice.

He smiled, pleased that I was showing him the respect that a commander deserved.

I'd've done almost anything he wanted, because I was his right then. That man had me and I'm not ashamed to admit it. If he wanted to cripple me or incarcerate me indefinitely or even if he wanted to kill me, that was his discretion. I could have been upstanding and proud and spit in that man's eye. But then who would have raised my kids? Who would have survived to bear witness against his crimes?

"That's good," he said. His hand on my shoulder felt like a bag of wet cement. "Now you just cooperate with us here and things might not get worse than they already are."

I held the "yessir" back in my throat. If I seemed too scared he would become brutal; bullies are like that.

"What were you doing at the Cain residence?"

"Looking for Elizabeth Eady."

"Who's that?"

"She's a woman that a man named Saul Lynx—that's L-Y-N-X—hired me to find."

"Find her for what?"

"He said that she had quit her job but that the lady who was her boss wanted her back. The lawyer Lynx worked for wanted to offer Betty some kind of retirement or somethin'."

"You didn't believe him?"

"I don't know what to . . ." I said. Then, with no warning, the commander leaped to his feet and hit me in the chest with a vicious uppercut.

The chair fell as I was knocked to my feet. I staggered back until I hit the wall and then crumpled like a crushed bug.

At first the only problem was that I couldn't breathe. It

felt as if my whole chest had caved in. With breath came a hurt so deep that it scared me. And then there was a noise like an angry goose honking at intruders into his harem.

After a few moments I realized that the honking was me trying to catch my breath.

"Come on, Rawlins," the commander said. He grabbed my shoulder and yanked me up.

The little man was fiddling with his tape recorder. The neat and pleated police officer stood at attention at the door. Neither one of them moved to help me. They wouldn't have moved if that crazy man had been beating me to death.

"Let me help you to your chair," the commander offered.

He dropped me into an empty seat and regained his perch on the table.

"What were you doing at the Cain house now?"

"Lynx offered me . . ." I started coughing phlegm from way down in my lungs. I must have coughed a full minute, but Styles didn't care. He waited patiently to continue with his interrogation.

"Lynx offered two hundred dollars up front and more if I could come up with Eady," I said at last. "I thought he was for real. Why would he lie about something like that?"

"I don't know," Styles said, prompting me.

When he brought his hand to his chin I put my arms up over my head and chest—and I wasn't the least bit ashamed.

"What about Albert Cain?" Styles asked.

"Who's that?" I asked, but I had a sinking feeling in my gut.

"He's the old man," Styles said. "Just died a couple'a weeks ago."

"I don't know nuthin' about him," I answered. "Lynx didn't even tell me about him. All he said was that the lady of the house wanted her servant back. All I was trying to do was to pay my rent. I didn't think that there was anything wrong with looking for a woman for her boss."

"You don't know anything about Albert Cain?"

"Not a thing."

"But this man . . . this, this . . ." He snapped his fingers thinking of the name.

"Lynx," I said.

Styles smiled. It was a genuine smile, friendly—one of the most chilling things about a natural killer is his smile. It was as if my submission filled him with glee.

"Lynx," he repeated. "He told you to go to the Cain place?"

"No. He wanted me to find Elizabeth Eady, at least that's what he said."

"But if it was the rich lady who wanted her, why would you look for her up there?" He sounded like a three-year-old wondering, without the slightest fear, why the ocean didn't rush up and flood the land.

"Lynx said that he didn't know the name of the lady. He said that a lawyer hired him."

"What lawyer?" There was a wolf grin on Styles's face.

"I don't know. He didn't say."

"What did he tell you?"

"Just that he needed to find Betty—"

"Betty? You know her?"

"Knew her. When I was a kid. A long time ago, in Texas."

"So that's why you went up to the Cains'? You knew this girl worked up there."

"I haven't seen Betty in twenty-five years."

"Do you know where this, this Betty might be?" He was trying to sound casual about it. But I could tell that Betty was the only thing he really wanted to know about.

"No, sir."

"And so if you don't know anything about her and haven't

seen her in all these years, then how did you know to go out there to the Cains'?"

"The check," I whispered.

"Yeah. The check," he said. "Now where'd that big ole check come from?"

"I found it at Marlon's house . . . down on Hooper."

Hooper? Styles mouthed the word silently. The question all over his face.

I was back in that outhouse—on my knees and surrounded by Marlon's dry blood. Styles knew I was lying but he wasn't going to expose me on a police tape recording. It was then that I knew that my life was hanging by a hair.

There was a long silence between us.

I counted the time by the throbbing ache each heartbeat brought to my chest.

Finally Styles said, "Thank you for your cooperation, Mr. Rawlins. Let me go and check this story out."

Commander Styles smiled and stood, then turned away and back again as if he had remembered one more question, I didn't see it coming at all. I suppose he just hauled off and hit me on the chin. My chin sure hurt later that evening when I woke up in my new jail cell.

My chest hurt too, and my arm and the back of my head. A big knot had swollen up above my diaphragm and my side ached awfully. He must have hit me after I was out. That's the only way I could understand it, all those aches and bruises.

"You all right?"

"Yeah, right," I answered.

There was a man standing next to my cot. He wore a tan shirt and pants of the same color with a dark belt. From my prone position he looked like a great big Boy Scout who had yet to earn his first merit badge. It was so funny that I started to laugh—and paid for it.

"Oh! Shit!"

"You need a doctor?"

"I'd settle for my one call."

The Boy Scout squatted down halfway, hands on his knees. Up close the white man's long face looked worried.

"I can get you a doctor," he said.

The sadness in his face scared me. I thought that I could see my death in his eyes.

"Please," I said. "Just a couple'a calls."

He stood up and went through a cell door, sliding it shut behind him.

There was a toilet seat next to my bed, I could smell it. I still had the urge to go to the bathroom but I didn't because I was afraid that half of my insides would come out if I gave them the chance.

It was a regular jail. Cells on either side of me and concrete floors. I was alone there too. The rest of the prisoners probably died in interrogation. That thought made me laugh again and the pain sent me to my feet.

The bars were cold to my grip. I liked that. I pressed my cheeks against the chilly steel. All I had wanted up to that moment was to get away from this job; to give it up. But now someone was going to have to pay.

"Mr. Rawlins?" The Boy Scout had returned.

"What's your name?" I asked him.

"Connor," he answered. "Are you okay?"

"Can I make my call, Officer Connor?"

His mouth opened into a smile and said, "Yes. Yes you can."

He went away for a few minutes and then returned with two young cops who carried truncheons.

There was a phone booth in a concrete hallway just outside the corral of cells. My first call was home. It rang thirty-two times before I hung up.

The next call was to the Horns. They had Feather and Jesus with them. I talked to Jesus but he didn't say anything back.

Feather got on the line then and said, "You got stuckted in trafferic, Daddy?"

"Yeah, honey."

"I got a red cherry on my head, Daddy. It gotsa funny face an' Juice wanted it but I wouldn't let him and he made a funny face too." Feather laughed.

"I love you, honey," I said.

"Uh-huh. Daddy, Mr. Horn here."

I told him that I'd been arrested by mistake but that I'd be home as soon as I could. I don't think he understood but that was okay because I didn't either. He was going to see after the kids. That's all I could ask for.

Mouse came next.

Etta answered the phone quickly. "Hello."

"Etta?"

"Easy, what's wrong, baby?"

"They got me down in the jail here in Beverly Hills. Mouse there?"

"Somethin' wrong wit' Raymond, Easy."

"Is he there, Etta?"

"No. He's out tryin' t'find whoever it was turnt him in. It's like he's all crazy-like again, Easy. He gettin' on LaMarque's nerves and I'm scared'a what he's gonna do."

"I'll go look for him when I'm . . ."

"You will?"

"But first I need to talk to Faye Rabinowitz. You got her home phone number."

"Somewhere here," she said. I could hear her going through drawers and shuffling papers. I could see her in the kitchen in her country house. She would be wearing a light nightgown and have a handkerchief wrapped around her head.

"Here it is, baby. What they got you in jail for?"

"I'll tell ya later, Etta."

"Okay. Here it is."

It was an Axminister exchange. Mouse's female lawyer was the only reason he didn't go down for second-degree murder. She worked with the ACLU and the NAACP. I only hoped that she would be in the mood to help me.

CHAPTER 12

Officer Connor was helpful like a Boy Scout too. He told me that Commander Styles (his real rank was captain but nobody, not even his superiors, called him that) was home until the next day. Styles had left orders to leave me alone in the cell. He didn't even want other prisoners talking to me, so they put me alone in a special wing designed to take the overflow on those special days when there was some kind of protest or other civil unrest.

But Connor didn't like Styles and he wasn't about to let a prisoner die while he was in charge of him.

"Men have died in here before," Connor told me. "But never when I was the one on duty."

It wasn't very reassuring to have Connor as my protector, though. He was a clerk with a big heart. Commander Styles would have eaten him for a snack before dropping me in the Pacific Ocean.

When I was alone in my cell I took off the mattress and loosened one of the twelve-inch metal stays that held the springs in place. It weighed about a quarter of a pound and even though it wasn't sharp it had a nasty snap to it when I swung it slicing through the air. If the commander wanted another piece of me I'd make sure he got more than he wanted.

I was willing to play the game, but that man was crazy. Insane. And no matter where I find myself I will not lie down and die without a fight.

At about midnight Connor came down to my cell with the guards.

"You got visitors, Rawlins."

"Who?"

"Come on," he said sliding open the cell door.

I had put the stay back under the mattress and couldn't get to it without letting the policemen see.

Connor took me to a small room where Faye Rabinowitz and a well-dressed white man were waiting.

I knew Faye. She was a white woman, definitely, but her skin ran toward the darker shades. She was slim and hardy-looking, like a weed growing out of a stone. Her eyes meant business and her nose flared slightly as if maybe she'd just smelled something not quite right. Faye wasn't out of her twenties yet but she'd never been a child.

Faye Rabinowitz didn't like anybody. Men were beneath her contempt and women were no good unless they did some kind of important job and talked hard. I'd met her when Mouse was indicted for Bruno's killing. She brought me into her office to answer her questions so she could be certain that I would stand up under cross-examination in the real trial.

"Why'd you take Raymond's case?" I asked after forty-five minutes of practice grilling.

"Because the law is shit," she said. She was only twenty-four at the time, one of the youngest people who had ever passed the bar. There wasn't a hint of makeup on her face and her hair was short and combed straight back.

"But you're a lawyer. You're part of the law."

Faye looked down at her watch. She was finished with me and couldn't have cared less about my questions.

It made me mad, the way she dismissed my presence as if I were no one and no good. She was trying to help my friend as if she were some kind of liberal but her attitudes were straight out of the plantation.

"So you're doin' this because he's some poor black man and he won't get a fair deal in court?" I really wanted to know.

"I don't care about your friend," she said, rising from her chair. "He's a killer and in a better world he'd hang. But the people who run this world have no right to put anybody to death. They're the ones who should die."

The man was older and dressed in three hundred dollars' worth of midnight-blue suit. There was a white flower in his lapel, giving me the idea that he'd recently been at some social gathering.

"Is this the man?" he asked Faye.

She nodded, somber as a Valkyrie pronouncing my fate.

The man, who was white-haired, turned his hard stare to Connor. "Why's he limping? Did he come in limping?"

"I don't know, your honor," Connor said. He might have hated Styles but he wasn't going to turn him in.

"Did you?" the judge asked me.

"Am I gettin' outta here?" I asked anyone who wanted to answer.

"There's not even a record of his arrest, your honor," Faye Rabinowitz said.

"Is that true?" The judge had nothing but questions for the Boy Scout.

"I'm just holding the fort, Judge Mellon. He was in the

cell when I got here. Somebody said that he'd been in a fight."

Judge Mellon. He was on the state supreme court. An outspoken critic of racism and champion of the rights of the poor. I'd read about him in the paper now and then.

The judge was silent for a few heartbeats.

"There's no paper on him, your honor," Faye said. "There's no reason he should be in here."

"What's your name?" the judge asked Connor.

"Connor, sir."

"Do you have a record of this man's arrest?"

"It doesn't appear so, sir."

"Do you know who brought this man in here?"

"I came on at six, sir. He was already in his cell," Connor lied.

The judge waited for his heart to beat some more and then said, "Let him go. And I want a report from your commander in the morning."

I could tell by Connor's hard gaze that he rued letting me use the phone. I hoped he could see in my eyes how sorry I was that he got into trouble.

"You should press charges," Faye Rabinowitz was telling me outside Beverly Hills City Hall. "The only way we can get some attention to this kind thing is if we can take it to court."

"Maybe later," I said. "Right now I got too much already to do."

"That's why the next man they bring in here will be killed. Because you have things to do."

"Listen, honey," I said in my deepest voice. I took her hand but she tugged it away from me.

"Get your hand off of me."

"Okay. Hey. That man up there is a stone killer. You can't stop him with a writ and lawsuit."

"I'm not afraid of any man," Faye Rabinowitz said. She was rubbing her hand as if to wipe off the residue I had left there.

"I know you aren't," I said. And then, "I was gonna call you even if I hadn't gotten arrested."

"Why?"

"I want to find out how it was the cops got on to Mouse."

"Why?"

"Because if I don't figure somethin' out quick, Raymond gonna be callin' soon and even you won't be able to help him out."

She gave me a quizzical look. Not friendly but opened up enough for me to talk.

"I need to find out about how the cops knew to go to his house that night. He thinks that it was the people in the bar that told. I wanna prove that it wasn't them."

"I don't work with the prosecutor's office. They won't tell me anything."

"The case is over. There gotta be somebody down there who'd talk to you."

Her stare was mean. A lawyer's loveless gaze combined with the stare of a woman who had no use for a man. She took a small address book and a golden mechanical pencil from her purse.

"What's your number?" she asked.

I told her.

"Call me in a couple of days if you haven't heard from me yet."

CHAPTER 13

When Connor emptied out my pouch of belongings I found that the check was missing. I didn't say anything about it, though. I was afraid that Faye would keep me there arguing until Styles showed up.

And Styles wanted to kill me. That was my working hypothesis.

The Horns were happy to see me. They wanted to keep Feather and Jesus overnight but when I looked in on the children I could see by their furrowed foreheads that they were having bad dreams, so I got them up and walked them in their underwear and blankets back to our house.

We had hot chocolate and bread and jam. At least Jesus and I did. Feather sat down on my lap, and after crying and showing me a three-day-old bruise on her knee, she fell fast asleep.

"Don't worry, Juice," I said to my son. "Everything's fine."

He gave me the thumbs-up.

We were late getting off to school. Feather just couldn't seem to get her clothes together and Jesus was no help for once. But by ten I'd dropped them both off and was on my way down to Avalon Boulevard, to a hole in the wall called Herford's gym.

On the way a hot wind blew into my face through the open window. It was strong and oppressive and made me think of hot days in the south. And that made me think about Betty. This wasn't the first time I had braved troubles for her.

After that kiss she gave me on the street I was always dogging her. I'd wait out in front of the flophouse Marlon lived in, because you never knew where Betty might be sleeping but Marlon almost always made it back home to his bed. Betty would show up at Marlon's around sunset and sit out in the hall on the first floor drinking and laughing with the men who lived there. It was summer and she always wore loose blouses so that she could fan her bosom more easily.

I hung around the front steps with the dogs and their fleas waiting to follow her wherever she went. I knew that she saw me but she hardly ever showed it; until one day, when she and Marlon were going down LeRoy Street. They stopped in front of a barber shop and then they both went in. I loitered around half the way down the street throwing stones into a muddy puddle and waiting to see where we'd go next.

"Hey, boy!"

My heart jumped so hard that it actually hurt.

"Yes, ma'am?" I shouted.

"Shh! Don't be shoutin'."

I ran up to her prepared to tell her that she was the prettiest woman that I'd ever seen.

"You know where Duncan's place is?" she asked.

"Yes, ma'am," I said, again too loud.

"Hush, boy! I ain't deaf. I want you to go over there and find Adray Ply and tell him that Betty could see him at twelve if he come over to Paulette's. You got that?"

I nodded because I didn't trust my voice.

"Okay then," Betty said. "You tell him that I said that he should give you a nickel."

Duncan's place was an old blacksmith's barn that went bust. I don't think that Duncan owned it or even paid rent; he just made a gin joint there because there was no one to tell him no.

It was an unsavory place. There were few chairs in Duncan's. The men either stood around or they sat on the floor and leaned up against the wall. Only men went in there, and all they did was drink. The smell was so sour and the language was so coarse in there that I started shaking the minute I walked through the open doors. There were men all around talking and vomiting and drinking. Two men were flailing away at a third man with their fists, and I tripped over a man who was either sleeping or dead in the middle of the floor.

"What you want here, boy?" Duncan, the one-eyed barman, hollered. His left eye had been gouged in a fight early in his evil life. The lids were sucked into the socket around a tiny black hole. The skin around that eye was badly scarred, but he never wore a patch because that hideous wound and his brusque manner were enough to dissuade many a tough customer.

"M-m-m-m-mister, M-m-m-mister Adray Ply," I stammered.

"What?"

I couldn't say another word. But I didn't have to because a tall man in a close-fitting charcoal suit came up behind Duncan.

The panther-looking man hissed, "You lookin' fo'me?"

"M-m-m-mister Ply?"

"That's right," he whispered.

The din around us seemed to recede.

Adray looked over his shoulder as if he were worried that people wanted to know his business. He grabbed me by the arm and pushed me out of the door. His grip hurt but I was happy to get out of that hell.

Outside he set me on a high step that led to a kind of utility door to Duncan's.

"What you want wit' me, boy?" His hoarse whisper scared me more than Duncan's eye.

"Black Betty say that she could meet you at Paulette's at twelve if you want." It was everything I could do to keep the tears out of my voice.

The smile that went across Adray's face was a purely evil thing. He forgot me and turned back toward Duncan's.

I was so scared that I could feel my insides trembling, but still, a nickel would buy a head-cheese sandwich on half a French bread.

"Mr. Ply, Betty said that you should gimme a nickel!" I knew it was a mistake as soon as the words were out of my mouth.

Ply turned and squinted at me. He put his oily brown face right up to mine. "You think I'm a fool, boy?"

I gave up on my mouth.

He grabbed me by the shirt with one hand and flashed out his silvery switchblade with the other. Then he lifted me up off of the stair.

"You think I'm a fool?" he rasped again. The men hanging out in front of Duncan's stood around, idly waiting for my demise.

I was nothing but scared.

He dropped me into a muddy puddle and I was up in a second and down the street so fast that I didn't even hear the laughter that I knew was bound to come.

I ran, hard and fast, all the way to the place I lived at that time. It was a little nest that I built in the back of a white family's barn outside of the ward. I crawled up into my hay bed and swore that I'd never go anywhere near Black Betty again.

And I was true to my vow—for at least three days.

There was a lock on the front door of Herford's gym but it was just a sham. Any burglar could have gone through it in less time than a regular person needed to work a key. Herford's had been broken into by countless thieves who had found that there was nothing worth stealing. They'd break into all the lockers and dump Clip's papers out of his drawers.

Papa Clip, who ran the gym, got tired of people breaking in and brought in a killer dog named Charlotte, after Clip's ex-mother-in-law. He put a tiny little typewritten note on the door that read, DOG, BEWARE. After getting Charlotte, Clip didn't even lock the door before going home. If you went in there off hours and climbed up the rickety stairway to the big workout room, you had Charlotte to contend with. "And Charlotte the dog," Clip would say, "is almost mean as Charlotte the woman."

Before I got up to the second floor I could smell the place. It was the combination of liniment, men's sweat, and a canine odor that was strong enough to hunt by.

There were maybe a dozen men working out around the room. Everyone was bare-chested except Clip and his father, Reynolds. Clip had on an old purple sweatshirt and denim jeans. He was a short bowlegged specimen who walked, it seemed, by swiveling his pelvis. Reynolds, who was at least eighty, wore a three-button cream-colored suit with a bright yellow-and-red ascot tied around his throat.

"Hey, Papa!" I yelled. And I was sorry the moment I had, because there came a deep growl and suddenly from a big refrigerator box in the corner a hundred and sixty pounds of teeth came hurtling at me.

I froze to the spot. The dog had already leapt, her open mouth aimed for my throat, when Papa yelled, "Charlotte!" I felt the breeze as the dog allowed herself to rush past me. She landed growling and sniffing around my heels. I don't know where Papa found that mongrel. It was some kind of cross between a St. Bernard and a mastiff. On all fours her head came up to my diaphragm. She was snarling with her ragged red maw open wide.

"Charlotte! Git!" Clip came over swinging a rolled-up

magazine at the dog's snout. All the evil flowed right out of her and she slouched back to her box whimpering.

"That fuckin' dog gonna kill somebody one day," the old man said, coming up behind Clip.

"I got my sign," Clip replied. "Law says you gotta have a sign you wanna keep a watchdog."

I wanted to tell him what he could do with that sign, but I kept it to myself.

"I'd like to see you say that to some judge." Reynolds Carpenter had run the gym before Clip did. Now he just hung around, living out his retirement.

"Hey, Clip, Mr. Carpenter," I said.

"Easy," Clip said. "What could we do you for?"

"I'm lookin' for Terry T. He still work out here?"

"If that's what you call it." Clip was disgusted. "If he come here and jump rope three days a week he think he ready t'be back in the ring. Shit! He lucky I don't th'ow his damn butt outta here. I swear if some good boxers showed up an' needed his locker I'd kiss him goodbye."

"He still makin' book?"

"Yeah," Reynolds said.

Reynolds was a gambler.

Most days, no matter what I was working on, I would have stopped and talked awhile. That's what made me different from the cops and from other people, black and white, trying to find out something down in black L.A. The people down there were country folks and they liked it when you stopped for a few minutes or so.

But I couldn't spare the time that day. I wanted to find Betty—and Marlon if he was alive. I wanted to end the whole thing and get back to where crazy animals, human and inhuman, weren't chafing to take a piece out of my hide.

"Okay then," I said to father and son. "I'll catch ya later."

"T might make a showup t'day," Reynolds said.

"Says who?" Clip asked.

"Ain't no race t'day. Ain't you ever noticed that T come in when he ain't got a race t'cover?"

"I don't know nuthin' 'bout no races or no gamblin'. I'm in the fights, that's what I do," Clip said.

"Yeah," Reynolds said and then he ran the pad of his thumb under his nose. All three of us knew that gesture meant a thrown fight.

There wasn't a manager or trainer or boxer who hadn't been close to gambling. Clip managed Joppy Shag the night he threw a fight to Tim "the Killer" O'Leary. Joppy was well past a shot at the title—the only thing he was selling was his self-respect. Joppy had told me that he and Clip took home thirty-five hundred dollars that night. He used that money to buy his bar.

I didn't hold it against Clip. At least when Joppy worked with him he took home a paycheck.

When we worked together Joppy ended up dead.

"What time he come in?" I asked.

"When it suit'im." Clip stared at his father while Reynolds examined his nails.

I left them like that. All around them men were throwing punches, feinting, doing sit-ups; all of them preparing for a war that they'd fight in the ring instead of on the street.

There was a little grocery store down at the corner. I braved the morning heat and got an *L.A. Examiner* and a Nehi grape soda down there. Then I sat down on a bus-stop bench across the street from Herford's.

All I was wearing was a pair of light cotton trousers and a short-sleeved shirt unbuttoned to the middle of my chest. The sky was so clear that it was hardly even blue. The sun shone down on me more relentlessly than Commander Styles.

Late morning in the summer is a time for old people. It's

the heat that gets them out. No matter how hot it is the old men dress up like Reynolds and go out looking for some corner to congregate on. The women are out to the store for margarine and collard greens.

One old man was walking down the block with the most dignified limp I'd ever seen. He strutted like he had some kind of knowledge denied to us younger fools. He was probably just proud that he'd lived so long. Because behind every poor old man there's a line of death. Siblings and children, lovers and wives. There's disease and no doctor. There's war, and war eats poor men like an aardvark licking up ants.

When I looked away from the old man I saw Terry T coming down the block. He was short and stocky, welterweight size. I'd seen him fight on a few starter cards. His fists were like hammers, insistent and right on the head. But he ignored the body, and that's something a boxer should never do.

"Terry!" I called.

He looked over in my direction and waved even though he didn't recognize me. Bookies know so many people, and they have to be welcoming because it's the man on the street that pays their salary.

He crossed over to me with a puzzled look on his face. Terry and I had been in various places, parties and what-have-you, at the same time but we'd never actually met. I knew who he was because he was famous for giving a good show in his first year in the ring.

"Easy Rawlins," I said to help him remember what he didn't know. "What's happenin'?"

"Not too much. I'm goin' to work out." He cocked his head over at the gym and flexed his biceps almost unconsciously. Like any good boxer he kept his head down.

Terry was sand-colored, which is not unusual in the black community. Some light-colored people felt that it was their duty to the future generation to marry somebody as light as they were—or lighter. Sometimes the prospective mate not only had to be the right color but had to have a special attribute like "good" hair or eyes-not-brown.

But there was always something about Terry. Maybe it was his buck teeth or the way he walked. It was as if he had the rhythm of a white man. A stride instead of a stalk in his gait.

"You wanna make twenty dollars?" I asked the young man.

His smile showed me three teeth capped in silver and two that were missing.

"I'm lookin' for Marlon Eady," I said.

Terry swallowed the grin and turned away from me saying, "Ain't seen'im."

"Hold up, man." I ran up beside Terry, and he stopped.

"What?"

"I heard you did his book."

"That's some shit. I hardly even know the niggah."

He made to walk off but I stood in front of him. I was close to a foot taller than Terry.

"I could go up to fifty," I told him.

"Get outta my way, man."

It was putting my hand on his shoulder, that was my mistake. Terry brought up his left arm to block me and then he threw a quick jab to my head.

That was okay. I could take a welterweight jab. I reached my arms out around to catch him in a bear hug, but Terry was too fast. He unloaded a half-dozen uppercuts to my middle, two of them landing where Commander Styles had hit me. I was on the ground as fast as I could get there and Terry was running down the street.

It was sort of funny watching a man run away after beating me to the ground. I laughed while holding my ribs.

"You okay, mistah?"

The dignified old man was peering down at me. He didn't look worried, just a little sad; tired of leaving dead men in his wake.

CHAPTER 14

I didn't take the old man's hand because I didn't want to owe anybody anything.

After about a minute or two I pulled myself up into a sort of stooping stance.

"You okay?" he asked again.

"What do you want?"

"You okay?"

"Yeah. Yeah, I'm fine."

"Them black mens over dere in that place always be fightin'," he said. I wasn't ready to walk yet so I let him go on. "I oughtta call the cops on'em. Always hittin' an' hurtin' an' bein' fools. That boy hit you is like that. He one'a them. But he don't know. No he don't."

"Don't know what?" I asked.

"That it's always a black man out there hittin' another black man so all the white folks could laugh: 'Look at that fool.' " The old man made like he was a pointing white man. " 'Beatin' the blood outta his own brother.' "

I don't think I even answered the old man. Nothing more than a nod anyway.

But I knew he was right.

Saul Lynx's office was on the boardwalk at Venice Beach.

I drove down there intent on taking out my anger and my

complaints on a white man. Lynx's office was in a small pink bungalow flanked by a Mexican bodega on one side and an empty lot on the other. It faced over a cracked concrete walkway onto the empty beach and flat gray ocean. Even in the summer Venice was empty. Motorcycle gangs, drug addicts, and wanderers were the only regular inhabitants. It was almost a poor man's beach back then.

Nobody answered my knock and the doorknob wouldn't turn.

At the back of the lot there was a slab cement wall with maybe fifteen inches between it and Saul's office. I scraped an elbow making it through the window.

His office was spare. The desk was just a table with a folding chair. No drawers. The tin trash can was lined with an empty brown paper bag. The floor was swept and newly mopped, clean enough to eat off. No file cabinets, but there was a small oak bureau that had a drawer and cabinet space. A bottle of red wine and a .38 were in the cabinet. A small stack of papers was all the drawer had to offer. I put the .38 in my pocket and carried the stack of papers to his desk.

Mr. Lynx was a hunter, had a license for small game in California. He was a veteran and he'd done some kind of work once for Crandall Industries. By the look of the bookkeeping journal he seemed to owe out more money than he was taking in. There wasn't anything about a lawyer or Elizabeth Eady or the Cains.

I could tell by his office that Mr. Lynx played his whole life close to the vest. I sat back in his two-dollar chair and rubbed my aching side. For some reason it didn't surprise me that Saul Lynx decided to come through the door at that very moment.

Everything he wore was the same except for the tie. This one was sky-blue, the kind of synthetic blue that didn't go with anything.

"What the hell are you doing here?"

It was almost worth the bloody elbow to see old deadpan Saul shook up like that.

"Thought I'd drop by an' tell you what's happenin'."

"Get up from there. You can't sit there." He glanced over at the cabinet.

I got myself up out of the chair, managing not to wince too much.

"What happened to you?" Saul asked. His whole body was leaning toward that cabinet.

"Have a seat," I said, gesturing at the chair.

There was a moment of indecision. Saul was wondering about the odds of him getting to the pistol before I used my superior size to stop and mutilate him.

Finally he put his smile back on and went to the chair.

"What do you have?" he asked.

"I met your friend."

His eyes asked, 'who?'

"Calvin Hodge."

Saul shook his head while pursing his lips. No.

"I met him out at the Cain residence. I had to go through a gate that said 'Beverly Estates.' "

"I don't know what this map lesson has to do with me, Mr. Rawlins." He sat back, secure again in his undertaker facade. "You want a drink?"

"No thanks. I don't drink." I smiled and took the .38 from my back pocket. I cracked it open to make sure that it was loaded—it was—then I cocked back the hammer and placed it down on the table. I can learn a lesson, even from a wild man like Styles. I placed the pistol closer to me than to him, but I was standing so he had the closer reach.

"It's gonna go off we go after it," I said.

Saul split his eyes between the pistol and my hand. A thin line of sweat formed across his upper lip.

"You see, it's at times like these that we truly are equals.

No bullshit now." I held up the lecturing finger of my left hand. I needed the right to go after that gun if I had to.

But I didn't think that I'd have to. Saul Lynx was a cautious man. He didn't have a thing incriminating in that office. And that was amazing, because even your most pious, God-fearing man has got something to incriminate him. That's just the way men are.

"What's this about, Rawlins?"

"Hodge hire you?"

He looked up at me, hefting that potato he used as a nose between blazing green eyes. "You're off the case. Keep the retainer."

"You don't want me t'find Betty?"

"I'd appreciate it if you left me my property." He nodded toward the pistol.

"Who hired you, man?" I asked.

Saul's shoulders twitched. That was as close as he came to lunging for that gun.

"I don't have to answer your questions. I paid you good money and you haven't produced a thing as far as I can see. You don't scare me."

I believed him. Mr. Lynx was a tough man. That's why his nose was so misshapen.

"Okay," I said. "I'll drop it 'cause I don't have anything in it. But if the cops come to me about Marlon or Betty or anybody else I looked into for you—I'ma give'em your name an' number."

Lynx didn't even shrug.

I snatched the pistol from the table so fast that he didn't even have time to blink.

"I'll send this back to ya," I said. Disarming desperate white men was becoming a habit.

He didn't get up to see me out the door.

Outside I realized how dark it was in Saul's office. He

didn't have any windows up front and the brightest lamp-light couldn't have been over sixty watts.

Out in front of the bodega was a big yellow trash can filled with popsicle sticks, cupcake wrappers, wine and beer bottles in sleek brown bags—and one large paper bag that seemed to be full.

I thought of Saul's clean floors and his neat trash can.

The bag had the rind of a pastrami on rye, an empty bottle of Dr. Brown's Cel-Ray soda, and various papers—some of which had Saul Lynx's name written on them.

I carried my find back to the car wondering why I bothered.

I guess some habits only die with the man.

CHAPTER 15

The kids and I went through the trash bag together. It was a little game we played. We took out our own trash can from under the sink and Feather looked for things I needed to keep so I could read them. Other things were all dirty and needed to be thrown away.

"How come you wanna be readin' 'em?" Feather asked.

"Because it's a secret and I'm trying to find it out."

Jesus helped his sister sift through the papers and food containers.

There was hardly anything worthwhile to be found. Just a few small sheets of paper with notes scribbled down on them. One had "Calvin Hodge" written on it with an address on Robertson Boulevard. I knew the building. I had already looked up Hodge's address but it was good to know for a fact that the two of them were linked. Another paper had “Elizabeth Eady” on it. It was also inscribed with the initials FL and Odell’s address.

There was a third paper that said simply “Ronald Hawkes” with a question mark next to the name.

“Daddy, I’m hungry,” Feather whined. “What we have for dinner?”

“Little girls,” I said in as close to a Boris Karloff accent as I could manage. I let my eyes grow big and developed a big hump on my back.

“Ahhhhhhhh!” Feather screamed with glee. She flew out of the kitchen. I came shambling on behind her chanting, “Girly arms, yummy good. Mmmmm.”

We went all through the house. Over furniture and under tables. Jesus joined us, making the little girl as happy as a human being can be. We went out the back door and all around the yard until finally a very tired, almost frightened little girl got caught between her two men in a corner of the back fence.

“Nooooooo!” she screamed but I grabbed her with my one good monster arm and hefted her up so that I could take big old monster bites out of her stomach.

But then I stopped.

“Ugh! Raw!” I growled to Jesus. “Gotta cook her. Put her in oven.”

So we threw the protesting little baby into the backseat and drove off to Mama’s Hacienda, where we had all kinds of tacos and burritos with beans.

I got three calls that night.

The first one was from a woman whose voice was unfamiliar to me.

“Mr. Rawlins?”

“Yeah?”

"I'm Gwendolyn Barnes. We met the other day."

"I'm sorry but I don't remember. Who are you?"

"I answered the door at Sarah Cain's."

"Oh yeah, the white girl with the tan." I don't know why I said that. I guess I was still angry about everything that had happened. "What do you want?"

"Miss Cain would like to see you."

"Where'd you pick up this number?"

"Mr. Hodge gave it to Miss Cain. He didn't think that it was a good idea to call you but she insisted. Will you come?"

"No thanks. They canceled my passport to Beverly Hills. I can't go back there for five years at least." I was only half joking.

"She won't be at that house," Gwendolyn told me. "She's at her farm. You take the Coast Highway almost to Oxnard but then take the exit to Lea. There's a yellow phone booth at the end of the road. You can call us from there." She rattled off a phone number and I jotted it down. "I can come lead you to the house from there. It's hard to find if you don't know the shortcut."

"Thanks for the directions, Miss Barnes, but I don't think I'ma be usin'em. You see, I don't have anything to do with your employer anymore. We're quits."

There was a muffled sound over the phone. I heard some voices and then some kind of commotion.

Finally I said, "Hello? Hello? I'm not just gonna sit here and hold the phone for you, honey."

"Just a minute," she said, exasperated with me. Then, "Miss Cain assures you that only she and I will be here when you come and she's willing to pay you six hundred and thirty-seven dollars for your trouble."

Must have been the loose change at the bottom of her purse.

"I don't think so, Miss Barnes. I'm not sure that I can afford any more of your boss's money."

"Please, Mr. Rawlins," she said as if I knew her, as if I owed her something.

"I'll tell you what. I'll sleep on it. If you hear from me tomorrow, let's say about two, well then you will. Okay?"

"Thank you. Thank you very much."

"Don't thank me unless I call."

I held down the phone button and thought about the women. I liked women, at least I liked something about them. I liked how they walked and smelled and how they looked at the world in a really different way than men. Because they were so different they were always full of surprises. But I'd had enough surprises.

I was still holding the phone when it started to ring again.

"Yeah?"

"This is Faye Rabinowitz," a crisp businesslike voice said. "Is Ezekiel Rawlins there?"

"That's me. It's pretty late, ain't it?"

"I just got home from work and I thought you felt some urgency about this matter. If it's too late . . ."

"Noooo, no. What you got?"

"I did what you wanted, Mr. Rawlins. I asked the prosecutor's office how my client was caught."

"And?"

"Why do you want to know?"

"I already told ya. It's because I want some kinda way of tellin' Raymond that it wasn't one of his friends turned him in. Maybe they got him on clues—I don't know. I'm tryin' to keep your client out of trouble."

"Well. There really isn't much to say. He *was* turned in. It was an anonymous tip. Somebody, probably male, probably Negro, called in even before the shooting was reported and said, I quote, "It was Raymond Alexander killed Bruno Ingram in the alley off Hooper. The Lord wouldn't let me be quiet on a night like this.' That's it. That's all they had. But that, along with the weapon, was enough for a conviction."

"Thank you," I said. "I'll do what's right."

"Hm," she answered.

After that we both hung up our phones.

"Hey, Raymond. How you doin'," I said when he answered Etta's phone.

"Yeah, Easy."

"You still lookin' t'see if somebody at John's turnt you in?"

"I been lookin' but ain't nobody in town who was there. It's almost like somebody warnt'em off." He paused a full fifteen seconds. Long enough to let me know that he suspected me. Sitting there at my kitchen table my life was in more danger than it had been in jail with Commander Styles. "But I told John that I better find me somebody quick or there will be hell to pay."

I couldn't think of anything more frightening than a face-off between Mouse and John.

"I want you to lay off doin' anything till I see what I could see."

"What you mean?"

"I got an idea, that's all. I heard somethin' and I wanna chase it down."

"Uh-huh. Well, you do that, Easy. But I'ma be doin' what I'm doin' too. Maybe we meet in the middle somewhere."

Jesus was standing around the kitchen table when I got off the phone with Mouse.

"How you doin', boy?"

He nodded at me.

"It's after eleven. Time for you to get to bed."

He smiled again. Jesus was always smiling at me. Ever since I took him out of a life of child prostitution he loved me. My first wife, Regina, had told me that there was probably something wrong deep down inside him; that there was a dark anger going to come out someday.

Maybe so.

But I wasn't going to treat him like a monster just because he was supposed to be one.

"You ever going to talk to me, boy?" I asked his back as he went through the door. He stopped for half a second and then kept on moving.

I was looking through the want ads at one in the morning when the phone rang again.

I could have been a plumber, electrician, mechanic, or salesman. Gotten up every morning at six-thirty and dragged myself in to work by eight. I could have said "yessir" and "no sir" and taken home a paycheck. I could have been promoted because I was a good worker; spent every day for the next twenty-five years going into an office or workshop, and then one day they'd put me out and in a year there wouldn't be a soul to remember that I had ever been.

"Hello?" I said into the phone.

Instead of an answer I got an earful of wet rolling coughs.

"Mofass?"

"Yeah . . ." He coughed some more. "Mr. Rawlins."

"How you doin', man?" I asked.

"Got this cold," he hacked. "But I'm okay."

"It's kinda late t'be callin', ain't it?"

"I need to talk," he said. I realized that he was whispering. Mofass's regular voice, even with the emphysema, was loud and hearty.

"Talk then."

"Not now. Tomorrow. You could come over here after ten."

"Okay. I got stuff to talk to you about anyway."

I folded the paper and put it in the trash. Maybe in a few weeks I'd get a job, but not that day.

CHAPTER 16

Mofass and Clovis had a big house on Peters Lane up in the Baldwin Hills. I'd had a house down the hill from there once but money troubles forced me to sell it and move down into the rental neighborhood. Grover and Tyrone came out at nine and got into a Ford Galaxy that was wedged in between a Cadillac and a Falcon in the driveway. They drove right across the yard and onto the street, leaving deep furrows in the lawn.

Clavell, Renee, Antoinette, and Fitts came out, one after the other, over the next half hour. They all got into different cars and went in different ways. Clavelle drove right past my car but I just held up a newspaper with my paper coffee cup in one hand and he didn't know me from any other laborer waiting for a friend.

Clovis was out of the door at nine forty-five. She said something into the house, I figured it was to Mofass. She shut the door, checking to make sure that it wouldn't come open. Then she looked all around the house and up and down the street.

Maybe she smelled me.

Finally she got into her Caddy and drove off down the opposite way from where I was parked.

I waited until ten and then went to pay my respects.

I had expected Mofass to answer but it wasn't him. It was Jewelle, a little cousin of Clovis's who was brought along with the rest of the family up to L.A.

"Good morning, Mr. Rawlins," she said as if having rehearsed the line in a grade-school chant. Jewelle was sixteen and already a senior in high school.

"Mofass here?"

"Uh-huh. He waitin' for you."

We went through the big messy house together. Men's and women's clothes were thrown everywhere. On the banister up the stairs, on the floor in the hall. There were empty plates on the dining-room table and cardboard boxes torn open and left on the chairs.

Thick drapes were pulled over the windows and all the lights in the house were on. There were newspapers spread out under a chair in the hallway with clumps of cut hair all over them.

"It's a mess," I said.

"You should see the kitchen," Jewelle said. "An' they want me t'clean it. They said I couldn't go to school until the house gets clean. Do that look like my hair to you?" She had turned and was looking me in the eye.

"No, ma'am," I answered obediently.

That got her to smile.

"Mr. Rawlins." Mofass was standing in the doorway to the den. He wore a dark purple robe that hung open to his navel showing his huge gut and his once powerful chest.

We all went in. The den in that house was also the office, so it was kept neat. All the furniture was mahogany. A desk, two file cabinets, and two chairs upholstered with red velour. One of the chairs was actually large enough for two. Mofass and Jewelle sat in that one.

That girl, who was looking more like a woman every second, grabbed Mofass's hand and squeezed it a brief moment before clasping her own hands together between her knees.

"What's this all about?" I asked Mofass.

"What you mean?"

"All this sneakin' around."

Jewelle wore a one-piece rayon dress. The dress was tan, two shades lighter than her skin. Her hair was hot-comb-straightened and lightened around the edges to a gold color that women were fond of in those days.

Mofass on the other hand was an ebony man with sad and sagging yellow eyes. He took two breaths for each one of Jewelle's.

"I hear you was down at Esquire the other day," Mofass said.

I stayed quiet.

He took twenty little gasps before saying, "I want my business back."

"Yeah? What you want me to do about that?"

"I need to get Jewelle here somewheres safe and then I need me some p'otection 'gainst Clovis's brood."

"What's wrong with you and Clovis?"

"She been stealin' from Uncle Willy," Jewelle blurted out. "She took everything from outta his bank account and she won't let him have nuthin'. Treatin' him like he was some crazy old man."

"She won't even let me out the house, Mr. Rawlins. I'm sick, but that don't mean I'm feebleminded, do it?"

"Naw," I said. I was thinking that maybe this trouble could help me. The first thing a black man and a poor man learns is that trouble is all he's got so that's what he has to work with.

"I still gotta couple'a bank accounts she cain't get into. She wants me to sign over my power of attorney. But if I do that then she could sell my stuff and . . ." Mofass paused for a moment. It had a melodramatic effect but I could tell that he was hurting, "... she got a husband that she done drug up from Dallas."

"What?" I tried not to laugh. Sometimes you're hoping that things will be different; that men and women will change over the years and become those good, if hard, folks that the preachers talk about. But it never changes. And if something does get good for a while you could be sure that it will turn sour before you have time to get any real pleasure.

"It ain't funny, man," Mofass wheezed. "Right down the hill." There were tears in his eyes.

"She there right now." Jewelle had snagged Mofass's hand again.

"So what is it that you need from me?"

"Take Jewelle somewhere safe."

"What for? Clovis is her family."

"Yeah, but she knows how close we is. She'd send her back down Texas or make her life hell up here. She'd think Jewelle helped me if I cut outta here."

Mofass was in his late fifties but he seemed older than that. He was from the old days when there was a black community almost completely sealed off from whites. He wore old-fashioned clothes. He belonged to a Negro social club that excluded poor blacks. Clovis got many of her investors from among Mofass's friends.

Jewelle was just a child. But give a girl child a hard life and you make a woman out of her faster than she can make babies.

I took my time looking at them. There was a smell in the house. "The stink of corruption," as my holy-roller voodoo grandfather used to say.

"Jewelle," I said.

"Huh?"

"Go make me some tea, honey."

"Uh-uh, I wanna stay here wit' you and Uncle Willy."

"You go on," Mofass said. He patted the girl's thigh and she gave in.

"You want lemon or milk?" she asked, pouting at me.

"I'll take it straight."

She went out of the door moving her hips in a way that I'm sure she was unaware of.

"What do I get outta this, William?" I used Mofass's given name because suddenly I was mad.

"County planner, Mason LaMone, and the Save-Co corporation." Mofass's yellow eyes seemed to infect the words he spoke. "They all been down here. I heard 'em when they thought I was upstairs asleep."

"What would men like that want down here, William?"

"You had a damn good idea, Mr. Rawlins. Damn good. The minute Clovis went down there with the application for permits, that sent shocks all the way up to the top man." Mofass raised his voice in excitement and then had to cough. It was a hard sort of hacking that sounded as if he were torn and ragged on the inside.

I watched him with little sympathy. His news meant that there was no way out of my real estate problems and nobody I could trust.

"So what?" I asked. "They wanna invest wit' us?"

Mofass shook his head slowly, not meeting my eye. Maybe he was afraid that if he looked straight at me while delivering his foul news I might take my rage out on him.

Maybe he was right.

"They got Clovis to work with'em. She done told them all about you and she give'em back all the papers they processed on yo' property. They started talkin', an' the next thing you know, they's this sanitation station they figure needs to be built. County planner in LaMone's pocket and LaMone in bed wit' Save-Co."

"LaMone," I said. "That the big real estate guy from downtown?"

Mofass stuck out his big lips and nodded. "That's why I called you, Mr. Rawlins. He was here last night. Him an' Clovis got a good ole laugh at how she was gonna make you spend yo' money to pay her to rob you blind."

"But why? Why'd Clovis wanna help the white man? We

could build Freedom's Plaza ourselves. We could own it ourselves."

Mofass shook his head again. "Not the way she seen it. Them men tole her that they was gonna take that land one way or t'other. Save-Co was gonna build an' they wasn't gonna have no Negro competition. An' they told her that she could manage the property by herself. You see? She don't need me no more, so that's why she wanna take my money now."

The spout from Jewelle's teapot begun to whistle somewhere in the big house. It was a weak and strained peeping sound; something like my complaint against Mason LaMone and the Save-Co Corporation—the largest supermarket business in southern California.

"So why call me, William?" I asked. "If I cain't beat'em then why I wanna help you?"

Mofass grinned at me then. If there was one thing I knew about Mofass it was that his smile meant money was somewhere to be had; money that he could trick out of someone.

"Maybe you cain't beat them white men, Mr. Rawlins. I don't know about that. But Clovis is usin' Esquire Realty to represent Freedom's Trust. And I own Esquire Realty. If you help me to get it back in my hands, at least you will get whatever profit Clovis made. At least that."

I'd spent years having little back-room meetings like that with Mofass; years of hiding, pushing Mofass up front like he was the one who owned everything. I did that because of the weight of black life down where I was a child.

The logic of my childhood had never proven wrong.

If a man wore gold chains, somebody was going to hit him on the head. If he looked prosperous, women would pull him by his dick into the bed and then hit him with a paternity suit nine months later. If a woman had money, the man would just beat her until she got up off of it.

I always talk about down home like it really was home. Like everybody who looked like me and talked like me really cared about me. I knew that life was hard, but I hoped that if someone stole from me it would be because they were hungry and needed it. But some people will tear you down just to see you fall. They'll do it even if your loss is their own.

They will laugh at your misfortune and sit next to you at misery's table.

"You help me take back what's mines and I will give you back everything that Clovis was gonna take," Mofass said.

"Yeah, uh-huh," I said. "But there's gonna be somethin' new this time, Mofass. I'm gonna be the new one representin' Esquire. You gonna send me in there t'talk t'them men."

"Oh yeah?" he asked, almost amused. "But I thought you liked to stay in the background, Mr. Rawlins?"

"Well, I guess it's time for me to get over that." I was thinking about my ex-wife, Regina. She left me because I couldn't be honest with her. I never told her about my property or how I got my money. I couldn't share my life with her and so our love died.

"Okay, Mr. Rawlins. You he'p me out an' I'll let you run the show on Freedom's Plaza. You know I cain't get around as well I used to no more anyways."

I nodded and we shook hands. Then I asked, "So what's with the girl?"

"What you mean?"

"I mean I ain't gonna help you with no statutory rape."

"It ain't like that, Mr. Rawlins," he protested. "JJ kinda starstruck wit' me 'cause I'm nice to her. An' they treat her real bad here, so when she see them treat me like that she feel sorry for me."

"Is sorry the only thing she feelin'?"

"Man, what you gonna do?"

I didn't know exactly what he meant by that. Maybe he meant that the world makes us and we just do what we have to. There he was, a prisoner in the house he paid for, and there was JJ.

"If I put the girl someplace she stays. At least until she's eighteen or back with her family."

"Sure." He nodded. "She need a home."

"It's gonna cost you, William."

"Whatever it take."

"Gimme a minute," I said, gesturing at the door with a motion of my head.

After Mofass went out I got on the phone.

"Etta?"

"Yes, Easy?"

"I need you t'take in a girl. She's a teenager and needs a little supervision and some help."

"How long?"

"I don't know."

"I don't know," she said, hesitating. "It take a lotta money to go feedin' a teenager, Easy."

"A man gonna pay for her board and he gonna pay you for your time."

"Well . . . does she really need help?"

"I think so."

Etta hemmed and hawed a little but she finally came around.

"Okay. Let's try it," she told me.

"Thanks, Etta. Mouse there?"

"Yeah. You want him? 'Cause you know I'm ready to kick his butt out the house."

"He still crazy?"

"Just cleanin' his pistol and mutterin' 'bout his five years."

"Get him for me, will ya?"

While I waited, Jewelle brought in my tea.

"Get your bags packed, honey. We're gonna put you somewhere safe for a while."

"Wit' Uncle Willy?"

"No, honey. No right yet. First you're goin' to stay with some friends'a mine out in Compton."

"I wanna stay wit'—"

"Go upstairs and pack, girl. I don't care what you want. Don't you know that William is sick and that this family'a yours might try and hurt him? He cain't be worried 'bout you and them too."

"Hello," Mouse said in my ear.

"Hey, Raymond."

Jewelle had turned away.

"What's up, Ease?"

I recited the magic words. "I need your help, man."

"With what?"

"You remember Mofass?" I told him the whole story, emphasizing the part about being cheated out of my idea.

"Help Mofass for me, Raymond," I said. "He'll pay ya and then you could help Etta with the bills." And I'd have time to keep him from killing any innocent people—including me.

"All right, uh-huh, sure—but I gotta know somethin' first."

"What's that?"

"You the one told them men about me?"

"What men?" I hoped to sound more certain than I felt.

"Don't you be fuckin' wit' me, Easy. You know what I'm sayin'."

"I know them men," I said in the dialect and song of my childhood. "An' ain't one of'em bad enough or fool enough to give you up to the cops."

"Uh-huh. Here you is sayin' you want my he'p an' the whole time you pullin' a load of shit," Mouse replied.

"I'm lookin' for the one turned you in, Ray. I am. You wouldn't wanna kill the wrong man."

We were children in a schoolyard arguing over a ball.

"I don't give a shit," he said simply.

I thought about Hawaii again. I wondered, for a brief moment, if a man could escape his fate.

I knew the answer but I wondered just the same.

"Work with me on this one, Raymond." He and I had been friends ever since I rolled into Houston in a boxcar—hungry, homeless, and only eight years old. We kept each other alive way back then.

"How many days you want for this job wit' Mofass?" he asked.

"Just a few days," I said. "That's all it'll take."

"I could use some money. You know Etta won't get up off'a dime. Shit. I thought I was gonna have to get out here and rob somebody."

"Take Etta's car and come on over to . . ." I gave him Mofass's address. "Mofass and a girl gonna be there. Take Mofass over to Primo's and tell him that I need him to keep him a day or two and then take the girl out to Etta. Tomorrow you go back and get Mofass. He's gonna need a lawyer." I smiled to myself. "A good lawyer."

CHAPTER 17

I don't know why I went out to Oxnard. Maybe it was because of Mofass and the feeling I got that I was in charge again. Maybe it was because I didn't want to look too deeply into Mouse's problems. There was no easy way out of Mouse's difficulties. I knew from hard experience that when he wanted somebody to die it was like destiny.

Maybe it was because I never learned to respect women.

If I knew that a man was dangerous I'd be wary, because a man can be a serious problem. I wouldn't necessarily be afraid of a man—still, I'd take him seriously. But a woman never called up fear in me. I've seen at least a dozen women kill men dead but I'd still laugh if one was to threaten me.

So when Gwendolyn Jones called me the only thing I took seriously was the promise of six hundred and thirty-seven dollars. Now that I was dealing with Mouse and he was promised cash I knew that I had to have some kind of reserve just in case Mofass was low.

And everything felt right about going there. The sky was blue over a dark ocean. Cool air blew into my window for the first time in weeks. The gulls sang their blues note and wheeled around. I was almost happy.

The Lea exit led down a long lane through strawberry orchards, finally coming upon rocky ridge that looked over the ocean.

A big yellow shack was perched on the cliff. There was a hole, roughly the shape of a telephone, cut out of the door. I pulled up next to the structure, parked, and lit a cigarette. The taste of tobacco and the cool sea breeze soothed me.

You couldn't see the land below, because the cliff jutted

out over the water. The ocean was rolling in like some great, dumb migrating animal.

The chill of the breeze brought a grin to my face. I got out of the car and went right up to the edge of the cliff. It was beautiful. Even more so because of the troubles I had right then.

The ocean and wind told me how small my problems were; how stupid I was to get involved with other people's troubles when there was so much beauty to be had. All I had to do was to look out and see the ocean, or go home and watch my children grow. I laughed and told myself to remember that the next time somebody comes pushing money at me.

I was ready to get back in my car and go on home. Tomorrow I could take the kids out of school and have a picnic at Pismo Beach.

But then I heard something, or almost heard it. It was a sweet sound. Behind me was a high rocky hill. A path wended through the big shale boulders and tall brown grasses. And way up at the top of the hill a solitary bicyclist was coming down the path shakily, but not so shakily that she couldn't wave and call out, "Mr. Rawlins!" I wouldn't have understood her at that distance if I didn't know my own name.

Gwendolyn Jones rode down the hill on her red J. C. Higgins three-speed. I watched her all the way down until she came to a stop in front of me.

She was even prettier than before in her hot-pink-and-white checkered shorts and pink tennis shoes. Her socks and V-necked T-shirt were white, except there was a tiny pink satin bow at the angle point of the V.

"Hi," she said with an innocence that couldn't be faked. "I was waiting for you. I knew you were going to come but I thought I might have missed your call because Sarah needed help with her bath." Gwendolyn crinkled her nose with loving disapproval. "Sometimes I think that she can't even blow her nose without somebody to help her."

"You always call your boss by her first name?"

"Well," she said. Gwendolyn's smile was so friendly that it called up images of my childhood, before my mother died. "It doesn't *feel* like she's my boss really. You know, it's kind of like we just have different chores."

"Different paychecks too, I bet."

Gwendolyn dismounted her bike and stood before me, holding on to the handlebars.

"Will you take me?" she asked.

"Say what?"

"Up to the farm. It's pretty far and it's mostly uphill. I can put my bike in your boot."

"My what?"

"The trunk, silly."

While I was folding the bike to fit over my spare tire I took a whiff at my armpits. I smelled like a man but not too strong. I was thankful for Johnson & Johnson baby powder because I didn't think that Gwendolyn could take anything too strong.

Maybe a kiss.

"You have to take the dirt road that goes out around the other side of the phone booth." She pointed at the slender path that went around the mountainside.

The road, if you could call it that, was textured with deep, hard ruts that were excavated by the drainage of the previous winter's rain. It was a slight pass that snaked its way upward around the coastal mountain. There were times that it seemed as if a deep rut might crumble and that we would go rolling down into the sea or one of the wild valleys below.

Gwendolyn put her pink-shod feet on the dashboard. I

tried, with some difficulty, to keep my eyes on the road and off those long brown legs. The car lurched from side to side, scraping the bottom now and then. I'm not a vain man, nor am I pernickety about my belongings, but I do like to keep my vehicle clean and in decent condition. Driving on that highway took away any trade-in value that my car might have had.

As we went inland the heat rose. Flies and gnats zipped in and out of the open windows. A stream ran in the gully beside the road. From all around a rotted odor arose. Birds, hidden in the decayed shrubbery, sounded like people being throttled down below.

"How much longer till we get there?" I asked.

"About a mile and a half." Gwendolyn pointed toward the top of the hillside and said, "There's smooth road starting there, and then it's not too much further."

"I sure don't understand this."

"Understand what?"

"How come somebody rich as Miss Cain would have a house way the hell out where they cain't even drive without messin' up their cars."

"Oh?" Gwendolyn mused. "We *could* have gone around the other way. That's paved, but it takes too long."

I couldn't even say a word. Here I was entrusting myself to the hands of a working woman—a black woman!—and she put one of the biggest investments in a workingman's life on a drive to ruin. If I had said a word I might have had to punctuate it with violence. So I kept my silence, bumping and jerking on that haphazard road.

When we reached the graded path I pulled the car to the side and stopped.

"Why are we stopping?" Gwendolyn wanted to know.

"I wanna talk to you before we get to the house."

"About what?"

I was staring hard at her. All kinds of feelings bubbled in

my head. I wanted to know about Betty, and maybe Marlon; I wanted to know why Miss Cain called me before I had to go in and hear her lies (I say lies because, back then, any white person had to prove themselves to me before I could consider trusting them). I wanted to get to know Gwendolyn too. I wanted to know why she said "boot" instead of "trunk."

"Where's Betty?"

Gwendolyn looked down into her lap, and so I put a finger under her chin to lift her eyes back to me.

We were both breathing hard.

"I don't know." She tried to pull her head back down but I wouldn't let her.

"Okay. I'll buy that. But what's goin' on here? Betty's just a maid, a house cleaner. Ain't no reason for lawyers and detectives and hundreds of dollars bein' paid just to find a house cleaner."

"Betty . . . Miss Eady was a part of the household. Our house wasn't like you say. I mean . . . everybody was close. Betty had been with the Cains since before the war."

"Why are the cops askin' about Miss Cain's father?"

"I don't know. All I know is that Mr. Cain died. He died and then Betty was gone and everybody was upset. The police came out to the house and then, the next day, Mr. Hodge came. But nothing happened. It's just that the police are still looking into something and the will is caught up in court."

"The police are looking into what?"

"I don't know. The man who came out from the police said that everything seemed to be natural, you know, the death, but that there has to be an autopsy. But the police doctor is taking a long time. The regular coroner is too busy or something and so they got this consultant. Anyway he's taking a long time."

Gwendolyn tried to move her head again. When I held on

she moved her hand to mine. That didn't work either but she kept her hand there, holding the fleshy pad under my thumb.

"So what's all this about Sarah Cain's husband—Hawkes? She still married to him or what?"

"No. No."

"No what? She not married?"

"Yes."

"What you tryin' to say, girl?"

I liked her fingernails digging into my hand.

"She's married but they're separated. She hates him but she can't divorce him because of Arthur."

"What's he got to do with it?"

"When they broke up, Sarah and Ron, Arthur was only ten. He stopped eating and lost fifteen pounds. The doctors said that he was going to die. They had to put him in a hospital for two months. It was then that Sarah promised never to divorce. It was that promise that kept Arthur alive."

"Damn. And where is this guy Hawkes?"

"Nowhere. She won't let him near the house. I think maybe he sends a letter to Arthur now and then but he's never around."

"What happened with Ron and Sarah?"

"He was awful. Just as bad as Mr. Cain was. Sarah had one of them on one side and one on the other. They both pulled until she almost broke. But Mr. Cain was the stronger and he made Ron leave."

"How'd he do that?" I felt Gwendolyn's chin push against my fingertips.

"He just told him to go—that's all."

I pushed her head up a quarter of an inch. "No it's not," I said.

"I don't know. Really. Ron got into trouble and the police arrested him. That was after Sarah's mother, Cassandra, died. Sarah came home and Ron never came back. We heard that they let him go but he never came back."

I leaned forward until my face was only inches from hers. "You know why I come up here?" The more she talked white, the more the street came into my voice.

"No."

"Because *you* called me." Maybe it was true. "If that white woman woulda called I'da hung up the phone."

Gwendolyn didn't answer, so I took the hand that was holding mine and kissed her fingers, kind of sloppy, and then looked into her eyes.

"Kiss me, girl."

She did, as well as she knew how. It was a dry little peck on my lower lip.

"Now watch," I said. I pressed my tongue into her mouth. She was shocked at first but then she softened, put her hand to the back of my neck.

She needed serious practice but her heart was in the right place.

After our little lip tussle I leaned back. She took a last kiss from my mouth and then drew up her knees to her chin, between us.

I didn't know if it was an invitation or a barrier so I asked, "You wanna go down there now?"

While shaking her head, no, she said, "But we have to."

CHAPTER 18

We drove for a long way through a dark grove of avocado trees, crushing the pulpy fruit and giant seeds that littered our way. The trees had been planted in long rows that ran away from the road at perpendicular angles. In some of the long shadowy corridors men, women, and children, dressed in ghostly white clothes, worked. They were Mexican mainly with a few Negroes and a handful of Japanese. The men were armed with slender wooden poles that had jagged tin cans attached to one end. They'd lift the cans into the trees, snagging the black alligator pears. After they'd gotten a few they'd lower the pole for the women and children to pick from. Then the men would lift their farming spears again while the rest arranged the fruit in large wooden cartons that had been stacked along the way.

Down one tree-lined alley came a large wooden wagon riding on two giant, lopsided wooden wheels. This wagon was drawn by a skeletal white horse. Big men ran behind the rig hefting the boxes of fruit up into the wagon bed.

I stopped the car. "Jesus."

"What?"

"It's like I drove out of California, back through the south, and all the way into hell."

"What are you talking about?" Gwen asked. I decided to call her Gwen after our teenaged kiss. She was really surprised. "This is just an orchard. It's part of the Cain farm."

"This is the farm we're goin' to?"

"What's wrong, Mr. Rawlins? Mr. Cain didn't like all that modern machinery kind of farming that's coming up now. He liked to think that the food he produced had human sweat attached to it." There wasn't a hint of irony in her voice.

"What about them kids?" I pointed past her nose down a twilit lane. "Don't you think that kids should be in some kinda school?"

Gwen's eyes pitied me. "They can't even speak English. How can they go to school?"

"Where you come from, girl?" I wasn't so much angry as I wanted to cry. "That's children out there. It's against the law to have children workin' like that."

"They're just helping their parents out. They're not getting paid or anything."

I turned away from the sight and looked out into the road ahead. It's a good thing I looked before putting my foot on the gas because I could have run them over.

It was a man seated on a magnificent black mare. The horse was well groomed and clean. You could see that she ate well and was exercised daily. There was a white patch at the side of her jaw that looked like foam flailing from her mouth as if she was moving at a fast clip. The white spot matched her bright leather saddle.

The brown man astride her wore blue jeans, a blue shirt, and a back-sloping tan cowboy hat.

"Hi, Rudy!" Gwen yelled. She got out of the car waving and running up to rub the horse's nose. "Hi, Beauty," she said to the mare.

"Gwendy, where you been?" Rudy asked. He was peering into the car to get a good look at me, so I decided to climb out and oblige him.

"This is Easy Rawlins, Rudy," Gwen was saying. "He's up here to help Sarah find Betty."

"Pleased t'meetcha," I said. It was a phrase I reserved for white people and others who might not have sympathy with my dialect.

Rudy just nodded and stared at me. He was a young

man, Mexican and a cowboy. I was willing to bet that he had played the kissing game with Gwen out among the avocado trees too; and that he heard the way her voice puckered around my name. I could see by the way he was staring at me that I had managed to make one more enemy in the world.

"We better get goin'," I said to Gwen.

Gwen gave us both a puzzled stare and then climbed back into the car. I got in myself and inched ahead. Rudy was still there before us. The mare got a little jittery but Rudy held her in place.

So I let the car jump ahead half a foot.

That got Beauty to raise her front hooves but Rudy dug his heels into her side and pulled on the reins until she was back in place.

"Rudy!" Gwen yelled out of the window, waving at the silent cowboy. "Move back! Get away!"

Right at that moment an insect stung me behind the left ear. I growled and threw the car into reverse, gunning the engine as I did. The car flew backwards, throwing dirt and pebbles at the mare's legs. All of this was too much for the horse and she took off—running twenty feet or so down one of the rows of trees. Before Rudy could get her back around I changed gears and hit the gas, leaving him my dust to navigate in.

"What's wrong with him?" Gwen shouted while trying to see out of the back window.

After about a mile the avocado trees gave way to lemon groves. More migrant workers were out there plucking and climbing and baking in the sun for pennies an hour.

Another fifteen minutes and the road became paved.

The Cain farm was lovely. Painted gray like the inside of an oyster shell is gray and surrounded by yellow roses that were actually golden.

I parked in the driveway, amazed at the beauty and isolation that money could buy. The road we had taken through the orchards had been a broad semicircle that brought us back to the ocean.

Gwen wouldn't let me help with her bicycle. She yanked and pulled at the heavy frame until it finally came out. She could have chipped or scratched my paint job but I didn't say anything.

For some reason I expected her to take me around the back door. There she was half naked in the eyes of most churchgoing black folks, with me, a big and black field Negro up to no good and getting worse. But we went right in the front, Gwen going in first. She banged her tire up against the door and it swung inward.

"I'm here with Mr. Rawlins," she shouted as soon as we were inside.

She motioned for me to go through an archway on my left. She went the other way, pushing at a door that swung open, revealing a large kitchen. Arthur Hawkes was standing in there. He wore a loose yellow shirt with gray Bermuda shorts and straw sandals. He raised his head and caught a glimpse of me just as the door swung, blocking my view. It swung back and forth once more so I caught another shot of Arthur. He was still looking at me.

Then I was alone in the foyer. There were paintings of ocean waves on the walls. Shimmering oils in heavy oaken frames. Waves at sunset. Waves by the moon. A hapless frigate trying to negotiate hurricane tides in a dark storm at sea.

I still had the salt from Gwen's lips on my tongue. Outside the sea rushed. I found myself getting aroused. The kiss and that opulence serenaded by the sea pumped desire into my heart suddenly.

My vow to remember the simple things in life—forgotten then.

Sarah Cain was just inside the archway door, sitting on a big pink sofa. A bottle of Gilbey's gin sat on the table.

Scattered around the bottle were crumpled wads of money. Maybe she *had* searched the bottom of her purse.

"Cigarette?" she asked, rising as I came into the room. "I'm sorry but all I've got are Luckies."

She shook the pack at me. "Have a seat, Mr. Rawlins."

There was a pink chair to go with the sofa.

"Drink?" Her hand, which I now noticed shook a little, drifted toward the gin.

"No thanks."

"You don't like liquor? We have wine."

"No, no. I love liquor. I love wine too, but you just go on and tell me what it is you want."

There was a big window directly across from the couch that opened onto the broad Pacific. The light coming in gave me a good look at Miss Cain. Her eyes drooped, not from being tired but from sadness—years of it. The smile she put on to entertain me was lost under the weight of those eyes.

"Nice house you got here." I wanted to say something about the children out in the fields, but the sadness in those eyes stopped me.

"Oh? You like it?"

"Don't you?"

Sarah Cain looked down at the floor under my feet.

"This is my father's house, Mr. Rawlins," she said. "It smells of him. Whenever I smell horse manure I think of this house. Horse manure and the smell of men out there picking fruit just so that Albert Cain could say that he ran a working farm."

"He's dead now," I said.

Sarah Cain hoisted the gin bottle, shaking slightly, and poured a squat glass half full.

"What?" she asked as if maybe I had lowered my voice or shifted into another language.

"He's dead. You don't have to keep this place for him. You could close it down."

She gave me the same pitying look that Gwen did.

"No, Mr. Rawlins. This is the one bit of property that's in my name. Not even the land, but just the trees. I only own the trees. The estate is all caught up in the courts, and so the only money coming to me is through this harvest. That bastard is laughing at me in hell."

"I don't know," I said. "He's dead and at least you don't have to be out there in that heat."

She wasn't listening to me.

"There was a man once," she said slowly, reminding me of Feather relating her dream, "who said no to my father. It was a freak fall; rainy and cold. The man, I don't remember his name, told my father that he and his men wouldn't work until the weather cleared. He said that the crops weren't worth pneumonia. And he was right. Our family has owned gold mines and oil wells and cattle ranches bigger than some states since a hundred years. What did he need with some lemons in a basket?"

"I don't know, ma'am. But I didn't come way out here to talk about that anyway."

"He brought men up from Ojai with rifles and they took that man—I think his name was Oscar, yes, Oscar." A brittleness came into her voice. "They took Oscar off to talk and a little later my father came back and told the other workers that Oscar took some money and left. Nobody believed him but he had all those men with rifles so they went back to work. That's what he did if you stood up against him. He'd take away your soul and kill it and tell you that it's all your own fault."

"Yeah," I said, mostly to myself. "I know."

"What? What did you say?"

"I said that I didn't come up here to talk about that. Gwendolyn said that you wanted to hire me for something."

"Oh. I'm sorry. Yes. Yes, of course. I'm sorry," she stammered.

We sat for a while then, listening to the waves.

"Mr. Hodge is an awful man and a smelly man," she said like a small child. "And I never have him in the house except when I have to. He was Father's lawyer, so I have to put up with him until the will is settled."

"Well, that smelly man is the one who hired me," I said. "What's he want with Betty?"

Gwendolyn came into the room then, wearing a calf-length maroon dress. She moved up behind Sarah and put her hands on the frail woman's shoulders. They both looked at me like guilty children who believe that adults know what they're thinking.

"Elizabeth was very close to Father. When he died she left us. I want her to come back."

"Yeah, well, you wishin' in yo' pillow didn't call the police down on me—it didn't cart me off to jail."

"You were arrested?"

"Yeah. And entertained by a man named Styles."

"Norman Styles?" There was a galaxy's worth of coldness in her voice.

"We didn't get to his first name."

The white woman rubbed her face like a day laborer wiping off the grit from an especially dirty job.

"I will pay you twenty thousand dollars in cash," Sarah said. "Just as soon as the will gets through probate."

"Excuse me?"

"Didn't you hear me? I said I will pay you—"

"Yeah, yeah, yeah. I heard that part. What I missed was what for."

"To find Elizabeth and to get us in touch with her. Mr. Hodge told me that he fired you. He said that he could find

Elizabeth another way. But I see no reason to leave you out of it. If you can find her I think you should. You seem to know something about her family and friends."

"No offense, lady." I reached over and took another cigarette from her pack on the table. "But your money killed Marlon."

"He's dead?"

"I ain't seen a body, but you could bet he's dead all right. Dead and dryin' somewhere out in the desert."

Gwendolyn started crying. Sarah got up and hugged the girl. It was a hug full of love and care. It made me feel lonely for my children.

"You go sit, honey," Sarah whispered to the sobbing girl.

Almost unable to walk, the maid made it to a chair.

"Mr. Rawlins."

"Yes, Miss Cain?"

"You have a choice, sir."

"Always got that, ma'am. Even when you die you got some kinda choice."

"Well, maybe that's true, but you'll die in the end, there's no choice about that."

I couldn't argue.

"I don't know why you keep talking about a check. I didn't write any check to Marlon—" She stopped in midsentence and cocked her head to the side like a wary bird who's just heard a thump in the air. "But . . . Betty's in trouble. And you're involved in it already."

"Excuse me, Miss Cain, but I'm not involved in anything. The only reason I came here . . ."

"Yes yes yes yes yes," she said, nodding away my words. "I know that you're not involved in anything that's . . . that's happened. But somebody might be thinking like that. After all, we're talking about some very important people here."

"So you sayin' that people like Betty and me couldn't

hardly expect a fair deal when comes to people like you and your father?"

"I'm just saying that I'd be willing to help if you'd be willing to . . ."

"Be your nigger," I said.

Sarah Cain recoiled as if I had struck her. "No!" she declared. "No! I don't feel like that! I never . . ."

"You did too. Yes you did. You offer me enough money to make most people sweat and then you show me how I'm so little that I better mind. Well, that might work wit' yo' people out there." I pointed behind me with my thumb to indicate the fields. "But it don't mean shit to me. Now I'm gonna get up and leave. I don't want your money and I'm not gonna do your work. That's it."

"But, Mr. Rawlins . . ."

"No." I shook my head and got up and went. I managed not to run. In spite of what I said, I *was* scared; scared to death of that white woman offering me help and offering me money.

I took a deep breath in the air outside. It relaxed me. I needed some relaxing after turning down twenty thousand dollars.

"Mr. Rawlins?" Gwendolyn had scooped up the crumpled money and followed me out to the porch.

"What do you want?"

"We need your help," she said, handing the money at me like a bunch of crushed flowers.

"You need help all right. This is 1961, honey. You shouldn't be working for some woman calling you a nigger."

"She's never said that. Never."

"Maybe not in so many words, but when a white woman start tellin' you how important she is an' how much trouble you might be in . . . that's her callin' you a niggah." There was a maniac in my voice. It felt like he was going to jump right out of my throat and strangle somebody. "And if she said it to me then she said it to you too."

"She was just making a point," Gwendolyn said—a great scholar of white folks. "She meant that you'd be in trouble with no way out because you're Negro."

"To begin with, we're both Negro, me *and* you. And the second thing is, she was threatenin' me with the fact that I couldn't contradict her in any court. If she says so then I'm gone—and she's gonna say so unless I slip on my chains and do what she want."

Somehow a discourse on racial politics seemed out of place at the sea. Gwendolyn was about to break down again. My arms went around her of their own accord.

"Please," she cried. "Please help us."

"Us? What do you have to do with it? What do you owe that woman?"

She pushed away from my embrace and looked at me.

"Sarah took care of me since I was young," she said.

"Now why she wanna do that?"

"She knew my mother, but, but my mother died. Sarah and Betty are the only family I ever had. And now Betty's scared and she needs help." Gwendolyn dropped the money and said, "Take it."

She inhaled an enormous sob.

I stood there gawking for a few moments, disgusted by money and the way rich people think that they can buy you. Then the practical man bent down to gather up the cash before the sea breeze could blow it away.

Gwen stood there sniffing and shaking but she let a smile break through when I picked up the cash.

"You'll help?"

"Maybe. But you know, I hardly see how I could help you. I mean, I don't know where Betty is and I don't know anybody that does. Somethin's goin' on here."

"What do you mean?"

"I mean, why would she just disappear like that?"

"I don't know," Gwen pleaded.

"You don't know nuthin' could help me find her?"

"She has a boyfriend," Gwen said hopefully.

"Uh-huh. Who's that?"

"His name is Felix. Felix Landry."

"You tell Hodge that?"

"Yes we did."

"What else you tell him?"

"That Odell Jones was her cousin."

"You tell him about Marlon?"

Gwen's eyes knitted. "N . . . no."

"Why not?"

"I . . . I really don't know."

"There's got to be some reason."

"Is he really dead, Mr. Rawlins?" She touched my forearm.

"Yeah, he's dead all right. I cain't prove it but I know it's true."

"He used to come stay with Betty when I was a little girl," Gwen said. "He did card tricks and made us laugh."

"Us?"

"He had a little nephew named Terry who'd come up and play with me. But he was too rough and one day they stopped coming."

"How long have you lived up here?"

"As long as I can remember."

"Do you know who your mother is?"

"I don't have one," she said clearly as a child might say to put away her nightmares.

She leaned heavily against the door and went into the house without another word.

I was glad for the solitude.

Arthur was waiting down by my car.

"Mr. Rawlins." He didn't put out a hand or smile.

"What?"

"What did my mother want from you?"

"Why don't you go and ask her?"

The pale boy tried to get serious with me. His eyes furrowed and his shoulders rose like hackles. He was a rooster flaring at a junkyard dog.

"You don't know what you're getting into here. This is family business . . ."

"Excuse me." I moved to go past him.

But before I could get by he swung, landing a perfect right hook to my nose.

I seized that boy by the front of his yellow shirt and lifted him up off his feet.

"Whoa!" he shouted, mistaking me for a horse.

My fist ached to hurt him but I just let go. He staggered on the brink of falling, so I gave him a little shove and he sat down hard.

I grabbed him by the back of his shirt with one hand and opened the car door with the other. As I pushed him I said, "Get in!"

He slouched sullenly in his seat but didn't move as I turned the ignition.

"Does this road lead down to the highway?" I asked.

Arthur stared dead ahead and caught up on his practice breathing.

I headed down the paved road, the opposite direction from the one I had come.

We drove in forced silence for the next few minutes. I'd driven all the way to a big wooden fence that was painted lavender. As soon as we were through it I stopped.

"So where you wanna go?" I asked him.

"You're the one driving," he answered: a petulant girl on a soured date.

"I'm gettin' tired of takin' this shit offa you people." I could see the Pacific Coast Highway down below.

"If you are, then why don't you just leave us alone? Nobody wants your help anyway."

"Your mother wants my help. She wants me to find Elizabeth Eady."

Arthur put his fists up against his forehead and pressed as hard as he could. He did that for a while and then he stomped both feet on the floor.

"What's wrong, son?" I asked him with a tenderness that I actually felt at the moment.

"Leave us alone, Mr. Rawlins," he answered. "Let Aunt Betty just go away. If you keep on pulling at it everything'll come apart."

Aunt Betty.

"Tell me why Hodge would be looking for your father." After tenderness, a slap.

"What?"

"I found the name Ron Hawkes on a paper in Saul Lynx's trash. Saul Lynx is the detective Hodge, and your mother, hired to find Betty."

Arthur sat up straight when I mentioned his father's name. Maybe it was all the emotion he had around that man. Maybe.

We sat awhile longer. The only sounds were the far-off murmur of the waves and the gurglings of Arthur's stomach.

"Tell me about it," I said at last. Soft again. That boy meant no more to me than a dragonfly impaled on a silver pin.

Arthur turned half toward me. I could see that the whole truth was there, just behind his eyes. I was so close, almost there.

But then I leaned a little too far and whatever truth

there was scurried back into the crevices and folds in his brain.

"I'm going to get out here," he said. He gave me a look as if to ask if I was going to let him go.

It would have been easier if I had been a man like Styles. I knew pressure points that would have had young Arthur screaming out to the wide ocean. I could have torn the truth from him. His white mother could threaten me but she didn't know the threat that I posed; she didn't see the crushing hurt in my hands.

But I wasn't Styles.

Arthur got out of the car and stumbled back up the road we had come down on. I got out too and was about to hail the young man. Maybe I'd offer him a ride back home. Maybe if I got them all in one room I could ask some good questions.

But before I could call out I saw a black horse racing down the hill. I had maybe forty-five seconds to make up my mind whether to stay and fight with the cowboy or to drive off.

I got in behind the wheel and waited until Rudy was almost on me. Then I hit the gas and fishtailed down the road, yelling and laughing as I slowly took the lead and left him to the stories I would tell friends, in the years to come.

CHAPTER 19

I called Primo when I got in.

"Hello," Primo said into my ear.

"You got my boy, Mr. Garcias?"

"He's here, Easy. How are you, my friend?"

"If I don't get killed I might be rich."

Primo's laugh sounded like two hands being rubbed together in greedy expectation. Mofass was coughing in the background.

"Let me talk to the man," I said.

Mofass hacked a little, then he wheezed, "Mr. Rawlins?"

"William."

"I wanna thank you for takin' care of JJ. You know Clovis woulda et that girl up."

"I don't know, man," I said. "That Jewelle is tough."

"She is that." I could hear something like a father's pride in Mofass's tone.

"I want you to do something for me, William."

"What's that?"

"You're gonna need a lawyer to advise you on how to get Clovis outta your hair."

"I don't need no gott-damned lawyer! Shit, I just go out there and tell them peoples I'm back and that *I* get the rent now and *I* sign the papers. Shit! Fuckin' lawyer steal yo' money an' then sue you for cryin' 'bout it." Talk about lawyers was the only thing that could get Mofass to curse.

"I'm payin' for it, Mo. You got to ask that man how to get your house back and how to put an injunction on Clovis so that she can't come around your property without getting arrested. A good lawyer could threaten her with criminal charges."

"Why I need a lawyer when I got Mr. Alexander with me? Nobody gonna fuck with Mr. Alexander."

"Think, man. Think. Clovis's brood don't know Raymond. And by the time they find out what he is he will have killed three of 'em."

"So what? I don't care if he kill'em all!"

"Okay. All right. Have it your way, Mofass, but you know

if Raymond kill somebody while he's workin' for you then you gonna get charged too."

Through Mofass's silence I could hear Primo's youngest running and screaming around the house. Primo and Flower had twelve natural children and three strays. The oldest was twenty-five with six kids of her own. The youngest was two.

"Who is this lawyer?" Mofass asked.

"His name is Hodge, Calvin Hodge. He got an office on Robertson." I gave him the address off the paper I found in Saul Lynx's trash. "Tell him your problem. See what he's got to say."

"I could trust him?"

"No. You can't trust this man worth a damn."

"Then why in hell I'm goin' there?"

"You're goin' there because I said to, that's why. Now listen up. Don't say my name to the man. Just ask him to help you. Tell him what your problem is but don't say my name. And after he talks to you, call me up and tell me everything he said. Every word of it. And keep your eyes open, William. I wanna know if he's got a safe and if there's chains on the door. I wanna know what floor he's on and everything else."

"I don't know, Mr. Rawlins, this don't sound right."

"You want me to put you back there with Clovis? 'Cause you know I didn't never have to take you out of there. You been knowin' all this time that she was cheatin' me an' you didn't call until you got wind'a this husband she got."

"I'm sick, man. I needed her. What could I do?"

"You could do what I ask you to."

"Sure, sure, Mr. Rawlins. Anything you say."

"Raymond will be by in the mornin'. You take him wit' you over to Hodge. Just tell the man your problem. Give him some money if he wants it."

"I don't know. I mean, I don't want no trouble."

"I'll call you tomorrow to find out what you saw," I said. Then I hung up.

I called Mouse next.

"... now remember, Raymond," I told him. "I don't want no trouble."

"Sometimes trouble just finds you, Easy."

"Listen, Ray. I need to know the layout of this man's office. He knows who I am, so don't let Mofass say my name."

"When this gonna be through, Easy?" he asked.

"Couple'a days. Maybe three."

"Okay. All right. I'll give ya that. You got three days. You understand me?"

I had phone directories for Los Angeles going back for eight years in my garage. Felix Landry wasn't in any of them. I called Miss Eto down at the library to search the directories of other counties. She looked, but Mr. Landry, if that was his name, was unlisted.

Ortiz, still shirtless and in the same pair of trousers, opened Jackson Blue's door and glowered at me. As a boy I would have gotten my face slapped for looking like that. No adult would take that kind of sass—not even from a stray.

"Jackson here?" I asked.

"What you want?"

"Nuthin' from you, brother. I just need Jackson a minute."

There was going to be violence between the two of us one day.

Sometimes you just know somebody, like they've been in your business for a whole lifetime. I knew Ortiz and the dark anger inside him. He lived in a haze of rage; probably couldn't even make love because he was so mad. That anger was a deep hole of despair that he lived in. I'd lived next to that hole since I was a boy. The recognition between us was like electricity. If he had been a woman we'd have ended up on the floor next to the bed. And if we ever had to spend five minutes alone one or both of us would end up dead.

"Easy?" Jackson was fully dressed. He had on a black-and-yellow plaid suit with a green felt hat. The brim of the hat was too wide for Jackson's spare face.

"You got a minute, Jackson?"

"Sure, Easy. Come on in."

I made a point not to touch Ortiz as I went past.

"I knew you was comin' back, Ease."

"Yeah? How'd you know that?"

Jackson hunched his shoulders and smiled with mock reserve—the closest he would ever come to innocence.

"I don't know, man. Maybe 'cause I got the best li'l money-maker"—he tapped the telephone box which sat on the couch next to him—"that you or anybody you know's ever seen, right here."

I could smell Ortiz's sour breath from somewhere behind me.

"Naw, man. I mean, it *is* a good scam, but them gangsters too much for me."

"So then what you want?"

"I wanna find Terry T. The boxer."

"Try Herford's."

"I need a house address."

Jackson knew where Terry lived, I could tell by the cagey way he looked at me. But he wasn't going to tell me—not straight out anyway. If he had information that I wanted then I had to buy it.

"I'm 'bout t'go out an' make a run," he said. "You got a car here?"

"I thought you had a red Caddy?"

"I do but this'll kill two birds with one stone. You got your car?"

"Uh-huh. But listen, Jackson, I'm in a hurry."

"Won't take long. I just got a few tickets to punch."

"All right. But just a few stops."

"Yeah." Jackson smiled and cocked his floppy brim. "Yeah. A couple or so."

"When you comin' back?" Ortiz sounded like a taciturn spouse. "You know we gotta do that thing."

"I be back, boy. Don't worry. Easy gonna cut my time in half."

We were a block away before I asked, "What's with that guy? It's like he wants to get killed."

"Ortiz is tough. So if you think you tough then he wants to set you straight."

"That ain't nuthin' but trouble, Jackson. Boy like that bound to come to harm."

"Yeah. But you know I could use his kinda trouble. Ortiz on'y know how to rumble and here I cain't even make a pigeon take off."

I had to laugh at that. I imagined little Jackson running after a pigeon and all it does is flutter and run.

We stopped at Ernest's barber shop, which had moved to Santa Barbara Boulevard. Ernest still ran a crap game in the back and played opera on the radio all day. He was an institution in the community. After that we went to a used-furniture store called Nate's.

Before we got to Juniper Funeral Home I asked, "So? Where do I find Terry?"

"Way I hears it," Jackson said, "Terry been outta town a whole lot lately. He even let go of his place down on Eighty-six."

"Outta town where?"

"Out in the desert. You know all'a L.A. is just a big desert."

"What desert?"

"I don't know, man. Desert."

"I saw'im down at Herford's gym a couple'a days ago. He got to be up here sometimes."

"Huh." Jackson scratched his high black cheekbone and peered out of the window. "It's right up here."

"What is?"

"Juniper's."

I baked in the car while Jackson went in to collect his money. He used collectors to get the money from all the people who played the horses through his phone scheme. A collector took in money for a couple of days and took a percentage before handing the rest over to Jackson, or Ortiz. Collectors changed every week or so to keep the police off balance. A collector was usually a working man or woman, like Ernest the barber, just somebody trying to supplement their income.

I was sweating and wondering what kind of business Terry could have had with Marlon to keep him out in the desert. Then I heard Jackson's excited voice coming out of the funeral home.

"I don't give a fuck what you say, man. I got it writ right chere that you owe me four fifty, not no two seventy-five." Jackson was backing out of the door. I thought about Lynx's .38 in my pocket but didn't reach for it.

Rollo Jones's big belly was forcing my cowardly little friend backwards.

"You callin' me a liar? Fuck you! Fuck you!" Rollo accented each curse with a shove from his belly. "You ain't gonna scare me."

"Easy!" Jackson squealed.

I got out of the car and stood by the door. Rollo stopped moving forward and looked at me. I held my hands up in a gesture of ignorance. I don't know what Rollo thought I meant by that but he stopped pushing Jackson, put his hand in his pocket, and came out with a wad of money. He peeled off some bills and exchanged a few quiet words with Jackson.

All this transpired on an empty sidewalk. The only thing that moved was the cars. There wasn't a pedestrian to be seen.

"All right!" Jackson slapped my shoulder and played bongos on the dashboard as we cruised away from Juniper's. "All right!"

"What was all that about, man?"

"Two hunnert dollars."

"That's how much he owed you?"

"Huh? Naw. That's how much Ortiz bet I couldn't collect what he owe us. He said I was pussy an' that the on'y thing a pussy could get was fucked. Well fuck him. Two hunnert dollars!" Jackson jammed two fingers before my face.

The vent was blowing hot air at me and I was having a tough time breathing. I pulled over to the curb and put my head down on the steering wheel.

"What's wrong you, Easy?"

"No no no no no, Jackson, what's wrong with you?"

"Ain't nuthin' wrong wit' me, man." He couldn't hide his smirk.

"Did you ever get that degree from UCLA?"

"Shit. Motherfuckers wanted me to study some kinda language. Uh-uh, man. I walk on the ground an' I talk like my people talk."

"But you could do somethin', Jackson. You're smart."

"Naw, Easy, I cain't do nuthin'."

"Why not? Of course you could."

"Naw, man. I been a niggah too long." He said it as if he were proud of the fact.

"You think that Martin Luther King is down south marchin' an' takin' his life in his hands just so you could be gamblin' and actin' like a niggah?"

"I ain't got nuthin' to do wit' him, Easy. You know I be livin' my life the onliest way I can."

"But Jackson, we can't be runnin' in the streets bettin' on each other's lives. We got to be men. We got to stand up for ours."

Jackson pulled off his big hat. Sweat was running down his face. It was one of the few times I ever looked him in the eye that he didn't smile.

"Terry got a pad on Twenty-second Street. House was abandoned. Terry just moved in. It's near a Renco station and a sto' called Happy Liquors. It's a pink house with blue flowers on a fence ain't got no paint." He said it all deadpan and then opened the car door.

He walked down the street, away from Juniper's. When he was half a block away I got the urge to stop him, to try and talk to him some more. I opened the door and got one foot on the curb, but suddenly I was weak, too weak even to call out after Jackson.

I sat there, holding my head and sweating, for long minutes. I couldn't stand, couldn't even sit up straight.

Jackson was sore on my mind. Life wasn't any more than a losing hand to him. And death was just another card to be played. All the money he made with his scams was shit through a goose. If he came to a friend's funeral he was full of ribald tales about how hard that man's life had been; then he'd try to *console* the widow or girlfriend left behind. There was never a tear, a regret, a dollar in the bank, a brick laid in a foundation, or a hope that pressed itself into Jackson's mind.

And if I were to tell him that his bad ways would lead to a bad end he'd just answer, "Ain't no such'a thing as a good end, brother."

And if I looked into my own heart I knew that he was right.

CHAPTER 20

I've never really been what you would call a friend to the LAPD. We were on speaking terms only because they needed my help from time to time. And also because I used to be fool enough to put myself in the way when somebody down in my community was getting the short end of the stick.

But the truth is that I did know some cops and Miss Cain's veiled threat made me want to set the groundwork for some kind of defense.

"Seventy-seventh Street station," a woman's voice said over the phone.

"I'd like to speak to Detective Lewis."

"Who's calling?"

"Easy Rawlins."

"Oh. Um. Just one minute please."

There was some static and maybe five seconds went by before I heard Lewis's voice.

"Rawlins? Where are you?" Arno Lewis, the resident Negro detective of the Seventy-seventh Street station, asked.

I knew when he asked that question that I was in deep trouble.

"At a pay phone." I was casual. "I got some trouble out here and I wanted to ask you somethin'."

"Why don't you come on down here and we'll talk about it."

"Why don't we talk on the phone? You know I got business to take care of."

"I can't really talk about police business on the phone."

"Who said anything about police business?"

"Why don't I drop by your house later on. We could talk after work," he said, ignoring my question.

"Right, okay. You got my address?" I knew he didn't. Only my best friends know my address and they wouldn't ever tell a cop. I wasn't listed in the phone book and I used my house, the one that Primo lived in down on 116th Street, for legal forms and correspondence. Primo and Flower held my mail.

"No."

"You mean it ain't in your records?"

"No. I mean . . . maybe it is. But why don't you just give it to me now and I'll be sure to have it later on."

I rattled off Clovis's address. I figured that a half-dozen police officers coming into her house shouting my name might help to keep her off of Mouse and Mofass.

"What time you getting home?" Detective Lewis asked me.

I imagined him; a tall Poindexter-looking kind of guy. He wore thick glasses and had the habit of pressing the bridge of his nose, between his eyes. I was willing to bet that he had his glasses off right then, concentrating every bit of his mind on the time he could get at me.

" 'Bout six," I said. "Gotta make dinner, you know."

"Well, maybe I could get a bite with you."

"Yeah," I said as simply as I could. "Come and get it."

I went over to Twenty-second Street. Right down the block from the Renco station and Happy's Liquors was a small weathered house surrounded by a fallen-down fence that was covered with a weedy vine of hardy blue flowers. The grass was straw and there were no cultivated plants in the yard.

The wind had brought trash from the street to litter the little front porch. Gum wrappers, leaves, gravel, and sand were scattered across the gray floor. There was a barrel there, I suppose to use as a chair, and a stack of small green umbrellas.

I knocked. I always knock. But there wasn't anybody home.

The door wasn't locked.

The house was as barren as the yard and porch; rough pine floors that some lazy fool had varnished without sanding; a mismatch assortment of furniture taken from the curb at trash-collecting time. A couch faced the wall and two wooden chairs were turned over. The shades were pulled and it was dark in the house. But it was still hot. Stifling.

Terry was in the kitchen; the whole back of his head shot off. He was wearing the same black jeans and T-shirt he had on when he decked me.

Suddenly I was sorry about the fight we'd had. Maybe if I hadn't tried to strong-arm him he would have talked to me, and lived.

Terry was on his back with his head sideways. His brain was a halo on the floor. There was dark blood spattered on his shoulders and down his chest. His eyes were wide and his mouth too. He looked as if he'd been trying to suck down one more breath before it was over.

Also on his chest was a string of green rosary beads. They were placed there. I knelt down to get a closer look and saw that they were wet, dappled with water, not blood.

I started to move the second I heard it. *It* was a heavy shuffle of feet. The sound came from behind me, and before I could rise, much less turn around, I felt a sharp pain, very deep in my back. I yelled and swung backwards with my fist. I connected with something hard and fleshy too, but before I could turn around there came a shock that started at the side of my head and ran all the way down to each and every one of my toes. There was a far-off gong and a giant wave crashing down on the shore.

I was running with a mob of black men. In pursuit of us were ravens and dogs followed by rabid white men and white women—the white people were naked and hairless. Horses with razor hooves galloped among them and a searing wind blew. We were all running but every black man trying to get away was also pushing his brothers down. And every man that fell was set upon by dogs with hungry rats dangling down from between their legs.

I ran so hard that my shoes wore through. Then my feet began to bleed and the blood made me slip. "Betrayed by your own blood," a familiar voice said.

My eyes opened before I came to. They were trying to let out the agony. I sat up and rubbed my head. It was wet. Wet with the brain and blood of Terry T. A number ten cast-iron frying pan lay next to me. A better swing and I would have been dead along with Terry.

That was too much.

The moaning started softly but soon built into a wail. I heard myself shouting out and I knew that I should stop but I couldn't. There was blood on me. Blood.

When I tried to stand, still racked by tears, a pain grabbed my shoulder. It was deep inside me and I knew I had been stabbed. I tried to grab the knife but I couldn't reach it.

It was the fear of death in the form of that blade that saved me.

I got up and stumbled into the living room. I was looking for something but I didn't quite know what. I went through a door and found myself in Terry's bedroom. He had a single bed with a thin blue-striped mattress on it. On the floor lay a stained pillow with no casing and a woolen blanket.

It was the blanket that I was looking for.

I draped it over my shoulder gently so as not to press against the knife. But even that little bit of pressure on the haft sent a high-pitched scream running down my spine. I had to lean up against a solitary chest of drawers to steady myself.

There was a framed photograph laid flat up there. And even though I was in terrible pain and in fear for my life I noticed that it was the same kind of frame that Marlon had for Betty's snapshot. I looked at the picture but I couldn't make out anything. I couldn't get my mind to focus on the faces there.

So I took the picture and stood up as straight as I could manage. Then I went out to the car trying to seem nonchalant, wrapped up in a blanket in hundred-degree weather.

The heat was nothing to me anymore.

I climbed into the driver's seat and sat back, jamming the knife a little further in. That sat me up straight.

My hand didn't want to do what I told it. It took me three tries to turn the ignition.

I had to get ready for a turn a full half block before I reached the corner.

And each block had its own special pitfall. Once I didn't see two little children playing in the street until it was almost too late. I hit the brake too hard and threw myself forward and then back against the seat. The jolt in my shoulder was so blinding that I had to stop for a while and rest on the steering wheel.

I don't know what Terry was doing with a wool blanket in the summer heat. I was getting light-headed but I was afraid to pull the blanket off. If one more thing changed I knew I was going to die.

A prowl car followed me for over two miles down Pico Boulevard. I don't know why they didn't stop me. I was cruising at about twenty-five, hunched over the wheel like I was making love to the thing.

But somewhere around La Brea they took off. Probably a real crime came in on the radio. I don't know. But it was just about then that I remembered about bleeding. Maybe I was bleeding too much. I stuck my hand under the blanket and brought it back covered in blood. My blood.

My foot was becoming uneven on the gas pedal. I would speed up and slow down, then speed up again. By the time I got to my block there was a bass sound thrumming in my ears. I turned into the driveway and was easing back toward the garage when suddenly I took a turn to the left. I don't know why. There's no turn in my driveway but I turned just as natural as if I did it every time I came home.

Jesus came running out after he heard me plowing into the side wall of the house.

"Go make Feather go to her room," I said, waving Jesus back into the house. "Go on! And bring me back my green coat."

God knows why I wanted that coat.

I had to move over to the passenger's side to get out of the car. By the time I made it to the back door Jesus had returned with the coat. He stood there looking at me, eyes wide. I lumbered past him, still wearing my blanket. I went through the kitchen and then into our TV room, followed by the silent boy.

"Go to the bathroom and get the witch hazel and the alcohol," I said. "And the gauze and some tape too."

Slowly, I let myself down into a perch at the edge of the couch while Jesus ran to get the things I needed.

"Daddy?" Feather was there at the edge of the room rubbing her nose and pulling at the hem of her little blue dress. She didn't run to me because half my face was covered with Terry T's insides.

"Go up to your room, baby," I said. My voice was thick and gravelly.

The man she was running away from wasn't her father. He was a real monster that had invaded her home.

Jesus came in with his arms full. I stood up and let the blanket fall off me.

"Juice, I don't want you to get upset, but I need something from you."

He was all attention.

"I'm going to turn around and you're going to have to help me. Okay?"

He nodded.

I turned around slowly and faced the wall. There was a copy of the Emancipation Proclamation that I'd bought from Woolworth's hanging there—gilded frame and all. It struck me that hanging that document up there was like an ex-convict displaying his discharge papers.

"Oh God, Daddy."

Jesus's hushed cry made me forget the frame. I even ignored the knife in my back long enough to smile at my son calling me Daddy.

"Is it a knife?" I asked him.

"It's an ice pick," he answered in perfect articulate English.

"All right, son," I said lowering myself down to my knees. "I want you to put both hands around it and pull it out the same way it went in. It might hurt me enough that I faint for a minute but that's okay. You take a wad of that gauze and press it against the wound until you're sure that it's stopped bleeding. You understand?"

"Yes, Daddy." And then he did it—all at once and with no hesitation.

"Uhh-ah!" I groaned. There came a bright yellow light,

not in my eyes but in the whole upper part of my brain. My body was being sucked upwards and I knew for certain what it was like to die.

But I wasn't going to die; not until I found Elizabeth Eady and the killer of Terry T.

The yellow light faded and with it my consciousness. I remember Feather calling and me wanting to say "Yes, honey?" but I couldn't and that simple fact was among the saddest things I'd ever known.

CHAPTER 21

When I came to I was afraid to open my eyes at first. Instead I listened to the sounds around me. The drip of the faucet in the kitchen; the rattle of the window in the Santa Ana wind. I felt a slight breeze that wasn't hot and a gentle stroke across my face. When I finally opened my eyes I saw Jesus using a washcloth to wipe the blood from my face. He was using a little plastic bowl filled with tepid water. I was laid out on the couch, with him next to me. On the floor at my feet Feather sat with her back to me playing with her doll, Roxanna.

"You be a good girl now, Roxy," I remember her saying. "Or you don't get no surprise."

There was a darkening knot under Jesus's left eye. I reached out to touch it and he drew back.

"What happened?"

"After the blood stopped I put some alcohol on it and you, you jumped like." There was a question in his voice, as if he were asking me if I had indeed jumped or was I mad because of something.

"I'm sorry. It musta hurt pretty bad."

"Yeah," he said. "It was real red in there."

I took a deep breath and noticed that the breeze was coming from the fan which Jesus had set at the foot of the couch so that it could blow over all three of us.

The green coat was over my feet.

I passed out.

When I came around Jesus was still there next to me. Feather was eating ice cream out of a bowl, just like the bowl Jesus used to wash me, and clutching her doll.

"Honey," I called out to Feather.

"Uh-huh," she answered, not looking up.

"Would you like to go on a trip to Uncle Primo's?"

"Yeah!" She stood right up from the bowl, wrenching Roxanna's arm. She was ready to go, and I couldn't blame her. The trouble I had brought into her house was too much for any little girl.

It was too much for me.

"Juice."

"Y-yes, Daddy?"

"Call Primo and ask him if you and Feather can come out there for a couple of days."

When Jesus got on the phone I had another surprise. He spoke Spanish! I guess it shouldn't have been such a shock; he'd lived with Primo's family from the time I saved him until he was five.

"He said okay." There was a slight smirk on Jesus' face. "He said that there's no room in the house or the garage but me and Julio and Juan-Baptiste can sleep out on the deck in the avocado tree."

Only children could make fun out of despair.

"You take Feather in the bus, okay?"

"Uh-huh." It was like he had always talked.

Feather was happy to go until they got out the door. Halfway through the front yard she started crying and running back to the house. Jesus caught her by the arm and picked her up. I watched them going down the street; Feather was hugging Juice and reaching back over his shoulder toward the house.

There was a bottle of Seagram's in the kitchen cabinet. It had been a gift from Lucky Horn and I hadn't had the time to bring it to one of my friends who drank.

I sat the bottle down on the coffee table and put the phone next to it. By now Officer Lewis knew that I wasn't coming to Clovis's house. She didn't know my real address, few people did, but Lewis was a good cop and I knew that he'd find my numbers soon enough.

The first call was to a hotel downtown. But the man I was looking for wasn't in.

The second was to EttaMae.

"Hello?"

"Hey, Etta. Jewelle get out there okay?"

"That's some girl you sent me, Easy. LaMarque's nose open so wide it's like t'bust."

"She just a girl."

"A girl who know where her pussy is." Etta always spoke her mind. That's one of the ten thousand reasons I loved her.

"Could you handle it?"

"Hell yeah. I been knowin' where my pussy is so long it might be gettin' time to move."

I knew she was mad at Mouse. Maybe, if it was five years earlier, I would have been fool enough to run after her again.

"Thanks for takin' her in, Etta. Mofass'll be happy she got a good woman like you lookin' after her."

The next call was to Primo. Jesus and Feather weren't there yet but Mofass and Mouse were.

"Yessir, Mr. Rawlins," Mofass wheezed. "He gots three locks on the do'. His file cabinets got combination locks in 'em and they's alarms on everything, even the windows.

"He a good lawyer too. Said that everything belongs t'me and that we could suck Clovis dry. Kick'em outta that there house an' close Esquire altogether. He says I could even take what money is her'n 'cause she couldn't prove that she made it without usin' my, uh, my capital. Shit, that lawyer could do some business. He gonna serve papers tomorrah at all her banks so that she cain't take none'a my money out."

Mouse had a different take on the man. "That's a tough ole cracker, Easy. He knew what I was the minute I walked in the door. He looked me up and down and leaned forward so's he could get to his pistol if he had to. He wear a pistol on his belt."

There are few things as beautiful as a glass bottle filled with deep amber whiskey. Liquor shines when the light hits it, reminiscent of precious things like jewels and gold. But whiskey is better than some lifeless bracelet or coronet. Whiskey is a living thing capable of any emotion that you are. It's love and deep laughter and brotherhood of the type that bonds nations together.

Whiskey is your friend when nobody else comes around. And whiskey is solace that holds you tighter than most lovers can.

I thought all that while looking at my sealed bottle. And I knew for a fact that it was all true.

True the way a lover's pillow talk is true. True the way a mother's dreams for her napping infant are true.

But the whiskey mind couldn't think its way out of the

problems I had. So I took Mr. Seagram's, put him in his box, and placed him up on the shelf where he belonged.

CHAPTER 22

The ice-pick wound had stopped bleeding. Still, I should have gone to the doctor, or at least I should have gone to bed. But instead I washed up as best I could and put on clean clothes.

When I backed away from the wall the siding fell down. A small burglar could have snaked into the house through the hole I left him. But the children were safe with Primo. All that was left was a bottle of whiskey and a gilt-framed copy of the Emancipation Proclamation. A thief was welcome to either one.

I went to a small residential hotel called the Piper on Grand in downtown L.A. The Piper was a hotel for poor whites. A lot of rural sons and a lot of criminals lived there. It wouldn't have been a surprise for a black man to get his throat cut just for walking into that place.

All around the lobby shabby men loitered, smoking cigarettes and talking in low tones. A prostitute in a purple satin dress and torn brown stockings came down the stairway just as I entered. She did a double take before sneering at my presence.

"Hey, Joey!" she yelled, her words straight out of Brooklyn.

"Wha'?" A bulbous man came down from behind her. The question left his eyes when he saw me.

I went on up to the front. A gaunt gray-eyed man towered behind the desk. I heard every sound behind my back. The scooting of a chair, the rustling of pockets.

The clerk looked right through me.

"You got an Alamo Weir here?"

No answer. Not even the recognition in his pale eyes that I was there.

"What you want, boy?" The bulbous man was next to me. His two-piece suit was too blue to be a natural fabric. His mottled shirt had the faded stains from many washings.

I could have killed the man. I wanted too. I hated him. I hated his fat cheeks, pink and raw because he'd just shaved. I hated the smell of the cologne on his unwashed body. I hated the little black snaps he had for eyes.

"I'm lookin' for Alamo, cracker," I said. I had to say it. I wasn't marching or singing songs about freedom. I didn't pay dues in the Southern Christian Leadership Conference or the NAACP. I didn't have any kind of god on my side. But even though the cameras weren't on me and JFK never heard my name, I had to make my little stand for what's right. It was a little piece of history that happened right there in that room and that went unrecorded.

The man pushed his right hand down into his front pocket. "Who's that?"

"Listen, brother. I'm here to meet Alamo," I said, then I slipped my hand into my own pocket. "It's hot. I bet you got a knife in your hand down there. But I got a thirty-eight. Now you could do somethin' an' your boys back there could back you up. But a gut shot will kill a fat man like you." I pointed down at his big belly. "That much we know."

The words came out of me effortlessly as if somebody else was talking for me.

"Easy?"

I looked up to see Alamo Weir come through the small lobby. Every man in that room was on his feet and pointed toward me.

Alamo was small and looked older than he actually was. His skin was wrinkled and discolored and there was a slight limp to his stride. His story about the limp was that he'd got into a fight with some Italian gangsters in San Quentin; he killed the main boss but was left with the gimp for a memento. I didn't know if it was true or not. Alamo was the kind of crazy criminal who lied, cheated, and killed. You never knew what might be true about him.

"Alamo." I looked around the room. "Friendly place you live in."

"Get outta here, Fatty," Alamo said to the blue-suited man. "Come on, Easy. Let's go get some fresh air."

Walking through that crowd made my heart race. Any one of them could have stuck a knife in me. The only thing I had to rely on was their respect for Alamo.

When we got outside he said, "Come on over to Dolores's," and led me across the street to a chili dog stand. I bought him four dogs with chili and sweet pickle relish and a cup of black coffee.

"Coffee's spicier than the chili." He winked at me.

There was a big plaster bench next to a concrete ledge that overlooked the parking lot next door. That was Alamo's office.

"What's the problem, Easy?" he asked between hot dog number two and hot dog number three.

"You know how to break into a place if somebody is trying to keep you out?"

He nodded and talked while he was chewing. "I used to like to break into houses up in Beverly Hills. Got all that top-notch security shit up there. I'd rob their bedrooms while they was sleepin', then I'd have dinner downstairs and play with the guard dog too. For a while, when I was flush, I did it for fun. You know, break in and take all the light bulbs.

"One time this broad wakes up and comes down. I had my shiv right there in my hand, you know?"

I knew. I'd spent two days in jail with Alamo.

"I was gonna cut her right on the neck but then, I don't know why, I just started cryin'. Cryin'! You know, I was bawlin' an' sayin' that I was sorry and that I was hungry. And please wouldn't she forgive me. And you know she comes up and hugs me!" Alamo laughed a laugh that would have done Satan proud. "I fucked that broad so hard that she still calls down here sometimes. Her husband's some kind of international banker. I been tellin' her that I could get him in a car accident and she could have my tough old peter twenty-four hours a day.

"You know, I killed a guy once in his car. I didn't know him—"

"So," I interrupted. You had to interrupt Alamo because he couldn't stop talking on his own. "You can break into a place that has security alarms and serious locks?"

"Can do."

"It's on Robertson at Pico. Right over a hot dog stand."

"Chili dogs?"

I nodded and then gave Alamo the exact name and address.

"When you wanna take it?" he asked.

"Soon as I can. Sooner."

"I'll call ya tomorrow, or the next day."

"I'm not gonna be home for a few days. Can I get a message to you?"

"Not up at the hotel. Couple'a guys been askin' around for me, so they don't say when I'm there, but you could try a bar called Remo's on First. They'll take the message. And I'll leave word with them and then we can get together and go in there."

"Don't tell'em what we're doin', though."

"Don't worry, Easy, I'm not a virgin."

He sure wasn't.

"Well," I said. "I better be gettin' on."

Alamo put his hand on my forearm.

"Don't be too mad at 'em, Easy."

"At who?"

"Those boys in there don't know what it's like. They ain't never seen what a white man truly is. They think it's all TV and *Look* magazine. They don't know that it's white men who cut off their balls."

I liked Alamo. He was insane but he had a clearer view of the world than most do.

"I don't hate'em," I said. "I'm scared of them. Scared that they might kill me for breathing air."

"You damn right about that."

CHAPTER 23

My next stop was Odell's. The front door of his house was wide open. I almost drove away. Another dead body would have done me in right then.

Two men in tan uniforms came out of the front door and went to the Diamond Ice truck parked out in front of the house. Each one hefted a fifty-pound sack of ice out of the freezer cabin and went back up to the house. Maude came out to hold the door for them.

"Just put 'em down on the kitchen table," she said.

They went in the house and Maude watched. When she turned back around I was standing there.

The men came back out, went down to the truck, and

pulled out two more bags of ice. They hustled past me and Maude as we kept up our stare.

The men made two more trips. Maude and I hadn't said a word. There was a wad of cash balled up in her fist.

One of the men, a young heavyset boy, came out of the house and went down to the truck. His partner, a small man with sparse gray hair and gold-framed bifocals, stopped in front of me.

"That'll be twelve-fifty," he informed me.

"Here you go," Maude said, handing him her wad of cash.

He counted out thirteen dollars and looked up at Maude. She nodded and he said, "Thank you," handing over a baby-blue receipt. He went down to the truck and they drove off.

"Havin' a party?" I asked.

"Icebox busted," she whispered. "Got almost two hundred pounds of beef we just bought in the tub."

"I need to see Odell, honey."

"He ain't here," she said.

"Where is he, Maude? I really need to talk with him."

Maude stood holding the screen door like a shield against me. I didn't think that she would tell me where he was, but I was willing to wait right there on the doorstep until he returned. Odell was going to talk to me this time—that was true.

Maybe Maude saw that in the way I planted my feet and the certainty in my voice.

"He down over at Martin's," she said. "He go over there every day to sit wit' him."

The prospect of going to Martin's almost kept me from seeking Odell out.

Martin lived on a nice block, Queen Lane. Mostly black professionals lived on that street. Accountants and lawyers mainly but there were a couple of doctors too. Martin had bought the place before arthritis took away his livelihood.

He had been a master cabinetmaker. All he needed was a pocketknife and a tree and he could make furniture so beautiful that you'd expect to see it in a castle somewhere.

We used to go to his workshop when we were children and he'd lecture us about life.

"Always own your tools," he'd say. "Your tools and your house. That way they cain't take it away from ya. Don't live on no paycheck and don't never ask the man for a thing. You got what he want right here in yo' hands." He'd hold up a chisel or a pile of freshly smithed square nails. "That way you gonna be a man. A'cause that's what a man is—it's what he could *do.* You-all be thinkin' that bein' a man got somethin' to do wit' women, but that ain't true. Woman compliment a man but he got to have his own if he wanna be wit' her. Shit! She wanna big dick what she need t'do is t'get her a horse."

Martin always made us laugh. He made us feel good about work and about who we were. Standing at his front door I realized that it was Martin who had defined my desire for property and my love of things done by hand.

Pea Williams, his ex-wife, answered the door. She'd been a beautiful woman in her youth but it was all on the outside. When the youthful beauty started to fade she just kind of fell in on herself. Her jaw muscles pulled back and her distaste for life came to the surface.

When she opened the door the sweet and sickly smell of disease wafted out of the house. A smell that poor people have to live with because they can't afford bed space in a hospital.

"Easy."

"Pea. I didn't know you were back."

"I ain't. I married Willis Murphy and moved to Seattle. But we come on down when we heard Martin was sick. You know our boys in the army, over in Germany, and they cain't come back home."

"That's good of you, Pea." I wondered what could have made such a sour and self-pitying woman come all that way to see after a man that she'd abandoned when his hands gave out.

"What you want, Easy?"

"Odell here?"

She didn't even answer, just turned away and went into the house.

There was a breeze off the ocean that night. The waters must have been loaded with seaweed because you could smell the brine if you breathed deep and stood still. Granite streetlamps lined the street and the barest trace of a mist was rising from the saturated lawns. I stood still for a moment imagining a chill when I was a child. The cold tickled me when I was a boy. I used to wonder if I was crazy for being out in the bayou, laughing at nothing.

"What you want, Easy?" Odell was behind the screen. His hand was on the latch, not to open it but to keep me out.

"I wanna show you something, Odell."

"What?"

"You got to come out here amongst the niggers if you gonna see it."

He stared at me a moment. It's always a little disconcerting when a flimsy waif of a man looks at you with an iron-hard stare. A powerful man looks like that and you can bet that he's thinking about swinging. But a thin man might have a gun, an equalizer.

Odell opened the door and stalked out.

"What?"

I pulled up my T-shirt and tore off the bandage Jesus had dressed the wound with. Then I turned to give Odell a good look.

"What the hell happened to you?"

"I got stabbed."

"How?" he asked. But his voice told me that he already knew the answer.

"Lookin' for your cousin. Lookin' for Betty. They wanna kill me for that, Odell. I been beaten and threatened, the police are after me, and now I been stabbed. All that because you sent that man to me. You blame me for Reverend Towne's dyin', but you ain't no better. That knife could have been in my heart."

"Sit down here, Easy," Odell said. He put a hand on each of my biceps and guided me until I was seated on the step. I was still weak from the knifing. I put my head down on my knees and closed my eyes.

I heard Odell go back into the house and then I dozed for a few minutes. After a while there was an argument at the door.

"I don't want him out there on my porch!" I heard Pea say.

"It ain't yours," Odell said, trying to bring down her voice with his.

Then the door opened and I felt a cool salve on my wound.

"You should go to a doctor for this, Easy."

"Goin' to the doctor might be goin' to jail right now, Odell."

He put a bandage on me and pulled my shirt down. I hadn't had so much mothering since I was seven.

"It's a clean wound. In the muscle, I think." Odell sat down beside me. "If it don't get infected, or the knife wasn't rusty, then you be okay. But you got to keep cleanin' it."

"What about Betty?"

"I'm sorry, Easy. I didn't mean to get you messed up in this thing. I mean, I thought that you could find Betty for them but I didn't know everything then."

"Every what thing?"

"I can't tell you that."

"This is my life here, Odell."

"I know, and I'm sorry for that, but there's things happenin' here. Things that you don't know about."

"You mean like Marlon?"

Odell stiffened a little but he didn't say anything.

"Odell, I'm in trouble here, man."

"Easy Rawlins!" It was a voice from the grave.

Odell and I both got up and turned to see poor old Martin standing there.

He was dressed in a white shirt, black trousers, and blunt-toe brown shoes. The collar of his shirt was way too big for his chicken neck and his pants were so loose that they had to be doubled over to tie them onto his hips with the belt. He held himself up with a cane in each hand. And those hands were shaking. He looked right at me but the effort to hold his head up was so great that he had to lower his head now and then to rest.

Odell and I went up to Martin and helped him to the banister at the edge of the porch. Once he was leaning he waved us off.

"I ain't seen you in years, Easy. Wasn't it at Jasmine's weddin'?"

"I think so," I answered. I'd never known a woman named Jasmine.

"Yeah, you was some boy, Easy. Smart as you could want and baaaaad."

I laughed. There was nothing to say about his cancer. Cancer meant that he was going to die.

"How'd you get Pea and her husband t'come down here, Marty?" I asked. "As I remember it she said she couldn't even stand to look at you."

Martin showed me a perfect set of front teeth. A skull's grin.

"Tole dem 'bout my in-surance." He spoke slowly, articulating each word.

"What insurance?"

"Twenty-fi'e hunnert dollars to be paid on the day that I die. Pea's the beneficiary."

"Really?"

Martin showed his teeth again and said, "No. But that's what I told'em. You know the minute they heard I was sick they rush on down. Pea come into my room every mornin' an' peer at me . . . then I open up my eyes and she jump." Martin laughed. He laughed even though he knew that he was dying.

Odell took his old friend's hand.

With his free hand Martin reached out to me. His cold claw felt as if it were siphoning off my living heat.

"It must be hard," I said.

"You know the hardest thing, Easy?" His voice was muffled like there was wet cotton down in his throat.

"What's that?"

He released me and held up his shaking hand.

"I cain't even raise up a pistol; cain't even pull the trigger. Odell won't do it for me. I know he cain't 'cause they'd put him in jail for it. An' Pea wouldn't do it—afraid that they would take her in-surance."

"Maybe they don't want to see you die, Marty."

"They call this livin'?"

"Martin!" Pea was at the door. "You can't be outside sick as you are. Odell! You should know better than to let him out here."

She bustled out and fussed around Martin. He let her take over, seemed to enjoy the activity. Martin had lived alone for many years and even though he'd never said anything about Pea leaving him I believe that he was heartbroken over it.

Now he had her jealously guarding over him. The greedy love of his money felt better for him now than no love at all.

Odell and I went down to the cars.

"I need to know what's goin' on, Odell."

He turned to me, his eyes were innocent like a hurt child's eyes. Odell had to be over sixty years old but he looked younger than I felt.

"I'm sorry, Easy. When this is all over you'll see that I didn't have a choice."

He got in his car and started it up. All I could do was watch him drive away.

CHAPTER 24

I didn't know where to go. I was afraid that the police would find my house. I couldn't stay at John's because everybody knew that we were friends. I didn't want to stay with Etta because if Mouse was there, and he got drunk, which he usually did at night, he might shoot me because I didn't pull those men he wanted to kill out of my pocket.

I drifted toward downtown trying to make sense out of what had happened. While driving I pulled the photograph from Terry T's bedroom out of the glove compartment and set it up on the dash to ponder it for clues.

It was another picture of Betty. This one was more recent. She was standing arm in arm with a dapper-looking man in the front yard of a little flat-roofed block house. Whoever took the picture must've been standing in the middle of the street. You could see the houses on either side. Behind them rose an electrical tower with a big gray flag hanging down in tatters on the other side. It was a photo showing a man with his woman and his house. But Betty and this man looked more like old friends than lovers. Her head was cocked back and she was waving at the camera.

You could see that she was no longer a young woman but even that little snapshot made my heart skip.

I was stopped at a red light when I heard her.

"Hey, mistah. Mistah!"

She wore a black top cut off at the midriff and a black skirt that would have been tight on most women. Her hair was black and hanging down into her olive face.

"You want a friend?" she asked, pushing her head and shoulders in the window on the passenger's side.

Maybe it was exhaustion but I thought I saw an honest sparkle in her eye.

"How much for the whole night?"

She frowned and then smiled. "Seventy-five dollars."

She had the face of a teenaged Mexican girl but her eyes gave her away. In her twenties anyway, maybe even thirty.

"You got a room?"

"Another twenty-two if you want a room."

"Come on then."

She grinned and rushed into the car all excited and beside herself, acting like a real teenager happy and pleased that I had chosen her. But as soon as we were driving she became serious, looking up and down the block for the police or maybe her pimp. I felt safe with her, as if I finally had someone to ride shotgun while I napped in the saddle.

"If you wanna go to El Lobo," she said, accenting the last two words with perfect Mexican-Spanish articulation, "it's a cost twelve dollars more, but they got a air-cooler right in the room. It's noisy too so they don't hear nuthin'."

When we got there it cost twenty dollars extra because the night clerk wanted a tip.

"It's not me, mister," the little bald white man said. "But I'm takin' a chance with a mixed couple."

"Mixed? Man, that ain't no white woman."

He hunched his shoulders and looked at me like I was speaking German.

Before we went in I handed my date four twenty-dollar bills. She gave me four ones and four quarters in change. Kismet.

The room was small and a full third of it was the air-conditioning unit: a large lead-colored box that had a three-inch hole throwing out a cool breeze. It made two sounds. One was the simple drone of a motor. The other was the sound of a loose chain slamming against the side of a metal wall. I imagined a little slave in there trying to pound his way to freedom.

I turned on the light while the girl/woman took off her clothes. She pulled off the top first. Her breasts were small but she had very large and well-formed brown nipples. Then she pulled down her skirt and kicked it off along with her black heels.

Her pubic hair was black and dense. It was dull from the dampness of sweat. It seemed to make sense that a whore's sex would be the part of her that perspired.

"You like her?" she asked.

Immediately I had an erection. After all my troubles and here one little suggestion from a nameless whore and I was ready. It was so ridiculous that I began to laugh.

"What's funny?" She lay back on the bed pulling up her knees and spreading her legs. She did it to cool down but if I wanted to look that was okay too.

"I was just thinkin' that your little lady there's been workin' pretty hard. . . ."

"I'm clean. I wash after."

I was in love.

"Listen, honey. You're beautiful. And I'd rather be with you than any other girl right now. But I need something."

"What?" She was suddenly suspicious. Maybe I'd come out with some handcuffs or thin cord that I wanted her to get intimate with.

I took off my shirt and sat down with my back to her. "Can you clean this out?"

Odell's dressing had loosened on my sweaty back. She pulled it away and crooned, "Oh, baby. What happened to you?"

"Cut myself gardenin'."

She got a towel and a glass of tepid water from the bathroom and then came back and pushed me down on my stomach. For the next hour she laved the wound. Her hair was a heavy mop moving back and forth across my spine.

Carmela Bonitas came from a small town down in the south of Mexico. Her father, a hardworking and good man, disappeared one day. He went off to look for day labor and never came home.

I started to care about Carmela when she told me about her father. My own father had disappeared. And when a poor man gets lost there's nobody going to care. If a poor man falls off the boat in a treacherous sea the captain will look out over the swells but he won't slow down to search. Why should he?

Carmela's mother had brought her all the way to Ensenada but something happened and her mother died or disappeared. Carmela was nine when she came across the border in the salt barrel of a food distributor's truck.

"He told me that it was for free but then he fucked me in a warehouse on top of a pile of rock salt," she said, the childish pout still in her face after all those years. "I gave sailors blow jobs in San Diego until the war was over and then I came up here with a soldier who married me. Bob Ridell."

Carmela had a son and daughter too. They lived with a

woman she paid down in a small California town called Placid. She sent money and visited on Easter and Christmas and the Fourth of July.

At some point I sat up and wrapped my legs and arms around her, from behind. She pressed back against me and laid a hand on either knee. Her thick black mane smelled of our cigarettes.

"What about your husband?"

"I don't know. I got my papers. But then he started drinking and getting mad. You know, he wanted to hit me. I tried to be good for him but he was just always mad."

"So you left him?"

She sat forward, away from me. "We used to keep the apartment door wide open, and one night, when he was slapping me, a guy named Ferdinand who lived on our floor tried to stop him, but Bob beat him up and took his clothes and threw him down in the street."

"Yeah?"

"Ferdinand was so mad that he come right through the door one night and shot Bob in his head."

"Damn!"

"When the police come I told'em it was a Negro." She pronounced the word as if it were the Spanish color. " 'Cause Bobby shouldn'ta done that to Ferdinand; that was wrong."

"Do you wanna hurt me?" Carmela whispered in my ear. I was half asleep after hours of talking. I told her all about my kids and my troubles. She listened and held me. I've never spent a better hundred dollars in my life.

"What?"

"You could fuck me in the ass if you want it."

"Why'd I want that?" I asked. Ashamed of the slight tremble in my voice.

"Because you're mad, but you're not like Bobby. You can't

just take it out with meanness. I don't mind. Men like it to hurt women. But if you know that and he's a nice man and lets you keep him from hurting you too much, then it's okay."

She kissed me in a way that let me know she knew everything that I wanted; even things I didn't know yet.

"I give it to you," she snarled.

I felt rock-hard down in the core of my body. I hadn't felt so powerful since I was young and too stupid to value my strength.

"Uh, no," I said, holding her back.

"Why not?"

"What time is it?"

"I don't know what fucking time it is!"

I got up and went to the window. There was the same gray light I watched over Saul Lynx's shoulder.

"I bet it's about six. If we leave now we could get to Placid by eight. If you called the woman who's got your kids they could be waiting for you."

I could have never made a whore smile in bed; I didn't know enough for that. But Carmela smiled for me then.

Mrs. Escobar let me use her phone while she and Carmela and the kids went to the park. I called Remo's restaurant but nobody answered. So then I went to sleep on the floor of her dining room. After a while I heard the sounds of children stomping and playing through the boards.

It's difficult to express how safe I felt at that moment. It was the safety of being homeless and nameless and not known, not really, to anyone. I slept on that plank floor better than I had in years. The children's hard-soled play and the chatter of glad Spanish filled my dreams. It was like being a child who hasn't yet learned to speak or to understand words. But he knows the sounds of happiness and love. And anything he hears good is his.

While I was sleeping there a red banner came into my mind. MERCHANTS LUMBERYARD. I thought about the lumberyard I wanted to start at Freedom's Plaza. And then I saw Merchants. The front door was boarded up and the banner they'd hung from the electrical tower was in rags.

Carmela and the kids and I had lunch in the early afternoon. We ate pork roast and potatoes fried with green chilis and garlic. There was strawberry pie for the ride back and the memory of smiling children who loved me because I had the power to bring their mother, like magic, out of season.

We exchanged numbers and I dropped her on a corner in Hollywood. We kissed.

"I hope I see you again," I said.

"Call me."

"I mean, I wasn't in the best shape this time but I could take it up again sometime soon."

She looked at me with twenty different replies in her eyes. The roulette of her emotions finally lit on a sad smile.

"Maybe," she whispered.

CHAPTER 25

I parked two blocks away and went to an outside phone booth on Hollywood. Somebody answered at Remo's but Alamo hadn't called in yet. It was only two o'clock, so I decided to drive down and see my dream.

But before I got back into my car a Ford Galaxy drove by, going east. The white man driving was corpulent, talking loud enough that I could hear him over the head of his passenger—a black haired woman who had her back to me. She was leaning toward the fat man with one hand on his shoulder—the other hand looked as if it might have been in his lap.

I couldn't be sure that it was Carmela.

I drove down Avalon until coming to the vacant lot. The lot that used to be Merchants Lumberyard. Now it was nothing but hard dirt, grasshoppers, and weeds. Behind that was an electrical tower. You could hear the energy hum through it; you could almost feel the electricity sizzle.

There were still a few shreds of the Merchants flag left. I took out the photograph of Betty and looked for the palm trees that flanked the steel skeleton.

I spent the next couple of hours driving up and down the streets that were parallel to Avalon around the vicinity of the tower. I'd been on every street for twenty blocks and was about to give up. Actually I had given up in my mind. But when I drove down Slauson Avenue on my way back to Avalon I decided to give it one more try.

The little bungalow was only two blocks back from the tower. I'd missed it the first time because someone had put up a small white picket fence around the yard and painted the coal-colored house a bright turquoise.

"Yes?" The man who answered the door had on loose yellow slacks and a bright seersucker shirt of a similar hue. His hair was long and straightened, combed back in greasy waves and going gray at the ears.

"Excuse me, mister," I said. I had over a dozen good lies to use. I was an old lover, an insurance man; I was a neighbor from another block, a friend with news from Marlon.

The man, who I recognized from the photograph, looked at me expectantly.

"My name is Ezekiel Rawlins," I said. "And I've come here looking for Elizabeth Eady."

His forehead creased into the same pattern of ripples that flowed across his scalp.

"She's not here," he said. His voice was a baritone, so resonant that his words could have come from a song.

"I didn't think so, but could we talk a few minutes?" I glanced past him into the house.

"What did you say your name was?"

"Ezekiel Rawlins," I said again. "And you?"

"You come to my house and you don't even know my name?"

"I'm sorry to bother you, mister," I replied. "But I started lookin' for Betty just to help out, and now, well, now I'm worried."

He didn't want me in his house. But he knew that he was going to have to deal with me. The minute I mentioned Betty I could tell that he wanted to know what I was all about.

"Come on in outta the sun," he said, pushing open the screen.

"Thank you, Mr . . . ?"

"Landry. My name is Felix Landry."

I liked Mr. Landry's house. It was a man's house. Solid furniture of dark woods. And open windows not overtaken by frills or knickknacks. The living room had two brown chairs and a cream-colored sofa with no pillows. The sofa faced a fake fireplace in which sat an open gas-jet heater. There was a large walnut cabinet that held a radio and no TV. The carpet was a blanket from New Mexico and the wall was decorated with crude oil paintings done from photographs of everyday colored life.

"You want something?" he asked. "There's some ham and a pecan pie."

"No thanks. Let's just talk."

"What you got to say?"

We were both on our feet. It wasn't like the standoff between me and Ortiz. We were two men worried and uncomfortable about what we had to talk about.

"Can I sit down?" I asked. And then, when we were seated, "It's like I told you, Mr. Landry. I'm looking for Betty."

"It's like I told you, Mr. Rawlins," he said, shaking his head. "Betty ain't here. She comes around sometimes but I cain't predict it."

"When's the last time you heard from her?"

"I don't know. A month?"

"Was she . . . was she upset about anything?"

"No, no. I mean no more than she ever is when she come down from up there." Felix stared through his wall up into Beverly Hills.

A spasm suddenly seized my shoulder and I winced.

"You mean up at Sarah Cain's?" I asked through the pain.

"What's this all about, Mr. Rawlins? I don't even know you but you here talkin' 'bout things that I don't never say."

"A man hired me for Sarah Cain to find Betty."

"Find her? She live with them."

"Not no more she don't. She's gone, and everywhere I look for her I find trouble."

I couldn't tell if Felix knew anything. The stern look on his face gave nothing away about what I was saying. But I got the feeling that there was a question he wanted to ask. He was wondering if I was the one to put his question to.

"I can't help you, man," he said at last. "I thought that she was still up there with them."

"Did she like workin' for the Cains?" I asked him, hoping to gain his trust.

"We don't talk about that too much. She'd come down here to get away from things, you know?"

"Get away? Was it hard up there for her?"

"Men always give Betty a hard time. They get around her an' start thinkin' like they bulls." Felix sneered. "They don't wanna know her, they wanna break her down; to take away what makes her so fine."

"What's that?" I asked.

"Her freedom," he said like I was a fool not to know.

"And you don't want to take it?"

"No. I love her for what she is." His words were so honest that I was ashamed for him.

"So you two is just friends?"

"Friends is the best thing you could be with Betty. Friends means that you love her and that you know her. Friends means you don't own her but you still there."

"Did Albert Cain think he owned her?"

"He does!" There were bitter tears in this strange man's eyes.

"Not no more he don't," I said in the ironic lilt of my youth. "He's dead. Been dead for over two weeks."

Felix swallowed hard and banked his eyes at me.

"You sure?" he asked.

"Pretty sure."

Felix brought his hands up to the sides of his neck. He rose up and walked toward the front door. A smile mixed in with a hint of fear played across his face. He came back to his chair and sat down for a few seconds but then he had to get up. He went around the room again. Then he pulled a yellow hankerchief from his pocket and spit into it.

"You say dead? That's the old man Cain?" he asked me. He came to a halt in front of the gas-jet heater.

I nodded.

Felix wrung the handkerchief so hard that I thought he might squeeze the spit out of it. "And did Betty go away before that or after it?"

"I don't know exactly."

Felix looked like a glad dog in a Warner Brothers cartoon when he laughed. He howled as if I had just told the funniest joke that he had ever heard.

"Goddam!" he cried, shaking his head with hilarity. "Goddam!"

Felix just stood there, bent over like an old man, squeezing that rag and laughing. It was scary. Scary to see that much hatred in a man. Scary because I had the urge to laugh with him. I bit my tongue to keep a straight face.

After a few minutes Felix got ahold of himself. He pushed out his tongue and licked his lips, then he sat down on the sofa next to me. He brought his knees together and placed his hands on them to prove that he was under control.

"So what can I do for you?" he asked, implying that I had just done him a great favor.

"You got any idea where I could find Betty?"

He shook his head, still smiling.

"No," he said. "An' I wouldn't say anyway, because if Betty wanted to go back to them then she would. But I will tell her that they lookin'—if she gets in touch with me."

"Why do you hate the Cains so much, Mr. Landry?"

"I don't hate'em at all. It's just him."

"Why?"

"Because," he said. "Because he took Betty an' broke her. Broke her because she was so strong. He had her by the short hairs for so many years that she didn't know how to leave even after he got sick."

"What did he do to her?"

"We never talked about that," he said. "All I could do was be here for her when she had a day off and he'd let her go. I'd cook up some chicken an' we'd play Fats Waller and dance right here in this room. I'd push all the furniture back an' me an' Betty cut that rug to pieces."

"She stayed with you?" I asked.

"Where else she gonna go? She didn't wanna do for nobody. She needed somebody to take care'a her. I'm the only one ever took care'a Betty." He patted the cushion between us. "I'd sleep right here and give her my bed. You know, I only sleep good when I'm out here on the sofa knowin' that Betty is safe in my room."

I wanted to ask, safe from what? But I knew that Felix wasn't going to answer any real questions. He just liked to talk about Betty. I imagined him all dressed up, walking around his tiny house talking out loud as if she were there. Asking her what she thought about the peach sauce and who her favorite big band was.

"I don't know where she is, Mr. Rawlins." Felix broke me out of my vision of his dreams. "But I'll tell her what you said."

I drove all the way out of Los Angeles County, all the way out to Riverside. I went so far that the roads became countrified as the sun went down. I pulled off the road into a vacant field and then I drove about half a mile to a place where Jesus and I sometimes set our nets for crayfish.

There was a stand of bay laurels and a big weeping willow that sat next to the little stream we fished in. The stream was dry at that time of year.

I pulled up under the willow and killed the light. The moon was just a sliver and the crickets were calling loud. There was a bitter scent from the laurels in the warm air.

I was thinking about Felix and his fierce platonic love and about Carmela and her offer of pain to me.

Every thought I had brought me back to Betty.

Three days after Adray Ply dropped me into the mud I was

on Betty's trail again. I walked half a block behind her and Marlon and whatever other man she was with that night. Sometimes a whole night would go by and I wouldn't even get to see her up close. But on other nights Betty would call to me, "Boy, come on over here," and get me to go pick up some cigarettes or a pint. I kept my shirttails tucked in for the first time because of that woman.

I remembered one night just like that one out in Riverside. Betty was out walking with a rude man named Rufus George. He was a redheaded mulatto with big muscles and freckles around his yellow face. They had left Marlon playing dice in an alley and were down among the tenements in lower Fifth Ward sitting on a crate and swigging moonshine from a bottle I got for them. I watched them from across the street passing the bottle and kissing back and forth over the neck. Rufus's big tongue looked like it was going to choke Betty. Finally she stood up and staggered across the street to me.

"Come here," she said, her voice as thick as Rufus's tongue.

I followed her across the street, past the crate that they had been sitting on, to an alleyway between two big buildings that stood high off the ground on stilts made from logs. Rufus was throwing a blanket he had down on the dirt there.

When he turned to us Betty shouted, "Rufus!" but with a little bit of a laugh in her voice. I looked at where she was staring and saw Rufus's big uncircumcised thing hanging out of his pants. It was a deep reddish brown and more than half erect. It seemed to me like an elephant trunk when the great beast was about to trumpet.

"You keep a watch out for us, honey," Betty whispered in my ear. Then she moved past me to Rufus. He folded his arms around her and her hands went down between them. Rufus beamed at me.

"You keep your eyes peeled for somebody comin'," he said. "And don't you be lookin' at us neither."

I always thought of that night as the first time I had sex.

I tried to look away but Betty kept calling out and I just had to make sure she was okay. At first I thought that they were play fighting. But then I saw the way that Rufus would touch Betty and how she would rub up close to him like a cat wanting a stroke. When they got passionate it scared me but I still couldn't take my eyes away. I split my watch between their lovemaking and the street behind.

They must have been doing it for an hour when Rufus finally got up off of Betty. She cried, "Oh!" and reached for him but Rufus was already beyond reach. He turned around toward me holding that elephant's trunk. He smiled at me while urinating a heavy splattering stream onto a flat rock. Maybe he was smiling because he thought I was in awe of his thing, but he didn't know that what I was looking at was Betty lying there behind him. She had her hands down between her thighs and was rocking from side to side. Every once in a while a shiver would run from her knees up into her head.

I could feel every bone in my body.

"I don't want you to hate me, boy," Betty was saying to me a little while later at the Cougar's Tooth Café. I took her there for a plate of sausages and grits with cheese cornbread and turnip greens. I paid for the meal with the twenty-five cents Rufus gave me for keeping watch.

Rufus had said goodbye to Betty after zipping up his pants.

"Where you goin'?" Betty was up on her knees.

"I got to get home, honey," he said in a deeply satisfied voice.

"What about me?" she demanded.

But Rufus didn't answer. He flipped me a liberty quarter

and walked down to the street under the light of the moon. I couldn't believe that he was such a fool to walk off from Betty like that.

"I don't hate you," I said. "I like you a *whole* lot."

Betty smiled and took my hand the way I'd seen her take her boyfriends' hands.

"I know I shouldn't't'a done that with Rufus, but you know sometimes a girl will see somethin' in a man that just ain't there. You know what I mean, sugar?"

"Uh-huh." I would have said yes to a plateful of cow pies.

"You a sweet boy, Easy. And you make Betty feel real good. You see, a man who really don't like a girl at all will make her feel good so that he could do what me an' Rufus was doin'. But then, when he finished wit' his business, he remember that he don't like you noways an' he pull up his pants an' leave you like somethin' in the toilet."

Betty was holding my hand so hard that it hurt but I didn't try to pull away. All I wanted was to be a man with Betty out under that building. I'd stay with her under there until the sun shined, until the cotton grew high, until water ran uphill.

The desire to help her came back into me the way it had all those years before.

I went to sleep remembering Rufus. A few nights later he came swaggering into Corcheran's bar looking for Betty. He found her with Marlon and Adray Ply.

Adray cut Rufus so bad that he died from infection a month later.

Betty didn't cry for him, and neither did I.

CHAPTER 26

I was startled awake by a cackle in the early dawn. Two crows were scrabbling in a thin film of dew that had formed on the hood of my car. I'd been sleeping sitting up behind the steering wheel. My left shoulder was stiff and I sent up a silent prayer that infection wouldn't get me like it got Rufus.

The crows stood so close to each other that their tails were touching. They were staring off in different directions—watching each other's back.

I wished that I had some kind of brother at arms to rely on. All I ever had was Mouse, and standing side by side with him was like pressing up against a porcupine.

When I roused, one of the crows took off immediately. But the other one cocked his eye at me and looked me up and down. His hard dull eye was the whole history of the natural world taking me in, sizing me up and classifying me a fool.

Even getting out of the car and slamming the door didn't rid me of my black angel. He just hopped to the side to keep his eye on my disgusting display of human sloth. He called out to his cowardly partner as I relieved myself against the trunk of the tree. He opened his mouth and spread his wings when I struck a match to light my cigarette.

"What you lookin' at?" I asked him after a while. He answered by jumping off the hood and pecking at a twig on the ground.

When I lowered myself back behind the steering wheel I smelled what those crows must have smelled: it was the smell of a sick animal, so weak that he couldn't even clean himself.

When I started the engine the crow finally took off. I saw him and his friend gliding over the willow as I drove back toward my life.

I went down to the YMCA on Main for an early-morning soak in the pool. After that I took a shower and a shave with a razor I borrowed from Amos Mackey—the towel man down there. I tried Remo's again but it was too early for them to be open.

I had time to kill but I couldn't think of rest. My mind was too agitated to read the newspaper and there wasn't anyplace to get cool. There were so many things on my mind; each one worse than the other.

I could have gone and talked to John about a solution I had about Mouse. But I didn't feel strong enough for that, so I decided to drive over to 52 Wilshire Boulevard where Save-Co had their southern California offices. At least Save-Co just wanted my property; as far as I knew they weren't a threat to my life.

It was one of those new buildings. White steel girders showing around green cement and blue windows. It looked something like a waffle that had sprouted various kinds of fungus.

When I looked at the directory I noticed that Mason LaMone had an office there. He wanted my money too, but he was just a solitary man. Maybe I could scare him into leaving my property alone.

"Yes, sir?" a handsome young white man with sandy blond hair said to me. He was sitting behind a desk in an office that had *Mason LaMone Realty* stenciled on the door.

"You LaMone?" I asked him.

"No, sir," he answered pleasantly. "My name is Carson. I'm Mr. LaMone's assistant."

"Get him for me, will ya?" I wasn't feeling very cordial.

"Whom shall I say is here?"

"Freedom's Plaza."

"What?"

"You heard me. You tell him that he's got Freedom's Plaza outside the door."

Carson got on the phone and delivered my message, more or less.

"Have a seat, sir. Mr. LaMone will be with you when he can."

I walked by Carson then, toward the door behind him.

He said, "Hey!" and jumped up—all six feet of him.

When he came toward me I held up one finger and said, ever so softly, "Sit down or I will break your head, white boy. An' I ain't foolin' wit' you."

Carson balked and I went on through the door to Mason LaMone's office.

It was more like a utility room than an office. Even though there was air conditioning in the rest of the building this room was hot. The window was propped open and that desert sun was pouring in. The floor was covered with gray linoleum tiles through which writhed thin red veins.

Mr. LaMone's desk was just a plain metal table, painted dark brown. There was no other furniture to be seen, not even a bookcase. There was a paint-stained black phone on the desk. From the phone ran a long knotted wire that snaked its way off to the cracked jack in the wall.

On the phone, seated behind the desk, on the only chair in the room, in a shaft of relentless L.A. sunshine—there sat Humpty Dumpty. He had a big upside-down bowl of a bald head with small ears and tiny-lensed glasses that were barely large enough to cover his big eyes. His mustache was gray down and his light green suit seemed to be sewn from baby frog skin, both bright and slimy.

"Excuse me, I have to go," he said into the receiver in a

husky whisper that sounded as if it could have carried for miles.

Mr. LaMone stood up from his desk on bright green frog-skin legs that were more like tree trunks than human limbs.

"Yes?"

"You LaMone?"

He nodded.

I wasn't prepared for such an odd-looking and intimidating man. Everything about him seemed calculated to throw me off.

"My name is Rawlins," I said.

He smiled and nodded. "I've heard of you. Yes I have."

"You might not have heard all there is. Not yet."

The door to the office opened behind me. Three more white men plus Carson came flooding in.

"Mr. LaMone!" Carson shouted.

"What is this?" LaMone said directly to Carson. His eyes were twinkling behind the sun-laced lenses.

"Uh, um, well, I brought the security guards when he, because he . . ."

"It's your job to guard the door, Carson," the great green egg rumbled. "Now go. Find Milo and bring him here to me." LaMone pointed at his feet with a wide forefinger.

"What about . . . what about . . ."

"I'll talk to Mr. Rawlins alone."

Only one of the security men would have given me any trouble. One was short and skinny, while another was fat in the gut and had small arms. The big, bearded guy might have had more muscle than me but he couldn't have wrestled with Saul Lynx's .38.

"Go on. Get out." Mason LaMone made a sweeping motion with his big hands.

The guards gave me hard stares as Carson herded them back through the office door. They were mad at the way

Mason was dismissing them but their anger was directed at me.

After all, I didn't pay their salaries.

When they were gone I faced LaMone. He was seated behind his desk again.

"I know what you an' Clovis been up to, man," I said. He wasn't even breathing as far as I could tell. "And I ain't gonna let you take away what's mines."

"I don't have anything to do with the county, Mr. Rawlins. They need a sewage treatment plant. What's that got to do with me?"

"You can't pull that shit on me. I got Clo's number now and I will bring the house down on both of you."

My threat didn't mean much to Mason LaMone. He took off his glasses and stared out with his big vacant eyes. "If that's how you want to spend your time, Mr. Rawlins, it's okay by me. I'm in business, that's all. When I heard that some investors were planning to build a shopping mall I went straight out to meet them."

Suddenly the egg was full of life. He got up and gestured meaninglessly in the air. "I found Miss MacDonald and opened a line of communication. That's what I do.

"Now I was upset to find that the county had to condemn that property." He pointed up to the ceiling for no good reason that I could tell. "I want to make money. A sewage plant won't make me a dime."

"But if they reverse the decision after they throw us out, that would open up the property at rock-bottom prices."

LaMone went back to his chair. He sat down and returned to his peaceful state. He cupped his big hands on the desk and contemplated them.

"I'm not a fortune-teller, sir. If the right chain of events occur I will exploit them. That's business." LaMone couldn't help but give me a little smile after that. Couldn't help but laugh at how he had it over some poor nigger who wanted to come up with the big boys and get his chance.

"Uh-huh, yeah," I said. "But I could read the tea leaves. I can tell you what will happen. I can tell you that Clovis MacDonald is gonna lose all the money that you gave her. I can tell you that if I lose my property and then by some celestial coincidence there magically appears a shoppin' center or some big store where that treatment center shoulda been, then there will come some terrible events. I can promise you that whatever comes up outta that ground, if it ain't mines then it won't be nobody's. Because if you insist on makin' me out a nigger I ain't got no choice but to be one. No choice at all."

Mason LaMone's smile dimmed. And where his eyes didn't care before I saw some little bit of concern, some worry. Where there had been a lifetime of clear skies set out before him, Mr. LaMone, the great green-and-white reptile egg, now saw a bank of clouds.

CHAPTER 27

"Yeah," the bartender at Remo's said. "He said that you was ta meet'im atta . . . atta . . ." He hesitated trying to read the note. "At nine out behind the hot dog stand that you told him about."

That was at twelve-fifteen. It was one hundred and seven degrees. The wind coming out of the east was a scythe of pain.

It was too hot to stay in my car and there was no place to drive until nine anyway. So I went over to a mixed bar on

Normandie called the Viking. It was a cool dark room that played old tunes and served food. I had deep-fried fish sticks with French fries and cole slaw. I almost asked for a beer but settled for ice water.

There was an *L.A. Times* on the bar.

Kennedy was considering resuming underground nuclear tests and Khrushchev threatened above-ground testing. Fallout in Alaska had increased three thousand percent and there wasn't a Negro in the world worthy of an article.

I hung around until two-thirty. Then I went to the phone booth and called John.

"I been tryin' t'call you, Easy," John told me.

"Ain't been home. What did you want?"

"I think you better drive by here tonight, 'bout nine."

"Cain't, man. I got some serious business and I don't how late it'll go."

The quiet on the other end of the line was John's rage. People didn't tell him no very often.

"I could make it in the mornin' if I ain't in jail by then," I said to fill up the silence.

"Make it nine in the mornin' then," he said and then he hung up.

I spent the rest of the day down in Santa Monica. I got barefoot and sat on a YMCA towel in the sand. But the sea didn't relax me and the bathing girls didn't make me smile.

I went to an army/navy store on Pico in the early evening. I got black pants, a dark blue shirt, and a pair of black canvas shoes.

I'd parked a few blocks west of Robertson, on Livonia, and was walking up the alley at eight fifty-nine. I was proud at being so exact and on time. That pride being a leftover from my army days.

"Easy."

In his drab-colored pants and black jacket Alamo was a wraith behind the trash bin. Slung across his back was a black-dyed long English rucksack. We were three buildings down from Hodge's office.

"You ready?" Alamo asked. He looked down at my hands and then at my feet. "Good shoes. Good shoes."

He gestured two fingers for me to wait and then he went ahead. I waited two minutes and then came on behind. The Robertson Professional Building faced Robertson Boulevard right at the corner of Pico. Alamo and I stood at the back of that building in a small lot for parking off of the alley. The parking was for the Cupcake Bakery, Ron Gordon Glazier's shop, and a stationery store that faced out onto Pico. The office building and the glazier's shop met at the angle of the backwards el.

"Shh." Alamo took two pair of yellow dish-washing gloves from his sack and handed me one. "Put 'em on."

There was a ladder propped up next to a window about midway between the first and second floors of Hodge's building.

Two more fingers and Alamo was up the ladder. The breaking glass was louder than some cannon fire I've heard. He was in and I was up and in right after him.

We were on the halfway landing of the stairs leading up.

We pulled the ladder in and took it up to the second floor, where we laid it flat against the wall. Alamo took a flashlight from his sack. It gave off a very dim light as if maybe the batteries were going bad.

We stopped at a door that had "Calvin P. Hodge, Esq." stenciled on it.

"This your boy?" Alamo asked.

"Yeah."

Instead of pulling his tools out and working on the door, Alamo went further down the hall to another office. This one said "Myna Goldstein, Fine Fabrics." Alamo took a pair of pliers that had a long flat nose. He closed the pliers and inserted the nose in between the lock and the doorjamb. Then he put his strength into it, trying to pull the pliers open.

"Gimme a hand."

I grabbed one side of the handle with my good right hand and pulled as hard as I could. After about thirty seconds the wood around the lock started to give. The bolt was pulled out of place and the door swung inward.

It was another poor office. Just a desk and a filing cabinet. There was a two-toned spider plant in a pot on the windowsill. While I improvised, propping a chair under the doorknob to keep unwanted noses out, Alamo went right to the wall that Hodge's office shared. He took two mountain climber hammers from his bag and handed me one.

"Let's get to it," he said. He started hammering away at the plaster wall.

We spent the next half an hour clearing away the plaster from the crossbeams that made the wall. Then we crawled through the triangular space and were in Hodge's office. No alarms to prevent going off. No fancy locks to pick.

Hodge's office was the same layout and size as Myna Goldstein's. But he had a large oakwood desk and plush carpeting. There were many plaques on the walls extolling his achievements and a glass-enclosed cabinet that had at least fifteen trophies that he'd won for hunting and shooting. There was too much furniture in that small room. I imagined that he once had a big office on Wilshire but he had to move when times got hard.

Mr. Hodge was a man on his way down.

Using hammers, a punch with a titanium bit, and a pair of metal shears, we opened up Hodge's file-safe in under thirty minutes. I found Albert Cain's file in there. It wasn't very thick. On a whim I looked up Saul Lynx and Commander Styles.

I expected to find Saul but there was only a slender folder on the commander.

While I searched, Alamo went through the rest of the office, taking whatever he could get in his sack and any petty cash lying around.

I was more than ready to go when there was a loud crash.

Alamo hissed, "Shh!"

We could see a light flashing into Myna Goldstein's office through the hole in the wall.

"Help me!" Alamo was grabbing the husk of the file cabinet. I knew right away what he was doing. Together we pushed the gutted file to cover the hole in the wall as well as possible. Then I took Hodge's typewriter and threw it through the bolted window.

Three different alarm bells went off all at once. Somebody shouted, "Police!"

Alamo was already through the window and I was right behind him. It wasn't until I grabbed the iron railing to let myself hang down the grated stairs that I realized my mistake. A pain went off in my shoulder louder than the alarm bells. I hit the roof of the hot dog stand and rolled right off of it, sprawling onto the sidewalk below. It was only luck that kept me from breaking a bone.

"You okay?" Alamo had me by the shoulders and was helping me up. His grip hurt so bad all I could do was nod.

"Half a block north of Pico, on Livonia," I said. Alamo was gone, running south on Robertson. I ran across the street intending to throw them off by heading east. When I got to the middle of the street they threw down on me.

"Halt or I'll shoot!" Right out of the movies. I never missed a step but in that one moment I could tell that the officer was still on the second floor of the office building. I weighed the chances of him hitting me with a pistol at that range.

I kept running.

At least eight shots were fired. Bullets ricocheted off the sidewalk around my feet. Everything inside me turned to water and I ran so hard that it seemed to me that I was invisible. I must have run seven blocks. The first four were a zigzag route away from my car. I had it in my mind that I wanted to confuse the cops, throw them off. But then I realized that they didn't know where my car was—they were after me.

I made it to the car quickly after that. Two minutes later Alamo was coming down the street.

I headed west on Olympic toward Santa Monica, figuring we'd cross municipalities so the police couldn't track us.

"Damn, that was close," Alamo said. He was wheezing from his hard run. "That was a close one all right."

My hands were sweating in the rubber gloves.

"I'll go down to Santa Monica," I said.

"You could drop me at a friend'a mines on Tuxedo Lane. Better if they don't catch no salt and pepper in a car," Alamo said. "When you wanna split?"

He was talking about the loot he'd taken.

"All I got was some papers to keep me out of trouble. That's all I want. You need me to pay you something?"

"Naw. Naw, but maybe we could go into business, Easy. You're good."

"Yeah. Good enough to spill out my blood on the street corner."

I dropped Alamo off half a block from his friend's house.

The desire to be home overwhelmed me. I couldn't imagine a hotel or even a friend's house. I wanted my chair and my lamp.

It was a fool's move but I had to go home. I drove around

the block twice. There were no suspicious-looking cars parked out front or down the street. The lights in my house were off. That didn't mean much—the cops could have been laying for me in the dark. But that was an expensive proposition. I'd have to be a real top ten for them to spend that kind of money on overtime. I finally pulled into the driveway and took my chances with the front door.

CHAPTER 28

The first file was labeled "Norman Styles." There was deposition indicating a charge of battery and sexual assault on a Mr. and Mrs. Bradley Rosen on North Stanley. The charges were dropped and Styles sued to get back pay for the time that he was suspended from the Beverly Hills Police Department.

He was questioned about an accidental death in 1954. The question concerned a prisoner (named John Doe) who died in his cell. John was drunk and disorderly before and after his arrest. He committed suicide by hanging himself from a leather belt.

The inquisitors wondered why John also wore suspenders.

Commander Styles also did private work for Mr. Hodge. He was a bodyguard for various Hollywood celebrities and businessmen. He was a security consultant on two occasions for meetings between men who were only referred to by first names.

The last page in Styles's folder was an old arrest report from the Beverly Hills Police Department. On July 14,

1939, Marlon Eady was arrested on burglary charges. He'd been arrested at the house of Albert Cain.

Cain's file said almost nothing. There was a medical report, all in Spanish, from a place called the Sisters of Mercy Hospital in Mexico City dating from 1940. From my little bit of Spanish I couldn't make out what the treatment was—the patient was Jane Smith.

There was a legal letter from one lawyer, Bertrand Fresco, requesting a transfer of legal documents for Cain. That letter was dated June 4, 1959. I supposed that was why Cain's file was so slim—everything else was with the new lawyer.

The phone started ringing somewhere near two in the morning. There was a slight chance that it was an innocent call. A wrong number or maybe an old friend who'd gotten drunk and sad. But more likely it was trouble. Another brick in my cell.

I didn't want to answer but it might have been about the children or maybe Jewelle.

"Yeah?"

"What is it, Easy? Did I do somethin' to you?"

I could tell from the first word that he'd been drinking. "Odell, man, I got enough problems right now. If you got somethin' t'say then get it out."

"I got somethin' t'say all right. Yeah. We been friends since you was a boy, Easy. I took you in my house when you didn't have nuthin' to eat and nowhere to sleep. I used to give you money when I didn't hardly have nuthin' myself. And then you turn it around an' shit on my shoe."

"What are you talking about?"

"Reverend Towne . . ."

"Odell, I know we got to talk about that one day, but there's things happenin' right now—"

Before I could finish Odell cut me off. "I know that! I know that! First Marlon gets killed. Betty's only brother, and you know she loved him somethin' terrible. And now you done killed her son."

"Her son? What you talkin' 'bout, man?"

"Terry."

"The boxer?"

"He was hers. They let him live down here wit' the Tyler fam'ly but he was hers. And you killed him."

"I did not kill Terry Tyler."

"How could you say that when I know you did?"

I waited a moment, confused by the force of his accusations. I didn't know if I was guilty or not. Maybe I had killed Terry. Not by my own hand, but maybe he was killed because of me.

"Who told you that?" I asked, coming out of my spell. "Who told you that I killed Terry?"

Odell went silent on his end of the phone.

"Odell."

"Leave us alone, Easy Rawlins. Stay out of our life." He hung the phone up in my ear.

I was down to his house by three, knocking at the front door. I rapped on it for five minutes with no reply. But when I started shouting the porch light went on and Maude came out dressed in a pink nightgown.

"Do you know what time it is?"

"Let me in, Maudria!" I yelled at the top of my voice.

A look of fear went over her and she shrank back from the door. I came in towering over her, looking around the neat and well-ordered house.

"I told you to leave us alone, Easy." His voice came from the side.

"Odell!" Maude shouted.

My old friend had come out of the door that led to his

kitchen. There was a double-barreled twelve-gauge shotgun hanging through the crook of his arm.

I put my thumbs up next to my ears. "I didn't kill Terry Tyler, Odell. I went to the house . . ."

"Odell, put down that gun!" Maudria screamed.

"... and I found him there. Somebody came up behind me and stabbed me in the shoulder and then hit me with a number ten cast-iron fryin' pan."

Odell's stare was too deep to decipher.

"And I know two things." Keep talking and keep talking. "One is that whoever stabbed me wasn't the one who killed Terry, and two is that whoever it was they told you about me."

"It was Betty!" Maude shouted. "Now, Odell, put down that gun!"

"Betty?" I wasn't even looking at Odell anymore. "Betty stabbed me?"

"She went to the house to ask Terry where she could find Marlon and she fount him there. And then she heard somebody and figured that it was the killer and she laid for'im an' stabbed him. When she told us what happened, Odell knew it was you."

"Where is she?" I asked Odell.

"We don't know," Maude answered. "She just called to tell us about Terry. To ask us to see that he gets buried."

"An' did she tell you about Marlon too?"

The guilty stare that passed between husband and wife was a testament to decades of honesty. Neither one of them could hide their guilt. I would have laughed if it wasn't so serious.

"Where is he?"

Both their heads retreated like a pair of turtles sensing a shadow from overhead.

"Naw. Here in this house?"

Odell let the shotgun hang down to his side and he

stumbled backwards. He was aiming to land in a chair but missed it and slid against the wall until he was crouching on the floor.

Maude ran to him.

"Oh, baby," she said as she knelt down and put her hands on his head.

I watched my old friends for a while, unwilling to interrupt their sorrow. It was a pain that they'd been holding in for days and it needed a time just to be. Maude cried and Odell looked around for tears that wouldn't come.

"Where is he?" I asked again.

"Down in the bomb shelter." Odell's voice was weaker than Martin's.

One eye was wide open while the other one was a glistening slit. His lip was swollen and curled up from where it had been split. A dead man's snarl to be sure. He wore only a T-shirt. One hand was twisted backwards, pointing at his sad genitals. The other was at his side pushing away some overly friendly dog or errant thought. He lay on three burlap bags that were wet. On his chest and knees two other bags were laid.

"Ice," Maude said. "To keep him from goin' bad down here."

"What happened to him?"

"They beat him, Easy."

"Who did?"

"Some white men. They wanted him to tell'em where Betty was, but he didn't know. They like to killed him. He played like he was dead and when they left him he stoled one'a their cars and used up his last mortal strength to drive to us." Maude's voice had a myth-making tone to it.

"Where's the car?" I asked.

"Odell drove it a couple'a blocks over."

"When did all this happen?"

"Right after you was here."

"Who was it that beat'im?" I asked.

"He said that it was the po-lice, Easy." Maude's eyes opened in the kind of terror that poor people have for the cops.

"Did you call the doctor?"

Maude shook her head. Tears welled up in her eyes. "He died right away, Easy. I seen enough dead men to know. We didn't know what to do, because of the cops, so we took him down here."

Odell stood at the door more gaunt than I'd ever seen him while Maude and I talked.

"Where's Betty, Maude?"

"I don't know. She wouldn't say where she was."

"You tell her about this here?" I asked while pointing at the icy corpse.

"No," she sobbed. "She was so broke up when she told us about Terry we thought that more bad news would kill her."

"What you gonna do with him?" I asked.

"I don't know. He needs a burial. He's got to be put in the ground," Odell said.

"You can't take him to an undertaker unless you want to tell the cops about him."

"I can't do that."

"I could dig you a hole right down here. We could have a service for him right here."

"We'll see," Odell said. Then he stumbled back up the basement stairs.

"Where's Betty?" I asked Maude. "What's she runnin' from?"

"Will you bury him, Easy?" was her answer.

"Yeah, yeah, honey. Just keep him cold a couple'a more days until I can get some things worked out."

CHAPTER 29

I was up with the sun again. In the morning the fear of the police returned. Policemen are working folks just like anybody else. They'd drop by the house in the early morning and maybe even at midnight but unless they were really upset they'd go home and go to bed in the wee hours.

I was down to my old house on 116th Street by six.

The yard was different. I kept neat little islands of flowers in a sea of thick St. Augustine grass when it was mine. But a family with so many children as Primo had couldn't maintain a proper lawn. The ruthless feet of innocent children pound everything down into soil. Flower, Primo's Panamanian wife, had grown a large garden where the children weren't allowed to play. She had a dozen tomato bushes and rows of three-foot onion stalks that sported brain-shaped waxy bulbs full of seed. Where I had my potato patch she grew beans. Nine-foot giant sunflowers bloomed all along the front of the house.

The avocado tree was trimmed back a little but it was still there. I could see the platform that Jesus slept in.

It was no longer my yard but it was still a yard full of life.

The front door was wide open. Flower was rolling out tortillas on a flat board in her lap. I could smell the bacon, eggs, and potatoes that she'd use to fill the tortillas for the children's lunch bags. Feather loved the lunches from Flower. She'd told me more than once that she was going to be fat and black like Flower when she grew big.

Primo wasn't doing much. He sat in the stuffed chair that he had in the kitchen keeping Flower company. He looked hungover. But he always looked like that in the morning.

"How's it going, my friend?" Primo asked.

"Never good enough. How's all my people out here?"

"Kids okay. But that Mofass is sick," Flower said. "He's always coughing and spitting." She made a distasteful face. "You think the kids can get it?"

"Naw. He's got lung trouble from smoking those damn cigars."

"Daddy!" Feather came running in with Jesus standing behind her.

"Hi, Dad," he said. Flower and Primo acted as if they didn't even notice. As if they were thinking, "Well, he just didn't talk the first fifteen years of his life. He must not have had anything to say."

We caught up, the children and I. Feather wanted to know when she had to come home.

"We got a big party on Saturday, Daddy. Can you come?" she asked me.

"Sure, honey." I really did want to.

Children paraded in and out of the kitchen for the next hour and a half. Eddie—who was ambidextrous and a heart-breaker at fourteen—came in proudly in his fake leather jacket and Keds tennis shoes. Rafeleta and Helen wore homemade dresses, red lipstick, and brass rings. Cindy stayed all morning. She was only a baby, really, and the one Primo loved best. She and Feather sat on Primo's knees taking turns kissing his calloused hands.

I think my little girl was actually trying to make me jealous.

The children consumed gallons of milk and stacks of tortillas. What my little family ate in two weeks was depleted in that one morning.

"I bet they got a file with your family's name on it down at Vons market," I said to Primo.

"I love to watch them, my friend," he said while he tickled the girls. "I love it."

Mofass was up by eight.

"Well, yeah, Mr. Rawlins. Mr. Hodge gonna work out fine. He got all kindsa papers wrote up to block Clovis right outta my business. He servin' them papers on the bank today and he's sendin' her family a notice of eviction from my house. Then he gonna close down the office on Crenshaw altogether, and if that don't finish it we gonna get a writ to keep 'em away from all my properties—even them ones that the white men owns."

Mofass looked ten years younger and healthier. "You know, I told Mr. Alexander I don't even need him no more."

"You what?"

"I paid him," he said in his defense. "I gave him just what he asted for. I don't think he was worth no two hundred dollars, but . . ."

"Mofass, how long we know each other?"

"Long time. Ten years, more."

"Then don't you think you should know to ask me before you do somethin' like fire Mouse?"

"Ain't nuthin' wrong wit' it. I didn't need'im. Why should I be payin' the man when I don't need'im?"

What could I say? Anything I ever did with Mofass turned out like that. His mind was so small when it came to money that it was actually no mind at all.

I shook my head and went away from him. I said goodbye to the children and drove on down to John's place, Targets Bar.

CHAPTER 30

John's bar didn't open until noon but I would have found him there even if we hadn't had that appointment. Men like John and me didn't have lives like the white men on TV had. We didn't roll out of bed for an eight-hour day job and then come home in the evening for *The Honeymooners* and a beer.

We didn't do one thing at a time.

We were men who came from poor stock. We had to be cooks and tailors and plumbers and electricians. We had to be our own cops and our own counsel because there wasn't anything for us down at City Hall.

We worked until the job was done or until we couldn't work anymore. And even when we'd done everything we could, that didn't mean we'd get a paycheck or a vacation. It didn't mean a damn thing.

I knocked at the back door. John answered in shirt sleeves and an apron.

"Hey, John."

"Easy."

"What's up?"

"I got some people I need you t'talk to, but first I got to make the chili for lunch."

I followed him into the back room. The kitchen was an afterthought in the bar. It was once just a storage room where John kept his booze. But now the little room had a two-burner stove and an deep lift-top icebox. He had a butcher-block table out in the hall that led to the bar. There was a great pile of chopped onion and green peppers there. John grabbed up the whole mound of the peppers in his two hands and carried them quickly to a big aluminum frying pan that was smoking from overheated peanut oil.

I stood in the hall while he stirred the sizzling vegetables.

"Mouse been by here?" I shouted into the smoky cave.

"Yeah."

"He been actin' a fool?"

John stopped a minute and turned to me. "I keep a loaded gun in every room since you called me, Easy. On'y reason I ain't gone to Joe Teegs is you."

You paid, somebody died—that was Joe Teegs.

"He been askin' questions 'bout the night they arrested him. An' he knows that I warned all them boys was here. He know you the one told me."

John came back out and returned with a handful of onions to add to his peppers. He took the onions and peppers and dumped them into a ten-gallon pot. After them he poured in three big cans of chopped and stewed tomatoes, a ten-ounce can of powdered chili, some garlic powder, and a heaping tablespoon of cumin. Finally he came out. There were tears flowing from his eyes. I knew that it was the onions and not fear. John had let fear out the back door many years before.

I had a question to ask John but before I got around to it there came a weak knock at the back door. It wasn't a regular kind of knock but more like a code; three taps, then two, then three again.

John went to the door and pulled it open. The three men came in quickly, looking around but managing to keep their heads down at the same time. Two of them wore hats.

"Easy," the big one, Melvin Quick, said.

I shook hands with him and his two friends, Clinton Davis and Malcolm Reeves.

"Come on into the bar," John said. He led the way down the hall and then made us wait while he closed the venetian blinds in the bar. I didn't say anything about it but I wondered what Mouse would have thought if he was sitting outside and saw those blinds close like that.

John's was a big room with black and white tile on the floors and walls, like they have in the fancy restaurants in New Orleans. There was a Blackstone bar with high stools and round linoleum-topped tables for the lunch and dinner patrons. They used to play music at John's but he'd calmed down as he got older and wanted to get to bed by midnight.

John remained standing while I sat with the three fugitives.

"These boys wanna talk to you, Easy," John said. "Anybody want somethin' to drink?"

"I take a scotch," cross-eyed and tiny Malcolm said.

"Rye for me," Clinton Davis added. Clinton was handsome. He had a razor-thin mustache, half-white features, and skin the color of coffee with two teaspoons of heavy cream mixed in. I once knew a woman named Corrie Day who was always mad at herself because every time Clinton called she'd come over to his house. When I asked her why she just didn't say no she looked at me like I was crazy. "And turn down somebody look that good?" she asked.

"We heard about Raymond." That was Melvin trying to sound brave. I couldn't help but think how he was the same size as Bruno Ingram. He was a simple day laborer with a face the size of a dinner plate.

"Yeah?" I asked, not friendly at all. "Then why you all here—in L.A.—together?"

"We scared about Mousc," Malcolm chirped.

"Naw, man, you ain't scared. You be in Chicago or Mexico if you was scared."

"We cain't run, Easy," Clinton said. "We got people here."

John brought Clinton and Malcolm their drinks on a cork-lined tray.

"You might have them," I said. "But let Raymond see your ass and they won't have you."

They were all afraid. Frightened to death. I tried to keep the disgust out of my face. I understood fear. And I knew better than anybody in that room what Mouse was capable of. But still I came from a place where to show your fear was like asking for death. It was suicide; a sin.

"So what you boys want then?" I asked.

"Well." Handsome Clinton was the spokesman. Maybe they thought that he could charm me. "We got three hundred dollars. And we thought that you could take it, you know, and pay Raymond and keep what's left for you."

Three hundred dollars was half the year's rent for any one of those men; it was also Joe Teegs's price tag. They were telling me that they would spend that money one way or the other. Killing Mouse was a hard proposition, because they knew that I was Mouse's friend, and even though I wasn't known as a cold-blooded killer, they knew that I might take it hard if Mouse showed up dead.

"So you wanna pay me to save you from what Bruno got?"

They didn't nod exactly but the assent was all over their faces.

"I got to know somethin' first."

"What?" Malcolm asked.

"Which one'a you called in on him? I got the police call at my house, so I know what was said. I just don't know which one'a you said it."

Melvin looked at Malcolm and Clinton studied both of his friends.

Tears formed up in Melvin's big eyes. "Ain't not one'a us stupid enough for that, Mr. Rawlins. You were there. You remember. We was all right here. John called the ambulance and they called the cops."

Some people say that they can tell when a man is lying. Those people are fools. You can never trust what somebody tells you is true. Maybe one of those men snuck off to a phone and turned Mouse in. But I couldn't tell.

"Where's the money?" I asked.

Melvin came out with a thick wad of mainly small bills.

"Two hunnert eighty-seven dollars," he said.

"I thought you said three hundred?"

"Here." John, who had gone back to the bar, pressed a button on his cash register and took out a bill. He brought it over to me.

Taking that twenty-dollar bill was a changing point in my life. Up until that moment I used what talents I had to trade favors with my neighbors and friends. It was rare that I would take cash from one of my peers—especially from a close friend like John.

I felt myself becoming cut off from the human debt that had been my stock in trade.

I peeled off seven dollar bills from the wad and handed them to John. His solemn face reflected the weight of that thirteen-dollar transaction.

I cleared my throat and said, "All right! Listen up! I need a week wit' you boys close to the ground. Don't go home. Don't go to your jobs, your families, your girlfriends, and don't never come here. Don't go drivin' down the street or to no stores where you know people. If you can leave town, then leave; better, get outta state.

"Mouse will kill you on sight. He will kill you. He won't yell your name or ask was it you. You cain't talk to him, deal with him, or make him understand. So put on them hats and get outta here. Call John one week from today. He'll tell you yea or nay."

"But I wanna . . ." Malcolm started.

I stopped him by pointing my finger into his cross-eyed stare. "Ain't nuthin' for you to say, brother. I told you everything you need to know. Don't do what I say and you dead. Do it . . . well, do it and there's some kinda chance.

"Now pick up and move out."

The men gazed over at John but they found no sympathy there. It wasn't that we were disgusted with these men. It was just that we were in hard times and the smell of fear made us angry and ready to fight.

They left quickly after that, thanking me and John by shaking our hands and muttering. Good-looking Clinton didn't want to let go of my hand. I glanced away from his pleading eyes to ease my shame for him.

When they had gone I asked John, "When's the last time you seen Raymond?"

"Two days."

"An' he's lookin' for them, right?"

John nodded.

"Then why you get them to come here if you know he gonna be lookin' here?"

"This is my place, Easy Rawlins." He pointed at his heart. "I have anybody I want here and there ain't nobody gonna tell me no."

John turned away and went back through the swinging doors, toward his kitchen.

I followed him.

"Did Raymond ask you about some girl named Sooky?" I asked. I'd been thinking about the young people I remembered in my dreams.

John was pulling a pink paper package of chopped stew meat from the icebox. "Sooky Freeman? Reverend Rowel's niece?"

"She got a boyfriend named Alfred?"

"Used to have. They broke up and she married Theodore Mix."

"You see her that night Bruno got shot?"

John looked me right in the eye. "Why?"

"I think they mighta been in the alley when Mouse killed Bruno. Maybe they know something."

It wasn't a pleasant thing to face off with John. He was a little older than I but John reminded you of a bison. He was big and strong by nature. His black face was like that of a dour African god sculpted from ironwood.

"Why you askin', Easy? What you gonna do to Sooky?"

"Just trust me. All right?"

John didn't swing so I guessed that meant okay.

"Did you see her or Alfred the night Bruno got shot?" I asked again.

John went back in the kitchen and threw down the meat into the frying pan. Then he came back to me.

"Yeah, yeah. I saw 'em both. They was out in the street fightin' like always."

"What time was that?"

"What is this? You a cop?"

"Was it around the time Bruno got it?"

John's nod was a small thing. Like a bullet in the brain.

CHAPTER 31

The police were waiting for me outside the bar. Two uniformed white men standing around my car. I thought about going back down the alley but one of them saw me and pointed. "Hey!"

My odds at dodging bullets were going down so I decided to go meet my fate.

"Hello, officers."

One was fair and handsome. The other looked like a fish.

His big ears were almost parallel to the ground and his eyes were glass bowls.

"Ezekiel Rawlins?" the looker asked.

"Yes?"

He smelled of cedar and his face was scrubbed so clean that his ears, forehead, and cheeks glistened—without sweat.

"You're under arrest," he informed me.

Officer Fish was a wizard at slapping on cuffs before you could think.

"Get in the car," the pop-eyed policeman whispered.

I obliged him but he pushed me when I was off balance stepping into the cage of the backseat. I barely got my foot in before he slammed the door.

" 'Scuse me, officers!" I yelled as we cruised down Central. "What's the charge on this here!" I was feeling playful. Maybe it was the lack of sleep. Maybe it was that I had just given up like so many men I'd known, putting up their fists against billy clubs, bullets, and hatred.

The handsome cop turned and said, "Murder," in a bland tone. "And conspiracy."

I was quiet for the rest of the ride.

Detective Lewis met us at the front desk. He told the uniforms that he had me now and we went back to his office—Quinten Naylor's old office. Quinten was the previous black detective that they had at the station. He was kicked upstairs somewhere. I hadn't seen him in years. But you could still make out the outline of Quinten's name under the black letters that spelled "Detective Arno Lewis."

Lewis took off my cuffs when we were secure behind closed doors.

"I'm under arrest?" I asked as soon as the door closed.

Lewis was a tall, lean man. His box-shaped head was high on the pole, as Martin used to say about skinny men.

Lewis took off his thick black-rimmed glasses and pressed the bones over his eyes. "You're almost gone, Ezekiel."

Suddenly there was a little animal trying to claw his way out of my chest. I had to catch half a breath to sound normal.

"What's the problem, man?"

"Sit down."

"I don't wanna sit down. I want you to tell me what the problem is."

Arno sat. The thing that made him a good cop, probably the best cop I'd ever met, was the fact that he couldn't be intimidated. He didn't mind if I stood over him in that small room. Because that room was his office and he was boss no matter where you were.

"I've two complaints here, Mr. Rawlins." Lewis tapped a manila folder with his exceptionally long and bony point-finger. "Both of them concern murder charges."

"Shit!"

"The second one came in after you pulled that joke on me with Clovis MacDonald. Oh, by the way, Clovis says that you kidnapped her boyfriend and her cousin. Anyway, the second complaint is that you were asking around Herford's gym about Terry Tyler. He was found murdered in an abandoned house yesterday morning."

"I was lookin'," I said. "I admit that. But I didn't find'im. What else?" I found myself sitting on the chair across from Lewis.

"Captain Styles of the Beverly Hills police tells me that he's investigating a murder and that you are hiding information pertinent to the solution of that crime."

It struck me that all black policemen who want to rise in the ranks have to learn how to speak like half-educated white men.

"What murder?"

"A man named Albert Cain."

"He was murdered?" I asked more to myself than to Lewis.

"Captain Styles said that the circumstances of his death were 'suspicious.' He thinks that you know about it."

"I never met the man. I sure in hell didn't know that he was killed. I heard that he died. His family hired me to find one of their old employees."

"Who is this employee?"

"Elizabeth Eady."

Lewis wrote down the name.

"What about Tyler?" Lewis asked.

"He was a bookie an' I wanted to lay down a bet. That's all."

"If that's true then why do we have a report that a man who fits your description and he were practicing fisticuffs out in front of Herford's gym two days ago?"

"That was nuthin', officer. Just horseplay. He's a boxer, he was just showin' me some moves."

"We're going to have to arrest you, Easy. And turn you over as the Beverly Hills Police Department has requested." Lewis didn't dislike me. He was a cop and I was a suspect, that was all. He wasn't going to beat me or humiliate me unless he had a good reason. He didn't mind that I was lying. Everybody lies when you drag them down to jail. He would have lied if they took him in.

"Arrest away, officer." My heart was beating so hard that I was sure Arno could hear it. "But you wrong on this one."

"Wrong how?"

"When Saul Lynx hired me—"

"Who?"

I told him about Lynx's early-morning visit.

"Anyway," I continued, "when he hired me I went up to talk to the family. I mean, I didn't know who they were, it's just that I heard about them, if you see what I mean."

Lewis didn't understand a word of what I said, but he was a patient man.

"When I left them this Styles guy took me down to jail. He didn't say a damn thing about Cain bein' murdered. Not a damn thing. And now, all of a sudden, he was murdered. Not even that; he *might* have been murdered. That ain't right."

The thing I liked the most about Lewis was that you could see when he was thinking. Something about Styles, or the way the complaints came in, bothered him. I could see it.

"You're not saying that you think that Styles has got something to do with all this."

"I don't know, man." I hunched my shoulders for him. "You got some desperate people here. I know that more'n twenty years ago when Styles was a sergeant he arrested Marlon Eady, that's Elizabeth Eady's half brother. Styles arrested him but then the arrest sheet never made it into the files."

That sat Lewis up straight. "Where'd you get this?"

"Askin' questions."

"And who should I ask about it, Ezekiel?"

"I don't know, brother. I don't know." I was coming dangerously close to giving Lewis a reason to want to hurt me but I wanted to keep quiet on what I'd had out of Hodge's file a little longer.

"If you want my help then you've got to help too," Lewis said. "You know nobody from here to City Hall wants to hear about a cop gone bad. They'd rather see you on a short leash, or in a pine box."

Lewis wasn't anything like Quinten Naylor. Naylor was idealistic, believing that law was a virtue and that the police were the tools of good. If a cop went bad, Quinten hated him. But Lewis knew that the law is just the other side of the coin from crime, that they're both the same and interchangeable. Criminals were just a bunch of thugs living off what honest people and rich people made. The cops were thugs too; paid by the owners of property to keep the other thugs down.

His threat was meant to save me from a wrong word that might end my life.

"I don't want no trouble with Styles." I rubbed my bruised chest while I spoke. "I talked to him once and that's enough, but I ain't goin' t'jail neither. Not for him."

I was on the edge of a shallow grave out past the county line. The darkness was at the corners of the room. All Lewis had to do was throw me in a cell and make a phone call; he'd never even have to think about me again.

"You know I don't want any trouble, Rawlins," he said. The light made his glasses into bright opaque planes. "A cop's name on a corruption charge hurts everybody. Nobody wants that."

"Let me go, man," I said as clearly as I could.

"What do I get out of that?"

"When you get in the bed in fifteen years after this, after you retire, you won't have my blood on your hands. That's what. You'll be able to sleep through the night."

"I sleep like a rock now."

"But everything gets soft. Everybody gets old," I said, and then, "I swear that I ain't done a thing wrong. Miss Eady is a black woman and there's a whole lotta people wanna see her. But I'm the only one don't want to hurt her. You let me walk now and I'll owe you one. You turn me in and Styles will kill me. Ain't no play to that brother—he will kill me."

"But what if I let you go and then, come morning, I find out you were in it? Yeah, you were in it but now nobody knows where you are. Styles tells my boss he warned me and those two nice white boys who took you in here say that they arrested you. Whose ass is in the sling then?"

Logic is the most frightening talent that a man has. A man with logic can see death coming where a fly only sees a shadow. I saw death in Lewis's reasoning.

"It's my ass, Mr. Lewis," I said. "I don't have a thing to do with these people. They asked me to look for a friend and I did. That's it." There was so much more that I wanted to say but there were no words.

"Where do you live, Rawlins?" Lewis asked.

I knew it was a test so I rattled off my real address.

Lewis regarded me for a moment or two and then nodded. He took a scrap of paper from the desk and pointed a floppy corner at me. "We got this about an hour ago. It's your address."

"So can I go?"

"Okay," he said. "For right now."

I was up and out of the door before another breath could pass.

There was a phone booth right there in the station but I went three blocks away to make my call out on the street.

"Raymond?" I asked when he answered the phone.

"Yeah? Easy?" He was still asleep. Most days Mouse slept until noon.

"Sit tight, man. I think I got a line on the one turned you in. It wasn't none'a them men in the bar."

"Who is it then?"

"I don't know yet. But just hold on, 'cause I think I know how to find him."

"How?"

"You got to trust me, Raymond."

There was a long silence on the line. The only sounds were our breath and the occasional car down Central.

"Don't you be fuckin' wit' me, Easy."

"I ain't fuckin', Ray."

" 'Cause you know I'ma kill me somebody. That is true."

"I'll talk to you tomorrow. I promise."

I took a bus back to John's.

Out the window I watched Central Avenue pass by. There weren't many people out in the street. In the early sixties nearly everybody was working. On the bus there were mainly old people and young mothers and teenagers coming in late to school.

Most of them were black people. Dark-skinned with generous features. Women with eyes so deep that most men can never know them. Women like Betty who'd lost too much to be silly or kind. And there were the children, like Spider and Terry T once were, with futures so bleak that it could make you cry just to hear them laugh. Because behind the music of their laughing you knew there was the rattle of chains. Chains we wore for no crime; chains we wore for so long that they melded with our bones. We all carry them but nobody can see it—not even most of us.

All the way home I thought about freedom coming for us at last. But what about all those centuries in chains? Where do they go when you get free?

CHAPTER 32

I picked up my car and drove over to Brenner's Lumberyard, where I bought a heavy spade. Then I drove back to Odell's. He was sitting in a straightback chair with his hands on his knees. I went downstairs and sledgehammered out a piece of the concrete floor in the basement.

That took the better part of three hours; the whole time Marlon winked at me from his icy bed.

The work took longer than it should have because I couldn't use my left arm at all. It took almost an hour to develop my one-handed sledgehammer swing, cracking again and again against the hard floor. It felt right. Ten blows and then a sliver of rock breaks out. Then a long crack to work at.

After three hours I had cleared away a piece of ground that was four feet by three. The clay soil was almost as hard as the concrete. The spade nor Odell's broad-tined pitchfork could dig into it.

Maudria borrowed three hoses from her neighbors. We screwed them together and snaked the thing down to the hole. I let water dribble into the soil and kept stabbing at it, one-handed, with the pitchfork. It was the best I'd felt in a long time. Hard work is good for a man. It's something he can do without thinking or worrying.

I got so tired that my fingers tingled. It was nine in the evening but I just kept jabbing at the earth. Finally the spade slid in.

By midnight the hole was four feet deep. Maudria had gone up to lie in her bed. Odell was sitting in the kitchen next to the basement door.

His hands were in his lap, palms up; his glass-bead eyes staring down into the tangle of fingers, trying to make sense out of a world that would never make sense.

Odell was a religious man. He went to church and prayed and rejoiced. Eternal life came to the man who took the heavy blows of the Lord. But those blows hurt more in the later rounds. Sometimes a man just wants to give in.

"It's dug," I told him. "In the morning I'll get the cement and quicklime."

I made it into the living room, which also had a dining table against the wall for special occasions. The sofa looked comfortable but I climbed under the table with a cushion for my head. I felt safe under there on the hard floor.

I woke to the smell of coffee. Maude was standing at the stove.

"Breakfast, honey?" she asked me.

While I was sitting at the kitchen table I began to think of a question.

"Where'd you think Betty'd go if she was still around down here?" I asked.

"I don't know, Easy," Maude said. But then, "Well, you know, Betty always went for the men. Men who liked her, men who loved her, that was always Betty's weak spot." Her tone of voice was the only evidence I ever had that Maude didn't approve of Odell's cousin.

"You know any'a her boyfriends?" I asked.

"Uh-uh. We ain't hardly even seen Betty in all the years she been up here. Maybe she give up on men."

"Then what about Felix Landry?"

"What about him?"

"You know him?"

"Yes I do," she said in a proper tone. "He's first deacon down at Christ Church on Normandie. We go down there every once in a while."

"Landry live over near Avalon?'

"No. He got a little house right behind Christ Church. But, you know, he might have another house, 'cause he works for the post office and buys up little houses here and there. That's why I know you're wrong if you think that he's with Betty."

"How's that?"

"Because Deacon Landry is not beguiled by the flesh," she announced proudly. "He don't take to women. And 'cause'a that he don't waste his money. He buy houses and rent them to elderly churchwomen. And you know you can always tell one'a his houses because they all painted turquoise with a short white fence out front."

"All his houses rented out to ladies from the church?"

"I think so. I never heard'a no house near Avalon, though. That must be a new one."

"I'll go get what we need for the burial," I said. "Tell Odell that I need to take a drive with him when I get back."

When I got back to Odell's house he was dressed in country jeans and a blouselike green Hawaiian shirt. He was standing at the gate, tall and grim, with his key chain in his hand.

"Where we goin', Easy?"

"Take me to Felix Landry's house."

Odell took a half step backwards. His left eye squinted nearly closed and I was glad that he was nowhere near that shotgun.

"I think he knows where Betty is, Odell. I think she's stayin' in one'a his houses."

"This ain't no play game, Ezekiel."

"I ain't playin', Odell."

Odell drove a 1936 DeSoto. He'd bought it new, for cash, and had kept it in perfect condition. The plush leather front seat was like a sofa. I settled in remembering the first time I'd ridden in Odell's car; I was sixteen years old and so proud to be seen in that chrome-and-jet automobile. Even grown men looked at me with envy down the wide lanes of Houston's Fifth Ward.

People were looking at us that day too. They were pointing and smiling but that was because there weren't too many cars from 1936 out on the roads anymore.

We went down toward Manchester and then up Normandie. We finally turned down a little street called Carpenter and pulled to a stop before a tiny block house that was surrounded by a white picket fence and painted turquoise.

There I was again standing at some door I'd never been to before, a pistol in my pocket and a pain with every breath. It struck me at that moment that I was searching for death. Why else would I have been there?

But all those thoughts disappeared when she answered the door. Older now and a little heavier—she was still a beauty. Her left eye was bloodshot and swollen from my backhanded blow but that didn't take a thing away from her.

There was hate in her face for me.

"What you want here?" she asked in cast-iron words.

"Betty?" Odell said.

"It wasn't me," I said. "I was lookin' for Terry and I found him like you did. But I didn't do that to him."

"Betty? You okay, honey?" Odell asked.

The question broke her. She seemed to fall in on herself, backing up and bowing to the pressure of her grief.

I recognized the decor of the house. It was as if Felix were trying to re-create the same house all over again—inside and out. The couches weren't the same style but they were upholstered like the ones near Avalon. He had the same curtains and similar Mexican blankets on the floor. The walls even had the same kind of rough paintings on them.

"How'd you find me, Odell?"

"Easy figured it out. But we thought Felix might be here."

"Easy?" Betty looked at me again.

"Yes, ma'am."

"You that little boy used to follow me around?" There was almost a smile on her battered face. And then there it was, that look of appreciation that Betty had for the male sex. A look that was at once hungry and satisfied. Men communicated to Betty with their bodies and sex. She didn't care about our words or our hearts.

Here it was nearly thirty years later and I was almost in her thrall again.

Almost.

"Marlon's dead in Odell's basement," I said, and the spell she weaved out of instinct was shattered.

"What? Marlon?"

"I couldn't tell you on the phone like that, Betty," Odell said. "You just told me about Terry . . ."

"It's true?"

"We're gonna bury him," I said. "But I don't think he'd like to go without you there to tell him 'bye."

It was hard news. It would have put most people on their backs. But not Betty. She leaned against the wall for a few minutes while Odell and I stood there, half in the house. Then she went to the bathroom on the other side of the room. We watched her through the open door splashing water on her face. It might have been cold water because she called out loudly when it hit her face and chest. After that she leaned on the sink with both hands and sobbed.

When she came out again she asked, "How?"

"Cops," I said. "They beat him . . ." I was going to say, "... to find out where you was," but decided that I had brought her enough pain.

"I know it's hard, honey," Odell said. "But Marlon said that it was the cops who did it. We didn't know what to do, so he's down in our bomb shelter. We got to do somethin'."

Long minutes went by where we were silent. Betty sat down hard on a chair and just stared down around her ankles. There was a crow cawing outside. I wondered if he'd followed me all the way from Riverside to get a good laugh.

After a long time Betty held out her hand. I let Odell help her up and out to the car. I sat in the backseat. It was easy to sit back there feeling nothing, with my mind blank.

Odell and Maude had gotten the first four hundred pounds of ice delivered. After that Odell went out by car and got the bags, which he drove straight into the garage.

When Betty saw his cold corpse she cried, "Mary! Oh, baby!" She was the only one that Marlon took that nickname, Mary, from.

She went to him on her knees and took his half-stiff body into her arms.

We stood around her, sad but satisfied that Marlon's death wasn't anonymous. He had his sister with him. He was going out under the shelter of family love.

More than half an hour went by with our vigil. Finally Maude took Betty by the shoulders and drew her away.

I made a thick paste out of the lime with water and rubbed Marlon's body with it. When I was a boy on the farm down south we took care of our own burials as often as not. I'd learned young how to handle the dead.

The corpse wasn't fully stiff, and with work Odell and I managed to wrap him in a sheet and then fold him into the small grave. I covered the shroud with more lime and put what dirt back would fit.

Then I piled the powdered cement into a hill and gouged a volcano crater in its peak. I used the hose to fill this crater with water.

While I mixed the quick-drying cement Odell took a stance at the head of the grave.

"Lord," he called, hands clasped tightly before him. "We submit to your wisdom. After all we're only men, and women, tryin' to find our way in the darkness. We heed your words and follow them blindly because there is no right but your right and there is no law but you."

If we were in a church someone would have intoned, "Amen."

"Marlon Eady comes to you now, Lord. He sinned and he is saved. I believe that because you have said it. He came to me all bloody and broken and he called out to you, Jesus. He begged you and he died. We all die in your name and in your shadow praying for your light."

Betty and Maude were both crying. I looked down and stirred my cement.

"I ask you," Odell said as if he were talking to some celestial peer. "Let Marlon's load be lightened in your name. He will add to your immensity and celebrate your love."

Using my bad arm for a prop I shoveled the first heavy load of cement on the grave. I dug, swiveled, and dropped eighteen times and then I got down on my knees with a block of wood to smooth out the floor. It wasn't perfect but no one would notice unless they were to suspect. There'd be an odor for a while but the lime would eat through the flesh soon.

Odell, Maude, and Betty watched me work.

When it was over the rest of us left Betty downstairs to say goodbye alone. Maude started making lemonade in the kitchen. Odell sat on the sofa in the next room.

I went out on the porch feeling so tired that I was afraid to close my eyes. There was so much left for the living to take care of.

CHAPTER 33

I was on my fourth cigarette when the screen door opened. I expected Maude with her pitcher of lemonade. But it was Betty. Her eyes were bloodshot things not even able to be sad.

"Is it really you, Easy?" she asked almost as if she were afraid to believe it.

"Yes, ma'am."

She hiccoughed and then cried a moment, making a sound like a panting dog. For an instant her face had a thousand lines in it and then she was fine again—except for her eyes.

"I'm sorry for hittin' you and stabbin' you," she croaked. "I was just so mad . . . and when I seen you I just thought . . ."

I reached for my sore arm. "It's done."

Betty sat down on the porch chair. I leaned against the railing and looked up at her.

"Was you that Ezekiel-man that Felix said come by?"

"Yes I was."

"What you got to do in all this, baby?"

"Miss Cain hired me."

I expected that to scare Betty, or at least get her to talk. All she did was to shake her head sadly. She didn't even ask why.

"They want you to come back up to work for them."

"That job is done."

"What's this all about, Betty?"

She splayed a hand out over her breast. It was her touching the heart. The tears for Odell's sermon burned behind my eyes.

"He had TB," she whispered. "Doctors said he'd'a died, so we come up here. An' I had to work. I had to."

Two lime-green hummingbirds darted into the bougainvillea that blossomed at the edge of Odell's porch. They stopped sucking sap for a moment and cocked their little heads toward Betty.

"You went to work for Albert Cain?"

"After a while I did. I worked by the day for the first year but then I come to work for Mrs. Cain and she liked me."

Betty cried for a moment again. "I had a whole house out in the back and when Marlon was really sick I took him in. There ain't nuthin' wrong with that, now is there?

"Mr. Cain was an im-portant man," she continued. "What he said went with most people. And so when I was first there he come in one day an' says that he want me t'shine his shoes. An' I tells him that I was busy right then an' went on back to my work. I could see it that he admired me. People didn't say no to Mr. Cain, 'cause he had a mean streak—but I didn't care." Betty sat straight up in her chair and scowled. "And then one day he come up behind me while I'm makin' the bed. Now you know that ain't no kinda way t'be askin' me somethin'." Betty looked at me with the arrogance of a young woman.

I laughed.

"Anyway I liked his wife so I pushed him down on the floor and walked out. I went back to the house they gave me an' was puttin' my clothes in the suitcase, 'cause you know ain't nobody gonna disrespect me. But he come runnin' down an' apologizin' an' sayin' he was playin' when I knew he wasn't. He begged me to stay on an' I finally said that I would—at least until Mrs. Cain found somebody else. But then, for a while after that, he was okay. Maybe a little too nice or polite or somethin' but I thought he was just tryin' t'say that he was sorry."

"So what happened then?"

"By that time Marlon was better and had a 'partment down around San Diego. He had a job in the navy yards an' he was fine. Fine. He come up an' stay wit' me on his time off. But then one day he comes runnin' to me all scared. He wanted me to hide him. But where could I hide a man?

"Then the po-lice come. He come right up to my place wit' Mrs. Cain behind'im. He come bustin' in here an' th'ows me down and hits Marlon all in the face. . . . He cracked a bone in Marlon's neck."

"Who was the cop?" I asked.

"I don't know his name, Easy. Just a big ole redheaded white boy who smiled like he liked you and then he hit you in the head."

"So what happened then?"

"The cop took Marlon off in his police car. Then Mr. Cain come runnin' and he seen what was happenin'. He told me not to worry an' tore out in his car. In about a hour he come on back wit' Marlon."

"What was the cop after Marlon for?" I asked.

"They said that he broke into the house next door and took some goldware. The cop figured he come from here. I fount out later that the gardener put Marlon up to it. Told him he knew how he couldn't get caught."

"And that's it?" I asked. "They just let Marlon go?"

Betty noticed the hummingbirds. That shadow of a smile went past her mouth.

"Mr. Cain come up into my room the next night all drunk an' wavin' a piece'a paper around that he took from the police. He said that that paper costed him three thousand dollars. He was a li'l man wit' arms and legs that was too short for his body. They say that li'l mens yo' meanest kind 'cause they always think people be laughin' at 'em.

"He was wearin' a Chinee robe that was open up an' he didn't have nuttin' on under it." Betty's voice came out flat, with no real feeling at all. "He told me that I better make him happy or he was gonna send Marlon down under the jailhouse. He fucked me three times and then he went away. And then he come back a little later an' fucked me again."

"You didn't fight it?"

The look in Betty's eye was enough to silence my question but she answered anyway. "Fight him how? Hit him and then see Marlon put in jail? Kill him an' go to jail my own self?"

A huge potato beetle hoisted himself up on the porch. His bloated amber-colored and tiger-striped body was heavy enough to make a dragging sound on the roughened paint. His dwarf wings buzzed now and then—just a memory of flight.

"Next day he come up with diamond earrings and says how sorry he is. I took 'em 'cause I was scared that he'd'a hit me if I turnt him down. That's how he was." She looked down at me. "He said nice things and then if you didn't answer right he'd get mad. He used to slap me when he'd be fuckin' if I missed just the littlest word.

"But I took his presents and Felix and me bought five houses wit' what we could get for'em." The spite in Betty's voice was a bittersweet revenge. "I was savin' up for Marlon. He couldn't hold on to money a'cause'a them damn horses."

"Did you meet Felix through Odell?"

"Naw. Felix was the one drove me an' Marlon up here from Texas. I known him since then."

"Did you tell Felix about Cain?"

"No. I didn't want him to hear it. But he knew. He knew because he could see it in me. You know it was all the time, baby." Betty rocked a little. The motion of her body brought to mind the rhythm of unwanted sex. "Cassandra, that was his wife, hated me now. But she didn't say nuthin' 'cause he'd'a beat her up and down the stairs if she did. One time he knocked out one'a her front teeth an' wouldn't pay for the dentist. He said she was ugly inside and she should be like that on the outside too.

"He'd even beat young Sarah if she said somethin'. It was terrible for a long time. He roamed around the house half naked mosta the time. He always told everybody that I was the one he loved. That I had been drivin' him crazy the whole time I was there. And it was because'a me that he did what he did.

"I had twins by him. They call 'em fraternal a'cause they don't look alike. He took me down to Mexico City so I could give birth an' nobody would ask no questions. They let Gwendolyn stay up at the house." Betty's words slowed with sudden guilt. "They told her that her momma died and that they was keepin' her in her momma's memory. They sent Terry away a'cause he didn't want no men in the house. Not even a little boy. He made Sarah send Arthur to boarding school when she came back."

"How come you couldn't say that Gwen was yours?"

"He was afraid that it would get out about him havin' a colored child livin' right there in his house. An' anyway, that's just the way he was. He didn't want nobody to have nuthin'. But he knew that he couldn't take her away so I never see her. So he let us . . . let us . . . be friends." Betty shook her head. "She was always askin' if I knew her mother. And I'd tell her stories." That was too much for her and we had to be quiet for a while.

"What about Terry? Did he know about you?"

"Yeah, he did. Marlon told'im. He put Terry wit' the Tylers and I sent them what I could. I even went to see'im sometimes when Felix was at work an' I was visitin'. But I never told'im that Gwen was his sister. I tried t'get them to be friends but they was too different. Gwen was gentle and like to play like she was havin' tea with the queen and Terry wanted to rassle."

I was surprised and I wasn't. I had had it all worked out in my mind that Sarah was Gwen's mother. I thought that she had gone off with some black man to spite her husband and her father. And Terry, well, Terry didn't seem to matter much now that he was dead. It was hard enough keeping up with the living.

After a while I asked, "You said that Sarah came back from someplace. Back from where?"

"She run off with a man right when I was pregnant. Ron Hawkes. He was the gardener and she was the fool."

"She married him?"

"I cain't blame her, Easy. That was before Mr. Cain took sick. He'd hit that girl, do all kindsa mean things to her. It was really more what he said than what he did." Betty cast her eyes down toward the gross beetle.

"That's Arthur's father?"

She nodded. "That's why he so mixed up."

"Mixed up how?" My question must have carried more weight than I intended. Betty's bloodshot eyes became red slits.

"Nuthin' bad. Not that. He just empty like. Empty. Nobody really cared about Arthur around the house. His momma was always sick and kinda weak. She didn't really know how to take care of children, and so I mostly raised him an' Gwen. I used to let him run around behind me when I'd be cleanin' or whatever."

"Where's his father?"

"I don't know. He got inta some kinda trouble and had to go away. And Mr. Cain hated him ever since the first time he found him with Sarah."

"He didn't like that, huh?" I imagined some big rich man finding his millionaire daughter grinding down in the tool-shed with some trash.

I had been a gardener myself.

"Kicked her out. I tried to stop him but he wouldn't listen." Betty rubbed the back of her hand against her nose. "It killed Cassandra. . . ."

Betty started crying in a way that made her whole body vibrate. I waited for her to stop but she didn't, so I got up and hugged her. Her powerful arms went around my neck and she cried, "Oh, baby! Baby!" shamelessly and loud.

Maude came to the door, still sensitive to the attention

that noise might bring, but when she saw Betty in my arms she withdrew.

Betty in my arms.

For years after her kiss I dreamed of it, yearned for it. And there she was, filled with passion and calling out for love. But not my love. Not me.

I held her and ran my flat palms over her back and head. We slid down to the porch and she tucked up her legs so I could run my hands from her head to her feet; not a lover's stroke but a mother's. A mother whose child has come awake from a terrible nightmare.

After a long time she quieted down. Her head was against my shoulder and she even fell asleep. Her face became younger in sleep and the same brash girl who kissed me for a lark on the muddy streets of Fifth Ward came out. My body was aroused but my mind was in the ascendant. I thought right then that maybe Odell was right; maybe we did live forever in grace.

I decided to have a cigarette for that deep thought. When I struck the match Betty woke up.

"Oh!" She pushed away from me, hurting my bruised chest. She got to her feet, her fists loosely balled at her side.

I'd come from the same time and place. A place where if you showed a vulnerable belly you were bound to get punched.

So I didn't say anything for a while, just puffed on my cigarette and watched the air on Denker shimmer in the afternoon heat.

After three Luckies she started talking again. "He sent Gwen away to school in Europe and when she was here she played the maid.

"But I wouldn't let him touch her. I told him that I'd kill him if he ever touched my girl." There was passion in her threat. Even in her weakened state she wouldn't take everything. She wouldn't abandon her child.

"Why did you stay so long, Betty?" I asked. "He couldn't do anything to Marlon after this long."

"I couldn't leave after Cassie died. There was Sarah and her baby. Gwen wouldn'ta understood if I took her. He didn't want sex no more after Cassie passed, and I owed that woman somethin'."

"So you killed him?" It was the only question I really had.

"I ain't killed nobody."

"That policeman who caught Marlon, he says that Albert Cain was murdered."

"I don't know nuthin' 'bout that. In his older years Albert got feeble. I used to have to take him to the bathroom and feed him strained peas with a spoon. When Cassandra died, Sarah came back and started to blame Albert for everything. I kept her from hurtin' him. I didn't wanna see her mess up her life 'cause of him and his evil."

"Did Sarah kill him?"

"I don't know nuthin' 'bout no killin's. I didn't do nuthin' neither."

"Then why'd you run, Betty? Why are they after you?"

She didn't have any more to say. She took one step down the stair and stepped on the big beetle. He broke open, making the sound of a large nut being cracked.

"Why'd they kill Marlon, Betty?" I asked, but all she did was turn her back on me and walk into the house.

CHAPTER 34

Betty didn't want my help. She didn't want something simple like the truth or revenge.

What could I do anyway? If the cops had killed Marlon there was no court that would hear his complaint. The only revenge we could get would be personal—a showdown. But I wasn't willing to kill a cop.

I couldn't help Betty, so I traded one impossible task for another.

There was a little cat tail of a street off of Crenshaw named Ozme Lane. It was a cul-de-sac of cluttered matchbook houses that would have been impressive if they grew to five times their present size.

The mailbox in front of the puce ranch house with the fairy-tale castle facade read "Mr. and Mrs. Theodore Mix and Son," in black block letters. I knocked on the pink door, and soon after a bronze slat that was situated at about the height of my gullet swung inward. It presented me with a lovely almond-shaped eye.

"Who is it?" the eye asked, none too friendly.

"Mr. Hall," I replied.

"What you want?"

It was her. That voice was burned into my brain just as clearly as Bruno's last stand.

"Ted Mix live here?"

"Ain't that what it says?"

"I need to talk to him." Actually I had hoped that Ted would be out. It was Sooky that I wanted to talk to.

"Well he ain't here."

"Then maybe you can help me. You Sooky Freeman?"

"I'm Mrs. Mix, but I ain't got no time to listen to no pitch. The kids comin' home soon," she said. And then as an afterthought, "With their daddy."

"I ain't sellin' nuthin', ma'am. It's just that I got a letter from a friend'a mine, a fellah that we call Two-toes because of a birth defect he suffered. This friend, he's in prison, but he's comin' out soon and he told me to tell your husband that he wanted to talk to him about a friend that they had in common."

"What friend?" Sooky didn't know that Theodore consorted with criminals.

"A man that he called . . ." I snapped my fingers twice to show that I could hardly remember. "Called Raymond." I watched that eye double in size. "Raymond Alexander."

"What you want here, mistah?"

"Nuthin', ma'am. It's just that Two-toes didn't have Ted's address and he couldn't find a phone book up in jail. So he asked me to come on by to find out if Ted wanted to talk." I smiled as pleasantly as I could.

Sooky was shaking on the other side of the door.

"Ted don't know that man," she said.

"What man?"

"The one you said!" she shouted.

"Which one?"

"None of 'em. You go and tell that man that ain't nobody here name of Ted Mix."

"Why should I do that if Ted don't know my friend?"

The door came open. Sooky Freeman was a sight to behold. She was that sloppy kind of beautiful. Full brown skin with the sort of wide ample lips that could wrap themselves into a kiss. She had on a ratty housecoat and floppy slippers. She knew she was beautiful; so beautiful that here it was two in the afternoon and she still wasn't dressed or made up.

"Come on in here," she said.

I went through the entrance hall, which was about the size of a broom closet, into the living room—a closet with windows. When I sat down I had the feeling that I'd followed some little girl into her dollhouse for tea.

"What do you want?" she asked.

The fabric of her housecoat was worn and soft. Her figure stood out from under it almost as if she were naked. I thought for a second that I could take everything in that room. I could get Ted's wife and his house for just a promise. A promise tangled up in those lips.

But I didn't want any of it.

"Toes said something about a man named Alfred too. You know where he live?"

Sooky folded her arms underneath her breasts and then, when she saw how I admired the framing, she brought her arms higher to be more modest.

"It was Alfred," she told me.

"What you talkin' 'bout, girl?" I didn't enjoy what I was doing. I didn't enjoy it but it was easier than interring a murdered man or facing Commander Styles; it was easier than letting Mouse kill me for keeping him from killing three innocent men.

"It don't matter if you understand me. You just tell your friend that it was Alfred who did what he thinks I did. Tell'im that it was Alfred Broadhawk told."

"Told what?"

"That ain't none'a your business, mistah. You just tell yo' friend—"

"Hold up on that, honey. I'm right here." I pointed at my foot, which I then crossed over my left knee. "You got to deal with me. If you want me to be your delivery boy then you got to pay my fee."

"Pay you?"

I nodded.

"How much you want?"

"First you got to tell me what I'm gettin' into, then I'll give you the price tag."

"You don't know nuthin'?"

"I know the names and I know it's somethin' serious."

Sooky licked her lips and glanced over at the door. "Ted gonna be home soon, Mr. Hall. Why'ont you meet me tomorrow . . . someplace else."

" 'Cause by tomorrah you have a lie all sewed up. 'Cause by tomorrah you could have three brothers come knockin' on my head. I'll deal with Theodore if he comes."

Sooky looked at the door one more time before she started to talk. "Me'n Alfred used to go together—kinda. He was in my uncle's church. He never even really liked me but I was a minister's niece and he wanted to be part'a that. He wanted to be a minister himself. And so he went out wit' me."

"So? That ain't nuthin'," I said.

"Yeah, but we was always fightin'. He didn't wanna do nuthin'. A kiss was a big thing for him."

I shook my head, thinking, poor fool. Sooky couldn't help but smile a little at the compliment.

"So it took me a whole week to get him to take me to hear T-Bone Walker over at the Ace Club. He didn't wanna be where there was drinkin' an' loose women. He was afraid of it.

"So he didn't wanna take me an' then he wanted to leave after just the first set. It was hardly even eleven but he start yammerin' 'bout Sunday school and how he couldn't even look them kids in the face if he didn't leave."

"Go on," I prompted. I stifled a yawn too. I really was tired. Tired down into my bones.

"Then he wanted to go through this alley and I didn't want to. And then we heard shots." Tears started from her eyes. "And Alfred run to see even though I tried to stop him.

He came back and said that he saw Mr. Alexander with his gun standing over Bruno Ingram."

Sooky was crying. I understood. All she wanted was a good time, a good life, but the world wouldn't leave her alone.

"I told him to fo'get it," she said. "I told him that it was the Lord's worry, not his. But he didn't listen. He didn't listen. He drug me off to a phone booth and stoled the dime right outta my purse."

"What'd he say?" I asked. "What did Alfred say to the cops?"

"He told about Mr. Alexander and Bruno Ingram."

"But what were the words he said? What did he say exactly?"

"I don't know. Somethin' about the Lord wouldn't let him be quiet or somethin' like that."

That was all I needed. I didn't feel good about it. Sooky had told me what my friend needed to know. She'd put her mark on Alfred's grave.

"Fifty dollars," I said.

"What?"

"Fifty dollars to deliver the message and to leave out your name."

She went through every drawer and pocket in the house. Then she took out the change jar. She came up with thirty-four dollars and twenty-seven cents. I took it. I told her that I'd be back for the balance but I never went. I took her money because that cost would give her the hope that maybe I'd be an honest crook and do what I promised.

Who knows? Maybe I would.

She even gave me Broadhawk's address. He was living in a little shack of a house on Ninety-sixth Place. Using beach stones, dry grasses, and three made-up dolls he'd created a Nativity scene on the left side of his weedy brown front lawn. On the right side he'd constructed a ten-foot cross from weathered fence boards. The cross lay on its side leaning against the front of the house.

When I walked up near the reclining crucifix I noted that there was red paint splattered where the hands, head, and feet of Christ were supposed to be.

Plastered all over the front door were poor-quality color prints clipped from a cheap illustrated Bible. Calvary and its victims, Mary by the Cross, John the Baptist plying his trade, Jonah kneeling by the sea.

A nearly toothless old woman answered the front door. "Yes?"

"Mrs. Broadhawk?"

"Elma Jackson, mister." She smiled. "But Alfred Broadhawk do live here. He's my nephew. He live wit' us."

"Is Alfred home?"

"No, sir. Alfred out at church. He goes out every afternoon to help the Lord." The old woman pointed out at the yard. "Alfred made all'a that out there. He wants the Lord to be in every minute of everybody's day. Bobo don't like it too much. He says that the manger is for Christmas and that the Cross is for Easter and that in the middle Alfred should take that stuff down. But Alfred says that we got to remember the joy and the sorrow every day."

"Bobo's Alfred's uncle?"

"Not by blood," she said. "I'm Alfred's only blood in this world. Bobo's my common-law hus'bun. He work at the junkyard down on Redondo. Bobo could take anything you got apart and then put it back together better'n it was in the first place. He's kinda like a genius about machines I guess.

"You want me to tell Alfred somethin', mister?"

"No, honey. No. Just say that Mr. Hall was here. I heard about his Christian art and just wanted to take a look. You tell him that it's beautiful."

Elma's grateful smile shamed me. She took my hand and actually kissed it.

Maybe they would put a little statue of Judas out there to commemorate my visit.

CHAPTER 35

I was a free man, more or less. I had done my errand. I'd found Betty and told her what they wanted. If she ever called them I'd ask for my money. If not, well, that part of my life, life in the street, was over. Betty was with her friend. Odell and Maudria were as good as they could be, considering.

I was going to lay low while the cops sorted out the murders.

Marlon was in the ground.

And Mouse . . . well, I didn't know about Mouse. But at least I knew the answer to the question. I knew that the men he suspected were innocent. The truth has to mean something.

Truth and Freedom; two great things for a poor man, a son of slaves and ex-slaves.

My arm ached. I could feel the deep reach of infection in my veins. One thing was certain—there was no escaping Fate. Fate hauls back and laughs his ass off at Truth and Freedom. Those are minor deities compared to Fate and Death.

But I wasn't dead yet. Marlon was dead. I didn't know why but I was sure that it had something to do with Albert Cain and his demise. Everything about Cain stunk. He was a foul man and surrounded himself with his own stench. But that wasn't my business.

Saul Lynx was standing out on the curb in front of my house. He was leaning against the thirty-foot carob tree that had grown there, staring at the ground with his big nose hanging down. When I parked he looked up at me and smiled. It was a real smile this time.

"What the fuck you doin' here, man?"

"Turnabout is fair play, Mr. Rawlins. At least you didn't find me inside your house." His breath was fragrant with gin.

"We done already turned this around once, man. Now I'ma walk on in my house and you gonna climb into that brown piece'a shit you drivin' and that's gonna be it."

"You got my pistol?" he asked.

"You want it?" I threatened.

"They're ready to kill your girl, Mr. Rawlins."

I didn't want to hear it. I turned away from him and went toward my house. But he was right there behind me.

"It's the will," he said in a whisper.

I spun around quickly, making him slip in the grass.

"Don't you be fuckin' wit' me, man."

Mr. Lynx was a master of mildness. He hoisted his pathetic nose up at me, his eyes glistening like two cicadas. "Five minutes," he said, pointing at my front door.

"Come on then. Let's make it quick."

It gave me a thrill to pour the little detective a juice glass full of whiskey.

"Aren't you going to join me?" he asked.

"Not right yet. What you got to say?"

He leaned forward on the kitchen chair, massaging his knee with a cupped palm. "The cops dropped by a couple of days after you did. They wanted to know about Hodge and some guy called Terry Tyler, a boxer they said. They mentioned Elizabeth Eady, so I knew that it had something to do with you."

"You knew that when they said about Hodge," I said.

"No. I've done a lot of work for Mr. Hodge. It could have been anything."

"Uh-huh. So? What about the will?"

Lynx slugged back the whole shot. I was there, ready with number two. He ran his hands over his eyes and then gripped the glass hard enough that I thought it might break. "I'm four hundred dollars in the hole over this one, Mr. Rawlins."

That would have been a lot of money to Lynx. He wasn't the kind of man to have property or money in the bank. Saul Lynx was one of those men who always drive their car a hair above empty and two quarts low.

"I know a woman who works in records down in San Diego," he told me. "And she's got a friend who does the same thing in Beverly Hills."

I watched the whiskey slip down between his thin pink lips, imagining the burn in his throat.

He looked to the side as if to make sure that nobody had sneaked into the house and then said, "Mrs. Hawkes filed an injunction against the will through Hodge. The lawyer representing the will is a guy named Fresco. He's an old-time friend of Cain. Cain left all his money to Elizabeth Eady. Everything. House, suits of armor from the sixteenth century, everything. Seems like Cain started feeling guilty toward the end of his life. He'd done some pretty bad things to Miss Eady and he wanted to make amends."

"And so they wanna kill her." It wasn't a question.

"Not only her. I found out that this man, this Terry Tyler, is really Eady's son, and there's a brother out in the desert somewhere. For Christ's sake, the maid is Eady's daughter. If Elizabeth dies they're next in line."

"Nobody's gonna do all that . . ." I started to say "just for money," but I knew that was wrong.

"Terry Tyler's already dead." Lynx held out his glass for another drink.

I didn't say anything about Marlon.

"So you figure Hodge knew about the will and he's workin' for the family?" I asked, gazing at the dregs in the bottom of his glass.

"Hodge isn't the estate lawyer. The lawyer is an old business partner of Cain's. Like I said, a man named Fresco." The little man blinked and shook his head, the first sign of inebriation. "But we're talkin' fifty million here, at least. The money Hodge could get from that fortune would set him up for life. That's why he had me looking for the girl."

"Woman," I said.

"What?"

"She's almost fifty years old, man. She's a woman."

Lynx stared at me. He couldn't quite figure out what I meant. When he gave up he reached for the bottle.

But I took it away.

"We gonna do somethin'?" I asked him.

"What do you mean?"

"I mean that you didn't come here just to tell me some stories. You must got some reason other than gettin' pie-eyed for bein' here."

Lynx sat back in the kitchen chair. The way he looked around the room said that he was just realizing that he'd drunk too much. He brought his hands to his face and squinted.

"I want," he said slowly, "you to back me up on this."

"On what?"

He blinked again and squinted. Like most drunks he thought that if he took longer to think he'd come up with the thoughts of a sober man.

"It's got to be the woman. Sarah Cain. She's the one

going to lose everything. And so she throws her big money around and people start dying."

"Why not her son? He seems to get along with Hodge just fine. It could be him."

"Yeah," he said. "Yeah. But it's got to be one or both of them. But all we got to do is go down there and face them. Try to figure out what's going on."

I was thinking about Marlon; about how he'd said that the cops had beaten him.

"Why not just go to the cops?" I asked.

"Do you know a cop you can trust?" he asked back. His brilliant eyes shone like some ignorant serpentine god's. "There's been two murders . . ."

"Two?"

"Albert Cain was killed too. The police made that plain. And now this Tyler-Eady boy. And when it comes to that much money, you and me are just a couple of grease spots. No. I want to know my P's from my Q's before I go to the police."

"Why should I care?" I said. "You the one came to me. All I got to do is to tell the cops that."

"How do you explain to the police that you were looking for Terry Tyler and then fighting with him just before he was found dead? Yeah. The cops told me about that."

Saul wasn't smiling. He wasn't trying to rub my nose in it. And I appreciated that, even though I didn't take the threat seriously. I didn't think that the cops could take me down for anything. I was worried about Betty, though. I didn't want to allow those rich white people to murder her.

"What you wanna do?" I asked Saul.

"Go up to the house. Talk to the lady. Then we'll see." Saul got to his feet as if that meant it was time to go.

But I held up my hand and said, "Hold on, man. I cain't drive up there."

"Why not?"

" 'Cause of a man called Styles."

"Commander Styles?"

"You know him?"

"He's done a lot of work for Hodge. One time when I got into a fix up in the Hills he helped me out. When we shook he grabbed me so hard that he broke one of the bones in my hand." Saul cradled his right hand. "What's Styles got to do with you?"

"Hodge put him on me."

"Oh." Saul felt his liquor then. Without me having to argue he sat back in his chair.

"Coffee?"

"Yeah. Yeah."

I went to the four-burner stove and heated some water. When the water boiled I took out a bottle of instant powder and a spoon and put them in front of him with one of my coffee mugs.

"Milk and sugar?"

"Like a good woman," he answered.

"Say what?"

"Dark and sweet."

Saul downed four cups of the stuff, drinking it until he thought he should have been sober.

We decided that he would drive my car because there was more room in the back for my sore bones.

I took a cotton sheet from the hamper to use as a cover should Saul be pulled over for some innocent reason. I figured that if I lay down in the leg space covered with the sheet a sloppy cop might not notice.

"You been doin' this kinda work a long time?" I wanted to talk in the car. Anything not to think about what I was doing.

"Long enough," he answered. Then after a pause, "At

least I don't have to punch in and kiss butt. At least when I don't like how something smells I can take it out to the ash can."

"I didn't say nuthin'," I responded.

"No. But you can see I don't have much. But at least I got a little bit of pride. My family eats and the rent is paid. And if I decide that something is wrong I can do something about it. I don't belong to a paycheck."

"You married?"

"Yep. Met her down in Georgia when I was in the service. She worked in the PX."

I could hear his grin.

"You in the war?" I asked.

"Military police."

Sunlight moved to and fro across the backseat. It struck me that I'd never been in the backseat of the car. I had them vacuum it out at the car wash so I didn't even clean back there. Here was a part of my life and property and I'd never even looked at it.

"What about you?" Saul asked.

"What?"

"You married?"

"Used to be. I got a letter last year sayin' that the state of Mississippi granted my wife a divorce."

"Too bad."

"Maybe. Maybe not." I was thinking about Sooky, Betty, and Martin. Which one of them had the perfect kind of life that Saul Lynx bragged about?

After quite a while Saul said, "Here comes the gate."

I huddled down under my sheet and the car came to a stop.

"Private," a voice said. I couldn't tell if it was the man from the other day.

There was the rustling of papers then the voice said, "Security, huh?"

"Yeah," Saul answered. "Nasdorfs up on Fischer want something. Probably a burglar alarm for the kennel."

The men both laughed. Then there was silence for a minute.

"Hey, um," the guard said. "Any openings down at your company?"

"Always room for a good man. You got a card?"

"Uh, well, uh, no, not on me."

"Always have your card," Saul chided. "That way the boss man knows you got the goods. But that's okay this time. I'm not the boss. Write up your name, address, and position and I'll pick it up on the way back down."

"Hey, thanks."

"No problem."

When we'd driven far enough away I asked, "Why'd you go through the gate? We could have taken side streets in."

" 'Cause they got this unmarked car surveillance system up here. If they see a strange car they call it in to the gate. But now the gate knows we're here. So it's fine."

I was a fish out of his bowl.

CHAPTER 36

"Yes? Who is it?" Gwendolyn Eady said through the speaker in the gate.

"It's Easy, Gwen. Lemme in, willya?"

I sat up when we passed the gate, taking Saul's .38 from my pocket.

"Here you go, man," I said as I handed it over. There was a .32 in my other pocket. Small-sized death.

There was a fire-engine-red '57 Thunderbird parked in front of the house.

"Oh!" Gwen said when she found two men at the door.

"We need to talk, Gwen."

"Sarah's very tired, Mr. Rawlins. I don't think that it's a good time to bring in people that she doesn't know." She came out of the door to keep us from going in.

"This is important. It's got to do with Betty and you."

She didn't take my meaning. "Where's Betty?"

"She's fine." I was happy to see her relief. "Maude and Odell lookin' out for her. But Terry's gone."

Before that moment, Gwendolyn Eady was just a girl to me. But seeing the pain she felt for that wild boy, who she didn't even know to call her brother, made me have respect for her as a woman. I knew right then that I would come calling if I survived. Even before she nodded, holding back the grief, I imagined her and Feather riding a bicycle down that rocky dirt road near the sea.

She stepped aside and we came into the house.

Arthur and Sarah were standing in the entrance hall. They both had dark circles under their eyes.

"What is this?" Sarah Cain asked. "Where is Elizabeth?"

"Where she's safe from you," I said.

"What's that supposed to mean?"

"It means that we've come here to set things straight."

"What are you talking about?" Arthur wanted to know.

"He means," Saul piped in, "that we know everything that happened and that we're going to go to the cops with it. But first we wanted to give you a chance to explain yourselves."

"And who are you?" When Sarah's straw-colored eyes blinked at Saul they reminded me of frail butterflies in the rain.

"Saul Lynx, ma'am. I was employed by you, through

Calvin Hodge, until I realized that I was being used for murder."

Sarah reached behind to grab hold of Arthur's arm. Gwen drifted across the room toward them. They were the only family she knew, but she didn't know that they really were related. Sarah and Gwen were half sisters.

"Come into the sitting room," Sarah said.

We followed them down a long hall lined with suits of armor designed for tiny little men; even Saul towered over them. We reached a doorway that was flanked by two larger metal figures; maybe six feet each.

"What's this?" I asked. "Giants?"

"After the plague," Arthur said, distracted.

"How do ya mean?" I asked.

"The reason Europeans were so small back then was because of diet. They didn't get enough meat, protein. After the plague there were lots of cows but hardly any people. So people grew bigger and some of the biggest ones put on armor."

I didn't know if it was true, but it was a good story. I'd try it out on Jackson Blue if we both lived long enough.

"Come in, gentlemen." The sweep of Sarah's arm introduced us to a large room. The ceiling hovered twenty feet above. From it was a chandelier adorned with crystal balls big enough to see back to the beginning of time. The clear crystal was surrounded by red and blue teardrop glass. The floor was covered with an off-white and thick carpet. The walls were a marbled tan. It was a room that cost more than I was ever likely to make in a lifetime. There was a stand of fifteen-foot palm trees against the far wall. On wheels so that they could easily be taken outside for the sun.

The trees made the air fresh and friendly. But Mr. Lynx and I weren't after friendship.

We sat on a smoke-colored leather couch while the family

members spread themselves out on chairs sheathed in wolf pelts, heads and all, that sat here and there.

"So?" Sarah wondered out loud.

"We know why Terry Tyler was killed," I said.

"Who is Terry Tyler?" Sarah asked me.

"You know who he is," I answered back. I could see the truth slowly dawning.

"That boy who, who used to come play with Gwen?" Sarah was shaken.

"What has that got to do with us?" Arthur said.

"Arthur!" Arthur followed his mother's stare to Gwendolyn, who was biting at her lower lip.

"Sorry," the boy said. He got up and went over to her. He even put his arms around her.

"I'm sorry about the boy, but I really don't see how you can think that has anything to do with us." Sarah's eyes were strong again. They bored into me.

"But it's not only him," I said. "Marlon Eady had disappeared and Elizabeth is hiding in fear for her life."

At least I rubbed some of the arrogance off her face.

"And it's all because of your father's will." I was finished.

The silence was profound. Arthur released Gwen. Sarah sat perfectly still except for the tremor up the back of her neck—keeping time with her wild heart.

"It's true, Mrs. Hawkes," Saul Lynx said. "We have reason to believe that Elizabeth Eady and her immediate family are the heirs to your father's estate. Somebody killed your father and then they found out about the will. That's how we figure it."

"If . . ." She stammered a moment and then halted. "If . . . that's true, then you think it was me?"

"You killed Terry," I said, "her son, and now all that's left is her daughter . . ."

"No," Sarah said, holding her hand up to stop my words.

". . . Gwendolyn."

"What?" Gwen asked. She wasn't upset, just bemused.

"We haven't gone to the police, because there's no proof, and when there's no proof there's no case. But . . ." Saul was at a loss for words.

"But we know that you killed Terry and Marlon and that you plan to do in Gwen and Betty 'fore you through." I was mad enough to pull out my pistol, but I didn't. "But we're not gonna stand for that."

"My mother? Betty?" Gwen shook her head.

"Yeah." I stood up to meet her. "Here you are treatin' these white people like they loved you and when they just reapers cuttin' down your real people like dead grass!"

"Easy." Saul was by my side. "Calm down."

"This is ridiculous." Sarah Cain was up too. "Do you really believe that Arthur or I could go out killing people like that?"

"I believe that Commander Styles could do it. I believe that Calvin Hodge could do it."

"It's true? Oh my God!" Gwen put her hands to her face and backed away from everyone.

"No, honey," Sarah cried. But when she approached, Gwen fell down to the floor.

"Uh-huh! Now she see the light. Now she sees." I was ranting. Some deep hatred inside of me came out suddenly, evilly.

"No!" Sarah yelled. "It's not like that! We were only trying to help Betty."

"But it's true about the will, ain't it? It's true that Gwen is Betty's girl but you never let her know it." I wanted Gwen to know, to see the truth.

"We only wanted time to talk to Betty." Sarah was crying now too. "She ran away and my father was dead . . ."

"You thought that Miss Eady killed your father?" Saul asked.

"She, she ran. And then we found him dead." Sarah

turned to Gwen. "That's why Arthur called Styles. My father had had dealings with Commander Styles before, and, and we didn't want any trouble for Betty. We wanted everything quiet. It wasn't to hurt your mother, it was to keep her out of trouble. I had nothing to do with keeping secrets from you. That had to do with Betty and my father."

"Betty killed Cain?" The wind was out of my sail.

"Who's my father?" Gwen asked.

Nobody answered.

Right then a bell rang. It was the kind of buzzing bell that schools have to indicate the passing period between classes.

"I'll get it," Gwen said, comforting herself in the role of a maid. She pulled herself to her feet and staggered away toward the hall.

No one moved to stop her.

"So." Saul started thinking out loud. "You got Hodge and Styles in here to take care of anything, um, nasty. But then they find out that you're broke, that the murderer, if there was a murder, has inherited the money." He pushed out his lower lip and nodded, appreciating the complexity of the crimes. "If it was just her, if she was the only heir, then all they'd have to do would be to turn her in. But since it's her whole family the court might rule that they get the pie."

"No!" Sarah Cain was ready for another round. "No! That's not it! That's not what happened! I wouldn't hurt Betty. She's like my mother."

"But that could still make sense," Saul said. "Sure it could. Hodge and Styles want their piece, and the way they see it is that all Eadys have to go. They don't need you to tell them that."

"Calvin didn't come to me until after Father died," Sarah Cain said. "Somehow he'd found out about the will. Father had fired him and taken on a new lawyer, his old business partner Bertrand Fresco. Calvin said that we'd better find Betty and talk to her. That's all I wanted to do."

"Sure, sure you did. We believe you." Saul touched my arm to include me in his generosity. "But they knew that these people were going to lay claim to your fortune. They'd lose whatever you promised plus the blackmail they'd get later on—I mean if there was a murder and then a cover-up."

I had to admit that Lynx made sense. But there was something wrong, something I wasn't sure about.

"Did Betty kill your father?" I asked straight out.

"Yes."

"How?"

"He was suffocated. He was really suffering. Maybe she just wanted to help him."

The sorrow in her face forced a sudden truth in my heart. I came to a decision that I knew would follow me down into my grave.

The hurt must have shown in my face. Sarah mistook my deadly decision as having something to do with her. She said, "You see? You understand, Mr. Rawlins."

"I don't understand a damn thing. What I wanna know is what's goin' on. 'Cause if you so worried 'bout Betty and her family, then why didn't you tell Gwen about all this?" I looked around but Gwen hadn't returned yet.

"I was going to tell her. I was. It's just that it was such a shock. A terrible shock. You can understand that, can't you? He'd made sure that Gwen never found out about him."

"Why's that, Mrs. Hawkes?" Saul asked.

She looked at him as if he had just peed on the floor. "She's Negro. He couldn't let people know about that, not if she was still living in the house. That would be as if he recognized her."

"Bastard," Saul said through clenched teeth.

"And he had to keep her," I said. "Because Betty would have left if he tried to take her girl."

"Why didn't she just leave anyway?" Saul asked.

"We're a family here, sir," Sarah said. "She was afraid. Everybody in the house was afraid of him. He had an awful lot of power. Betty didn't want to leave Arthur and me alone. She took over for us after my mother died."

"Where's the girl?" Saul asked.

"She answered the gate. Maybe it was a delivery," Arthur said. I noticed that he'd turned a grim shade of green.

"Gwen!" Sarah shouted. She went to the door and yelled down the hall, "Gwen!"

"It's just a delivery, Mother," Arthur said. He was at a chrome-and-glass standing bar that came out from the wall, adding things to a tumbler of gin, or vodka.

"Let's go look," Saul said, and it struck me that this careful little man was like me, that he lived his life on hunches. Hunches are a desperate man's way to hope.

The front door was ajar and Gwen was nowhere in the house; at least she didn't answer our calls. She wasn't in the driveway or around the lawn.

"Let's break up," I said, taking Mr. Thirty-two from my pocket. Saul took out his piece too.

"What are the guns for?" Arthur asked. The most compelling argument that he was innocent.

"I don't know if you've been listenin', son," I told him. "But people want the dark side of your family dead."

Arthur went with Saul down around the Greek statues while Sarah and I went back down a lane of apple trees along the side of the house.

The lane opened up to a long tier of white marble stairs overlooking a dense green maze cut from a great stand of bushes. At the center of the maze was a large bronze statue in the likeness of a prancing bull. Beyond the maze was a white stone house with weeping willows on either side.

"That's Betty's house," Sarah said, so close to me that the whisper was like a lover's request.

"How do we get down there?"

"Through the maze. Father said that the maze was better than a lock because with that nobody could even find your house."

"Unless they just cut right on through." I was up on my mythology too.

"But those bushes are laced with barbed wire."

The maze was beautiful. Vines of delicate white flowers hung down, gently camouflaging the barbed wire. The path was paved with lava stones that had been cut into brick. At every turn there was a small metal statue of a realistic-looking insect. A termite, ant, or wasp—all about the size of a toy poodle.

When I saw the termite for the third time I knew we were lost.

"Don't you know your way through here?"

"I didn't usually go back here," Sarah said. "Father would go sometimes."

The thought of her father and Betty sent Sarah down the wrong road again and again. I made us turn left at the termite and then right at the copper-green preying mantis. He was leering at the spread-legged corpse of Gwendolyn Eady.

She was on her back. The skirt was all the way up to her waist. The bullet holes in her chest and over her right eye were small. A high-velocity .22 probably, the kind of weapon that a professional criminal would use; a professional crook—or a cop. Her hands were out to the side, fresh blood and skin under the fingernails. She'd fought hard with her attacker. Her shoes were badly scuffed and one was half off. Her dress was torn around the collar and sleeve.

I was down on my knees again, looking in the face of another dead innocent. Gwen's eyes were almost completely shut. She seemed to be just awaking from a nap. I put my face up next to her mouth to see if she was still breathing. I could get physically close but I couldn't get close to her in my mind, couldn't accept her any more now that she was dead.

A noise came out of my mouth, unbidden. A sob or moan. I remember it because I didn't have any feelings right then, it was only because of that sound that I knew my own sorrow.

Sarah had pressed back against the hedge. When I saw the shock in her face I went to her, putting my arms around her and pulling her head to my chest. Her forearms were bleeding from pressing against the wire. I remembered holding Gwen the same way.

It hasn't helped.

I led Sarah back to the house, saying stupid little things like "It's all right" and "It'll be okay." I put the grieving woman in a chair in the entrance hall of the house and went out to find Saul and Arthur.

When I noticed that the Thunderbird was gone I ran down the rich people's hill.

I found Saul crouched down in the front stair holding the back of his head.

"He sapped me," he said.

"The kid?"

Saul nodded. "I saw him drive away in the T-Bird. Then I passed out again."

Saul let his head hang loose.

"Gwendolyn's dead."

Saul let go of the pain and stood right up. "Where?"

"Out back. They got this kinda maze back there."

"You sure she's dead?"

I didn't answer and he didn't ask again.

Sarah was still sitting where I had left her.

"What can we do?" she asked when we got her into the front hallway again.

"You expecting anybody to come by?" That was Saul.

"No. On Thursdays and Fridays, Clementine comes in to help Elizabeth and, and . . . Gwen . . . We have to call the police."

"We can't," I said.

"Why not?"

Of course, if there's a violent murder right there in your house, you call the police. But not if you're the murderer. And if she hired the killer would she have had him come to her house?

"Do you know who did this?" I asked.

She shook her head. The hand she held up in front of her face was still bleeding from the barbed wire.

"You got somebody to take you in?" I asked.

"Up at the ranch."

"Could you drive yourself?"

"Gwen does the driving," she said hopefully as if maybe that simple declaration would bring the poor dead girl back to life.

"How about some friend? Somebody nearby?"

"There's Bert and Louise Fresco."

"That's your husband's lawyer, right? The new one he got after firing Hodge. They friends of yours?"

"They used to be."

"Used to be before he decided to do what's right and try an' give Betty what's hers—is that what you mean by used to be?"

She didn't answer. She just stood there shaking her head at us.

"Okay," I told the grieving woman. "We cain't leave you here. I don't think anybody wanna shoot you, but we can't be sure. So call them and we'll drop you off there. He can call the cops," I said, holding up a finger, "but you tell him about Styles. You tell him, okay?"

She nodded, a little.

She went to the phone and dialed Fresco, but no one answered.

"It's not good, Easy," Saul said. "We got to take her somewhere. It's not safe here."

"I guess we could take her to the police. Or call a cab to take her there. By that time we could be back in L.A. anyway." I was thinking about what Detective Lewis would say when he heard that I was at the scene of another murder.

"I can't go to the police," Sarah said.

"Why not?" I asked.

"I just can't go there."

"Where do you want to go?"

"I want Betty," she said, just like a young child who's tired and wants the person she loves the most in the world. I knew then that Sarah Cain didn't want to kill Betty.

"Okay, but I got one question to ask you before we go."

"What?" It was only a word but it told me that one more question, maybe even another breath, might destroy her.

"What's goin' on with your boy?"

"Why did he hit me?" Saul added. "Why'd he run?"

"I don't know," Sarah Cain said to the floor. "Maybe, maybe he was scared. Arthur's always been afraid of things. And you did have a gun."

"Saul," I said, prompting the little detective. It was the first time that I'd called him by his first name, and it struck me as odd. Somehow in that hard time we crossed over into being work friends. Dependent on each other, close.

"What about you and Ron Hawkes?" Saul asked.

"What does he have to do with it?" Sarah Cain might have been hurting but her hatred for her husband was healthy.

"Hodge told me that Miss Eady's brother was a pal of your husband. That they ran together. When he gave me the Joneses' name he also said that I should look for Hawkes."

"What do you know about that?" I asked the woman. "Arthur got all sick when I mentioned his father's name. He couldn't even talk."

"I haven't seen Ron Hawkes in over nine years," she said. "Arthur wants a father but he doesn't know what that man really is."

"What is he, ma'am?" Saul asked.

Instead of answering she looked down the long aisle of suits of armor.

"Where could Arthur have gone?" I asked.

"I don't know," Sarah Cain lied.

CHAPTER 37

Odell and Maudria weren't happy to see us, but what could they say? Betty wasn't there. Odell said that Felix had come and taken her home. Maude took one look at Sarah and took her into the bedroom to rest. She sat there at her side after that. I think that Maude needed to take care of that woman as much as Sarah needed to be taken care of.

I called Primo just to see how the kids were doing. Mofass was there and he wanted to crow but I wouldn't talk to him. I had too many things on my mind.

When I got off the phone Saul took me by the arm and brought me out on the porch.

"Leave me alone with Mrs. Hawkes for a while, Easy," he said.

"What for?"

"I think I know how to talk to the lady but I need to be alone with her."

"Okay," I said. "I got one more thing to do anyway."

"What's that?"

"Somethin' private."

Back inside the house I told Odell, "I think I'll take a spin over to Martin's house. Saul's okay. He wants to talk to the lady."

Odell smiled a sad smile. "Martin's hurtin', Easy. I can't hardly stand to see him in that kinda pain. All this other hurt I could see, but at least these people got some kinda chance. All Martin got is less every mornin'. He ask me every day to kill him. Just give him some poison don't hurt. He hurtin', Easy."

"There's a lotta that in this world, Odell. Lot of it."

"But a man like Martin is just too good to have to take it."

I could see the suffering down in Odell's heart.

It felt good to see my old friend's heart again.

Pea wasn't going to let me in but she relented when Martin struggled up out of his chair and came to the door. We both helped him out to the porch. He looked different, healthier in some way, but I couldn't tell why at first. Then I saw that it was his clothes; they fit him well around the neck and waist. The jeans were a little loose but other than that he looked fine.

"Little Willie's," he said when he saw me notice. "Pea's son with Willis. He's eleven years old an' his clothes was in the trunk and they fit me." Martin lifted up his arm and admired the checkered long sleeve of his flannel shirt.

"Where's Willis?" I asked. Pea had gone back in the house where she could sit in front of the fan.

"When Pea seen that we still hated each other but that I wasn't gonna die soon she made him go out and get a job."

"Doin' what?"

"He's a usher at the Baldwin Theater and a short-order cook at Silo's bar."

"Can I do anything for you, Martin? I mean, is there anything you need me to take care of?"

"I wanna die, Easy. I cain't take this."

"You hurt?"

He nodded. "But it ain't the pain. It's gray death."

"What's that?" I was a young boy again at the feet of a scientist and a craftsman.

"It's in my bones, Ezekiel. It's eatin' through me like a slow-worm. It's like gettin' et alive."

I took his hand and he was grateful but I knew he'd rather have me choke his bird neck.

We talked for about fifteen minutes, until Martin fell asleep. I didn't leave then. I didn't let go of his hand. Every now and then his eyes would come half open and he'd squeeze my fingers. I had some hard choices in my life but that was hardest one, ever.

When he came to I leaned over and kissed him on his cheekbone, then I whispered a magic formula in his ear.

"What?" he asked me. So I told him again. And then one last time.

I left without saying goodbye to Pea.

CHAPTER 38

Saul was sitting at the dining table in the kitchen eating ham hocks, mustard greens, and honeyed lemon yams. Maude stood behind him beaming at the way he could put away food.

Sarah Cain was at the table too. She was ashen and nauseated. The plate in front of her remained untouched.

"Easy." Saul looked up from his forkful of greens. "Mrs. Hawkes here has some interesting things to say about Arthur and his habits."

"Arthur hasn't done anything wrong," the pale woman complained.

"I didn't say he did," Saul garbled through a mouth packed with buttery yams. "All I'm saying is that Arthur came home late to the house with Marlon Eady and Terry Tyler the night that Albert Cain died."

"What?"

"That's it. What?" Saul said in mocking irony. "What were Marlon and Terry doing there then? Huh?"

"I don't know," Sarah answered. She pushed the food away.

"Honey, you got to eat," Maude said.

"I just can't."

"How did Arthur even know them?" I asked.

"It had to be Ron," she said. "Marlon and Ron were friends in a way. I mean, they went around together. Ron is a bully, Mr. Rawlins. He likes to push people around. Marlon was a mild man really. I always thought that it must have been my father who got Ron to set up Marlon. That was before Father knew about me and Ron."

"Did Betty know that Marlon was there, I mean the night that your father got killed?"

All Sarah did was shake her head.

"Do you know where Arthur is?" I asked.

She wouldn't answer.

"Listen," I said. "You don't have to tell me where he is, but do me a favor. Call him. Tell him that I know he was there with Marlon and Terry. Tell him that I'll help him if I can. Will you do that for me?"

She might have nodded.

I sat back and wondered at the possibilities.

Maybe Arthur killed his grandfather for beating him or his mother or Betty. Maybe Marlon killed him.

But I didn't care about that. For all I knew the police hadn't even officially called it a murder. All I wanted was for Betty to survive. I couldn't save her brother or her children, I couldn't save Martin. But maybe I could help Betty.

Saul and I parked across the street from the turquoise house.

When nobody answered my knock I called, "Open up, Betty. It's Easy Rawlins. Come on, open up." There was a panic in my body all of a sudden. My fists clenched up and the perspiration from the heat turned to free-flowing sweat. My greatest fear was that Betty was on the floor on the other side of the door like all of the other corpses I associated with her—spread-legged, brainless, toothless, and dead.

When the door came open I was prepared for any kind of mayhem.

But I wasn't prepared for Felix Landry. He wore tight tan pants and a white silk shirt that wasn't tucked in.

"You're not welcome here, Mr. Rawlins."

"We have to talk to Betty." I pronounced my words slowly

and clearly to let Felix know that I meant what I was saying.

He turned to the side and said to someplace behind the door, "You wanna see Mr. Rawlins, lady?" He paid attention to the hidden place for a moment and then turned back to me, "Betty don't wanna see you."

When he tried to shut the door my arm shot out to push it open. Felix was my height but he had a slim build. Still he grabbed me. He bared his teeth and snarled.

"Yeow!" I shouted when Felix's fingernails dug into my arm. Out of the corner of my eye I saw Saul reach for his pistol. Quickly I pushed both hands against Felix's chest. He flew backwards and the door swung open.

"Something happened to Gwendolyn!" I shouted before the violence could escalate.

Betty, who was still standing beyond the door, sobbed, "No," and then she shook, "No, no, no, no, no," all the way down to the floor.

Felix shouted, "Betty!" and ran to her side. Saul and I scuffled in but we didn't approach them.

"No!" Betty cried, and she socked Felix on the jaw, making the sound of two wooden blocks being slammed together.

Felix fell flat on his back. He wasn't completely out, though. He was writhing on the floor, trying to rise.

"Noooo," Betty beseeched with upturned eyes. She began to tear at her chest, ripping open the man's work shirt that she wore, revealing a large breast that looked as if it had never suckled a child. I tried to cover her up but all I did was to keep grabbing her like some rough kind of lover. Finally I gave up.

"Ahhhhh, oh!" she yelled. She began running around the room turning over furniture.

"*Noooooo!* Ahhhhhh! Oh Lord!" Dishes and plates went

flying from a scarred old maple cabinet. I ran to grab Betty by her arms from behind.

"Nooooo!"

I was holding Betty in front of a long slender mirror that was attached to the door leading to her tiny bedroom. Both of her breasts were out and she struggled with the strength of a mother fighting to save her child. With a great heave she pulled one arm free and let fly with a china cup that she'd grabbed. The mirror shattered in place, our images froze for a second in a thousand slender shards, and then fell to the floor, giving me the distinct impression that it was both of our lives that had been splintered and destroyed.

"Let me go!" she shouted. "Let me go!"

I obeyed her plea.

Saul backed against the wall. Felix made it to his feet for a moment, then tumbled back to the floor.

Betty started ripping the cushions off the sofa, tearing open the material and letting the foam rubber fly.

"Betty! Stop it!" poor Felix yelled. He staggered toward her. Betty turned to him in rage and terror. I was afraid that she was going to hit him again.

"It's her daughter!" I yelled at Felix. "She's dead!"

Felix didn't know what to make of what I'd said. But Betty did. Her shouts turned to pathetic sobs and she fell hard to the floor on her knees.

Saul went to her side and I went to Felix. I told him that Gwendolyn had been murdered.

We got Betty up and led her to the bedroom. Felix took off her clothes and dressed her in a nightgown. He surrounded her head with pillows and kept his body between the bed and me and Saul. All the while Betty was sighing and muttering to herself. I didn't understand the words but I knew what she was saying.

"I'm going to make tea now," Felix said.

It was about half an hour since we'd arrived at the house.

"Go make it," I told him.

"You two better be goin'," he said. His musical voice now a dirge.

"We should talk to Miss Eady," Saul said to me. "We should find out what she knows."

"What difference does it make? Who cares what happened?"

"Are you guys goin'?" Felix interjected.

"The hammer will fall, Easy," Saul said. "We're in this."

I knew it was true.

"Lady needs to sleep," Felix said.

"Listen, man," I announced as if I were addressing a crowd. "We've got to talk to Betty. We are going to do that. When we finish we'll leave you to it. Now if you want to watch that's okay by us, but we will talk to her, that much is sure."

Felix cut a glance at Betty in the bed, then sized us up. He knew that violence between us would only upset her more, but he was so angry that he couldn't move aside.

Saul and I went around him though, and that seemed to break the spell. Felix left. To make tea I suppose.

Betty was lying quietly in the bed with her head and shoulders propped up on half a dozen pillows. Tears were flowing from her eyes.

"Betty," I said.

"She's dead, Easy."

I took her hand.

"Were Marlon and Terry there the night Albert Cain died?" I didn't want to ask her but I had to.

Betty looked away and shook her head—no.

"You sure they didn't come in there with somebody else?"

No reply. Not even a motion of her head.

"Betty, we got to find the man killed your kids," I said. "He might be after you."

"I'm dead already. He already killed me."

"If that's true," Saul said, "tell us what happened so we can get him—for the memory."

I didn't know what he meant but Betty seemed to understand. "Marlon and Terry come in with Arthur that night. I was gettin' ready to go to bed." Betty looked from side to side, pitiful in her own bed now. "But I heard somethin' and I went to the stairs an' saw 'em comin' up."

"Did they see you?" Saul asked.

"No. I was scared at how serious they looked. It was the first time I ever seen Arthur stalkin' like a man. You know he just a baby. Why he wanna be walkin' like that?

"And then later, when I went in to check on Albert he was dead with a pillah on his face."

"And so you ran to make them think that you did it?" I knew it was true.

"I come down to stay at my house. I just told Felix that I was takin' a vacation. You know I only called Odell 'cause of Terry. I needed somebody to put him in the ground."

"Do you know where we could find Arthur, Miss Eady?" Saul asked in his undertaker's voice.

"He might be at his secret place." She was looking out past the wall.

"Where is that, Miss Eady?" Saul asked.

"Arthur was takin' his momma's checks an' payin' rent on a place on little Santa Monica."

"He told you that?" I asked.

"The landlord called about a year ago and asked to talk wit' Miss Cain. But she wasn't there. I told him that whatever check it was that Arthur gave him was okay. And then later when I ast'im 'bout it he said that he just needed a little place to get away."

"Did Sarah know about it?" I asked.

"After a while he told her. He said that he liked to go write poems over there."

The phone number and address were listed under Arthur Cain in the white pages. Nobody answered, so Saul and I drove over to West Los Angeles.

We went up to apartment thirty-nine but nobody came to the door. So we went back downstairs to number one—the super's apartment.

He was so tall that he had to stoop to put his head out of his own front door. "Yes?" he asked pleasantly. If he was startled to see a white man and a black man together at his door he didn't let it show.

"Mr. Manetti?" Saul smiled upward. We hadn't discussed how to approach this man but it was only natural that Saul would talk to the white man.

"Yes?"

"My name is Howard and this is my associate Mr. Grodin. We're here to pick up some furniture from your tenant, a Mr. Cain."

"Arthur Cain." The super had his hands braced against each side of the door, like Samson.

"Yes." Saul smiled. "Do you know if he'll be in soon? You know, I'm going to waste a half a day's pay on Mr. Grodin here if we can't get in there."

"Sorry, I don't know. Him and his father took off 'bout an hour ago."

His father?

"His father?" Saul asked.

"Yeah. Why?"

"Um, nothing. He did say that his father had rented the place for him."

"I doubt that, Mr. . . . uh?"

"Howard."

"Yeah, I doubt that, Mr. Howard. Mr. Hawkes didn't look like he could pay for a cup of coffee, and that dusty old yellow station wagon of his is just a pile of junk."

"Station wagon?" I couldn't keep quiet. "You said he drove a yellow station wagon?"

"Was it a Studebaker?"

"I think so, yeah."

"Come on, man," I said to Saul. "We got to go."

"What's going on?" the big super asked. "Who are you guys?"

But we were going out the front door. We were in Saul's car and headed back to Odell's house.

CHAPTER 39

I told Saul my fears on the way. The more I said, the faster he drove. We made it to Odell's house in less than a half hour.

At first I was relieved to see the familiar Studebaker out in front of Odell's; at least they hadn't made it to Betty. But then I was afraid of what we'd find in the house: Odell and Maude slaughtered and heaped on the floor.

I was already plotting my revenge when I burst through the front door.

They were all there. Odell and Maude with coffee cups in their laps, sitting on the sofa next to Sarah. Arthur was sitting in one straightback chair and there next to him stood Dickhead, smiling and talking.

Dickhead looked up at me, his eyes glinting with mirth. "Well hi. Surprised to see me here?"

Dickhead was standing behind Arthur's chair. His grin was so ingratiating that I was taken off guard. I saw him take the pistol out of the back of his pants but I didn't react. Maybe it was because I was so tired, trying to do so much.

"Watch it!" Saul ran into me with both hands straight out.

Thinking back on it now, maybe it was a mistake. Dickhead, also known as Ronald Hawkes, probably wasn't going to shoot. He just wanted to balance the odds. Saul hit me hard and Dickhead's gun barked, twice. The first shot winged Saul and spun him around, the second one got him in the back. Arthur leaped out of the chair at the first shot and the women screamed. Dickhead looked over at them for a second.

That was just the second I needed. I moved low and caught the vacated chair by the legs, swinging it high while staying down. Dickhead, in a moment of fear, shot the chair before it crashed into his head. I had to hit him three more times before he was all the way down, and out.

I pulled the gun from the unconscious man's hand, then I ran to Saul. His eyes were open like a dead man's but a choking sound came from his throat. I pulled the hair at the front of his head back toward the floor and held his nose closed, then I took a deep breath and filled his lungs with my air.

"Call an ambulance!" I cried between breaths.

Blood was coming out from underneath the little man. Sarah Cain brought me a pillow to put under his head but I put it underneath him, hoping to block up the wound in his back.

Deep breath, exhale, push. Deep breath, exhale, push.

The women and Arthur were making fretting noises while I worked. Odell called the ambulance. There was a commotion suddenly. Odell had grabbed Dickhead, but the bloody-headed white man pushed him down and ran for the door. I had his gun but I was thinking about Saul. I couldn't worry about the killer while there was life in my hands.

Everyone was shouting but I kept up my work. I did until I was light-headed but I still didn't miss a breath. I didn't know if Saul was dead or alive but that didn't even matter.

Somebody must have called the police after hearing the shots, because the cops came before the ambulance. Arthur wouldn't say a word but Maude described the car that they were in. Sarah gave them his name. Finally one of the policemen spelled me while the other one was on the phone to the police station.

I went out on the porch to get some air. Soon after that the ambulance drove up. They seemed a little confused about the address, so I went out to the curb to point the way. Three more police cars arrived at the same time. People were starting to come out of their houses to see about all the sirens and uniforms.

It was easy to get into my car and drive off. Nobody had asked me to stay.

I knew the police mind (at least I thought I did). If I had told them about the house he was going to they would have put me in jail. They wouldn't have gone straight to the address, because they never listen to criminal cant; and all blacks were criminals.

So I doubled back to Arthur's apartment. I drove like a crazy man, Dickhead's gun wedged in my belt.

I arrived at the same time as two police cars were pulling up. There was a Buick sedan on the curb in front of the building, blocking off the dusty Studebaker. I pulled up to the curb across the street and heard a man's scream—loud and scared. Then there were a lot of shots, at least five, and the cops began to move quickly and cautiously down the alley at the side of the building.

I waited a couple of minutes and then followed. The

policemen were standing at the far end of the dead-end alley looking down at the ground in the middle of a half-dozen overturned trash cans. Their pistols were all holstered.

I should have gone away, I know that. But there was just too much hatred in me right then. I moved up behind the cops. There lying between a scatter of green ale bottles was Dickhead. His arms and legs were every which way and his khaki shirt had turned the color of murky blood. His head rested on a shoulder.

"I shouted for him to stop," Commander Styles was saying.

He spoke patiently to a uniformed cop jotting in a notebook.

"I heard the APB on the radio. I'm Beverly Hills but I was down here looking for something for my kid's birthday. You know the shops in my town . . ." He didn't finish because he spotted me over the wall of blue shoulders.

The note-taking policeman looked up then too. "Hey! You! What are you doing here?"

The rest of the pack turned toward me.

"Uh, I just heard the commotion and come around the corner, officer. I—I didn't mean nuthin'." I was nobody and nothing.

"Did you see anything?" the policeman asked. But it was Commander Style's stare that I was answering.

"No, sir. I come back here after you did."

"Well, move on. Get out of here."

I backed up the first few steps, looking Styles in the eye. He smiled at me and the L.A. summer broke.

CHAPTER 40

Maude and Odell were alone by the time I returned.

"The ambulance took your friend to Temple, Easy. Miss Cain and the boy went on with'em," Maude told me. "He didn't look too good."

Temple Hospital. The place where my wife met her lover; my old friend, Dupree Bouchard. The place where my only blood child, Edna, was born. The whole place had a feeling of loss for me.

The front desk sent me to the intensive care ward. I got to the nurse's desk there and asked after my companion.

"He's in critical condition," the older Mexican woman told me. "They're operating on him now. His family are down the hall in the waiting area."

She pointed out the direction and I went. All the way to the hospital I'd been thinking about Saul, worrying about the white man who had put my life before his. And so I was surprised to see Sarah Cain and Arthur sitting in the hall outside of a door labeled *Intensive Care.* A few seats away from them was a young black woman who held an infant in her arms. Another tragedy case, I thought. Her brother or boyfriend was probably cut down in Compton or Watts over a dime bet or another man's woman.

Sarah Cain rose immediately and came toward me.

"Mr. Rawlins," she said.

"What you doin' here?" I wanted to slap her face.

"We came . . . we came because of Mr. Lynx."

"What you care about him? You don't know him."

Sarah Cain hesitated and I knew why she was there.

"You afraid he was gonna say somethin', huh?" I asked

her. "You afraid he'd say about Arthur and Terry and Marlon."

"Not just that. No."

I wanted to be mad. I wanted to hate her, but I couldn't. A woman had the right to protect her child.

"You got that divorce you wanted," I said.

"He's dead?" She actually reached out and touched my forearm.

I nodded.

"Arthur," Miss Cain said in a voice that meant business.

The young black woman was watching the doctor's station but now and then she'd steal a glance at me.

Arthur came up to us. His fresh complexion was marred by a few days' growth. "Yes, Mother?"

"Your father is dead, Arthur. He's dead." Sarah Cain's voice was full of emotion. There was joy there in celebration of the death of the man she hated; and a deep sadness for her son and herself.

Arthur for his part was past feeling. I could see in his eyes that all the violence and hate in his life had hardened him into a man. The kind of man who has nothing to give.

"Tell Mr. Rawlins what you told me," Sarah said, seemingly oblivious to the changes in her son.

"But, Mother, is that wise?"

"This man risked his life." It was a simple declaration. For bearing the best news that she had ever received I was, for a brief moment, her best friend. She would have shared anything, told me anything, because I had touched her deepest desires. I was the source of her joy.

"Dad got me together with Marlon." He went right into the story with no preparation or pretense. "He told Marlon about how Grandpa got him to set him up for that robbery and about what he did to Aunt Betty after Marlon was gone. He told him that Grandpa was Gwen and Terry's father. He said that Betty couldn't ever be free until

Grandpa was dead. Then he told me that I had to forge a check to Marlon, "for reparations,' he said, and I had to let him and Terry in the house that night. And after I did that and Marlon was gone he wanted me to call the cops, he even gave me the number to call. I didn't know what they were going to do."

"Was the cop you called Styles?" I asked.

Arthur nodded. "That's the one."

"Who told you about him?"

"Dad did."

"He knew Styles?"

"Yes. Grandpa sent Styles to tell Dad to stay away from us, but then they got to be friends. They were working together."

"Who told you about the will?"

"Calvin Hodge did," Sarah said. "He found out somehow and told us that we'd better make a deal with Betty."

"Some deal," I said. "And did Calvin call the cops on me when I left your house the first time?"

"I'm sorry about that, Mr. Rawlins," Arthur said.

"You called him?"

"I didn't know what you were doing there. You said that you were looking for Marlon, so I got scared. I didn't think that he'd hurt you."

"You knew he wanted to kill your grandfather. You knew he wanted to kill Betty."

Arthur shook his head. "I didn't mean to hurt Betty. I only wanted to get at Grandpa for hurting Mom." He turned to his mother. "For keeping you from Dad."

"I hate him," Sarah said. I was pretty sure that her father and husband were one man for her.

"So it was your father who killed Marlon and Terry and Gwen?"

"Dad was outside the house this morning. He told me that he wanted to talk to Gwen. He said that he wanted to ask her something about Betty. He wanted me to bring her out to the gate so Mother wouldn't get mad. But then you guys came." Arthur peered over at the operating-room door.

"Did he kill Gwen?"

Arthur stared directly into my eyes, not saying a word.

"He wanted my money," Sarah said in her son's place. "The fool thought that Betty was going to take everything. The only reason he wanted to be married to me was that he wanted to get bought off. But he couldn't get anything until Father was dead."

"And that's why he got Arthur to tell Marlon and Terry about the rapes." I was just talking out loud. "Marlon loved Betty more'n anything."

"Yes," Arthur and his mother said at the same time.

"What about Styles, though? Why'd he start sayin' that it was murder?"

"I don't know. He knew the coroner and got him to say that they were overworked so that a private contractor could do the autopsy. The report originally said that foul play wasn't suspected, so then the contractor doctor was free to say that it was a heart attack."

"Styles knew this doctor?" I asked.

Arthur nodded.

"Excuse me, but are you Mr. Rawlins?" The young black woman, with the baby cradled in her arms, had come up next to me.

"Yeah?"

"I'm Mrs. Lynx," she said. "They told me that if Saul lives it will be because of you. They said that he saved your life and that you kept him breathing for more than half an hour before the ambulance came."

"I wasn't watchin' the clock." My hand went down to hers. She held it next to her infant son's face. His lips pushed in and out. There was very little of Saul in his dark features but you could tell by the hair, a little.

"Thank you."

I went to the phone and dialed the Beverly Hills precinct.

After a little bit of work I got Officer Connor on the line. At first he didn't want to talk to me but after I told him I thought I could get Styles he wanted to listen. I told him everything I knew about the murders, including Styles's part in them. The only thing I left out was Marlon's burial.

"Styles has been sitting on the murder investigation and he's been working with the man he killed today. I'm gonna send you a copy of an arrest report that he buried over twelve years ago." I left him with the puzzle, hoping that he would work it all out.

After that came the wait. Miss Cain and Arthur went home at midnight, but Rita, that's Mrs. Lynx, and I waited until the doctor came out at three A.M. to announce that Saul had passed the first hurdle. If his body could fight off any secondary infections he'd probably live.

I drove her and the baby to their home in Redondo Beach and then I made the long way back to my house.

It was early morning again. The children were safe with Primo and I'd have them home with me again soon. My money problems weren't solved yet but I had some hope. And I was definitely sure that I'd never enter work that didn't have a paycheck and benefits involved. I was through with the streets. That was a younger man's game.

"Mornin', Ease." He was seated in my reclining chair, a gaudy Colt .45 resting on his knees.

"Mouse."

"I'm'onna kill me somebody today, man. Now either it's gonna be you and John or it's gonna be them boys turned me in."

"None'a them men turnt you in, Raymond."

Mouse laid his hand across the pistol. He couldn't help himself, I knew that. He needed to kill somebody, and even though it would hurt him he'd kill me if there was nobody else to blame.

"The man turned you in was a religious man. I found out from Faye Rabinowitz that he said God wouldn't let him keep quiet on a night like that when he called in. Them men in John's wouldn'ta said that. You could call Faye Rabinowitz. She got that from the prosecutor."

His fingers wrapped around the butt of the pistol and he lifted the silver barrel a quarter of an inch.

Three seconds before my death I said, "I know who did it."

"Well all right then." Mouse's grin was his relief at my survival.

I told him everything that he needed. "Just call this number and tell her that her husband's sick. That'll get the house open for ya and you could just walk in."

With every word I swore to myself that I'd never get involved with another man's problems again.

CHAPTER 41

Jesus and Feather had to spend another week at Primo's house because I collapsed in the front yard the morning after the shooting. Lucky took me to the hospital where they diagnosed the infection from my stab wound. Antibiotics saved my life from the bacteria, and seven days on my back were enough for me to decide how to go out and find a job that would keep me out the streets forever.

Saul Lynx lived. His wife nursed him back to health and he took a job doing security for WestBank in Santa Monica. I get together with him and Rita now and again. They're good people.

Officer Connor was able to get an indictment against Arthur Hawkes and Commander Styles, and Marlon Eady too—though he was never found to stand trial. Styles, the workingman, went to jail for his crimes. The fool had used his own pistol to kill Terry Tyler. I was sure that he was the one who helped Hawkes beat Marlon.

Arthur went free. His lawyers made Marlon Eady and Ron Hawkes the bad guys. "These hardened criminals misled the boy and blackmailed him. He loved his family, and if he had been aware of the evil of the men who used him he would have definitely turned away from them," the defense claimed.

The prosecution didn't fuss much.

The trial destroyed Betty. They hauled her up on the stand and asked again and again if she was aware of her brother's plotting. They made her seem like a whore who had beguiled Albert Cain.

These last accusations were used to break the will. Calvin Hodge did that. He was never implicated in the crimes. Maybe he didn't know anything about them. He was just a lawyer trying to make it through the muck. When the prosecution asked him about his relationship with Styles, Hodge said that he'd introduced Albert Cain to Styles but that he had "no entrée into their intercourse."

Hodge helped Mofass break Clovis's hold on his business. Actually Mofass got away like a bandit, because really it was Clovis who had built the business. Mofass just took it away from her and then became a kind of a recluse because of the threats her family put down. We tried for two years to keep Jewelle and Mofass apart. But finally, on the day she turned eighteen, they went off together.

They condemned Freedom's Plaza and bought up the property for the city. Then they found that the soil was unsuitable for a waste-processing plant. They sold the property to Save-Co with Mason LaMone as the managing agent.

I hired on to the construction crew that laid the foundation for the shopping center. No one ever suspected that it was me who put the extra sand in the cement that made it crumble only one year after the opening ceremonies. Nobody except maybe Mason LaMone.

She told the police that a call had come saying that her husband was sick at work. She hurried out to him. After all, what could happen in the house in just twenty minutes?

I don't know how it happened exactly. They found him behind the sofa. The shot from the Colt .45 had knocked him back and flipped him over.

Mouse had come in and asked him who had turned him in and Martin said that he'd done it. He said that the Lord wouldn't let him keep quiet on that. And Mouse shot him. A sixty-year-old man dressed in a small boy's clothes, but all Mouse saw was the man who'd turned him over. So he shot him and walked out of the empty house.